BOOKS SHOULD BE RETURNED ON OR BEFORE LAST
DATE BELOW

3/89

Public Library
North's Lane
MAESTEG, CF34 9
Mid Glam

13 APR 1989   3 1 AUG 1989

27 APR 1989   -8 OCT 1980

31 MAY 1989   15 SEP 1989

morgans   31 OCT 1990
1-5-89

11 SEP 1989

16 JUN 1989   29 JUN 1991

26 0

27 JUL 1989   10 MAY 1990 -8 JUL 1991

26   31 MAY 1990 -6 MAR 1992
                            Renewed
1 MAY 1990   -8 OCT 199   04-2-92
5 OCT 1990   14 MAR 1992

               29 JUN 1991

                            20 MAR 1992
                            25
                            14 MAY 1992

Author
FRIEDMAN, R.

AN ELIGIBLE MAN
Enw

Class No.		Copy No.	
Dosbarth	**F**	Rhif	2

MID GLAMORGAN COUNTY LIBRARIES

By the same author

The Life Situation
The Long Hot Summer
Proofs Of Affection
A Loving Mistress
Rose Of Jericho
A Second Wife
To Live In Peace

As Robert Tibber:

No White Coat
Love On My List
We All Fall Down
Patients Of A Saint
The Fraternity
The Commonplace Day
The General Practice
Practice Makes Perfect

Juvenile:

Aristide

An Eligible Man

Rosemary Friedman

PIATKUS

© Rosemary Friedman 1989

First published in Great Britain in 1989 by
Judy Piatkus (Publishers) Ltd of
5 Windmill Street, London W1P 1HF

British Library Cataloguing in Publication Data

Friedman, Rosemary, *1929–*
    An Eligible Man
    I. Title
    823'.914 [F]

    ISBN 0–86188–836–7

Phototypeset in 11/12 Garamond by
Phoenix Photosetting, Chatham
Printed and bound in Great Britain by
Biddles Ltd, Guildford and Kings Lynn

For Tony

'Alice had never been in a court of justice before, but she had read about them in books, and she was quite pleased to find that she knew the name of nearly everything there. "That's the judge," she said to herself, "because of his great wig."'

Alice's Adventures in Wonderland

Acknowledgement

Lines from 'Memory', by Trevor Nunn, incorporate lines from Eliot poems and are reprinted from *Cats*: the book of the musical with words by T. S. Eliot, with the permission of Faber & Faber Ltd.

'*Woo-waang, woo-wing, nong chow baah! Woo-waang, woo-wing, nong chow baah! Woo-waang, Woo-wing, nong chow baah! Woo-waang, woo-wing, nong chow baah! Woo-waang, woo-wing, nong chow baah!*'

On Christmas Day, His Honour Judge Christopher (Topher) Osgood sat wedged between two other members of his group in the sub-zero temperature of Beijing airport, where he had been for the past six hours. Huddled in his padded anorak, his Friendship Store hat (made of what he strongly suspected was cat) ear-flaps down, on his head, he warmed his hands round a cracked mug of green tea and listened to the unfathomable announcement that came with monotonous regularity over the public address system.

Topher closed his eyes. He had been up since five-thirty. The bus had broken down on the way to the airport, forcing them all to stand – like a crowd of extras in a scene from *Doctor Zhivago* – in the soft white flakes of snow that drifted down from a black sky. Delilah, eleven years old, the youngest member of the party, who had attached herself to Topher for the duration of the tour, dug an elbow into his ribs.

'"Why does the bicycle sleep all the time?"'

Rousing himself, Topher looked out of the window at the iced up Ilyushin immobilised on the bleak landscape of the runway.

'Why *does* the bicycle sleep all the time, Delilah?'

'Because it's "two tyred!"'

'I would never have thought of that.'

Bored with the enforced activity of the long wait, Delilah fiddled with the strands of hair which straggled from under her fluffy white beret. She had bought it in the market in Shanghai, since when it had not left her head.

' "What time do you go to the dentist?" '

'Leave the judge alone, Delilah,' her mother's potent Brisbane accents reproved the child. 'He wants to sleep.'

Topher closed his eyes again.

He did not want to sleep.

He wanted to think how it was that he had come to be spending Christmas Day, chilled to the marrow (despite the thermal vest Lucille had insisted that he wear), holed up in the airport of the capital of the People's Republic of China with a strange group of Australian school teachers.

He wanted to discover whether the past year had been a chimera, in which he had been a butterfly thinking he was a man, or if, on the other hand, it had been nothing but a bad dream.

Chapter One

When Topher Osgood opened his drawer and saw a rectangular empty space next to the dwindling pile of socks where his clean pyjamas should have been, he knew with sickening certainty that his wife had died.

That he was a supreme example of male chauvinist piggery – according to his surviving family, his daughters, Chelsea and Penge – he accepted. In his day a chauvinist had been one prone to an exaggerated and bellicose fondness for one's country, and chauvinism was not even remotely concerned with one's expectations of finding freshly laundered and folded linen in one's closet. The addendum of the farm animal, renowned for its unaesthetic lifestyle, its wallowing in the mire, was downright offensive. But then were so many of the epithets to which one was currently exposed. Only last week in his court a defendant had removed his denim jacket and appeared before Topher in a tee-shirt which had exorted him (he took the instruction personally) to 'Fuck Off'. He had refused to hear the case.

It was not only the expectation of clean pyjamas but his assumption of specific night attire which dated him. When Chelsea and Penge had lived at home, unlike their mother who had a selection of attractive floor-length gowns soft to the night-time touch, they had appeared newly risen from their beds in, it seemed to Topher, a random selection of whatever garments happened to be nearest to hand when they crashed out. There was no such thing as a *peignoir*, and certainly not a slipper, a disaffection they shared with their cavalcade of partners. Real men did not wear pyjamas.

1

The patch of emptiness in the drawer next to the socks reflected exactly the hollow area experienced by Topher in the region of his viscera. Since Caroline had died there had been a numbness within, a barren sensation which he would have been hard put to describe. Unpleasant as it had been, it was as nothing compared with the new awareness which now struck at what he could only imagine, in a confusion of metaphors, was his cerebral solar plexus.

There had always, since his marriage, been supplies of clean pyjamas, as there had been of clean shirts and bath towels. Buttons, where appropriate, had been firmly attached. He had been amazed to discover recently how fragile was their tenure. It was not that Topher was unworldly. Nor other worldly. He had, despite what Chelsea and Penge had to say, moved with the times. Domestic help was not what it had been and he had often given Caroline a hand. When she was tired as she had been sometimes of late, her deposits of youthful energy dwindling, he had done whatever was required of him. But when the cancer had come, like a thief in the night, to spirit her away, he had been totally unprepared.

Death had of course been discussed. In practical terms it had been anticipated. Equal shares of their worldly goods to Chelsea and Penge, notwithstanding their unsuitable liaisons. The only exceptions were the Chippendale mirror, to which Chelsea had a particular attachment (Topher shuddered to think where it would fit in the Wapping warehouse) and the Sheraton cabinet which Penge had had her eye on ever since they had brought it back from the King's Road.

When the subject came up, both he and Caroline had each declared their certainty that they would go first. In their heart of hearts neither of them, convinced of his own mortality, believed it. In the manner of most people who at some time or another imagined their loved ones dead, Topher had on occasion pictured himself a widower. Or thought he had. He had seen Topher Osgood, an object of both sympathy and pity, mourning his spouse, putting a brave face on things, but otherwise carrying on with his life precisely as he had done before his bereavement. There had even been times, when Caroline had been particularly annoying, that he had momentarily relished the prospect of his release from her incursions into his mental privacy or some of her more maddening habits, such as that of tidying up after him so that his clues were removed and he could not remember what it was that he was supposed to have been doing.

Once, he remembered, before he had been appointed to the Bench,

Caroline had accidentally thrown out his next day's brief. He had had to run along the street in his dressing-gown after the dustcart. Fortunately it had been in the days before a mechanical grinder masticated everything that was hurled into its revolving maw.

He thought he had been prepared, but the obscenity of death, when it visited so unexpectedly, so swiftly, caught him totally unawares. There had been nothing the matter with Caroline, who normally waged an ongoing battle with the scales, except that she was off her food. The minute amounts she did manage to eat disagreed with her. The doctor whom on Topher's insistance she consulted, had at first prescribed antacid tablets, then an X-ray, by which time Caroline was scarcely eating anything at all. The surgeon, to whom in due course she was referred, diagnosed a blockage. Waiting for her to come back from the operating theatre, Topher had passed the time wondering where he would take his wife to convalesce. The South of France, although indisputably south and therefore warm, had never been, either in his opinion or Caroline's, France. Jamaica was too far, and Madeira too dull. Ecuador and the nearby Galapagos Islands, which was of special interest to Caroline and on their list of places to visit, was appealing, but she would be tempted to chase after frigate birds or blue-footed boobies. The Costa del Sol was the Costa del Sol. Greece perhaps. Turkey possibly. He was bogged down in Bodrum when the surgeon came into the ante-room where Topher was waiting.

'Your wife is still in ITU.'

It was no more than Topher had expected.

'We opened her up.'

The man seemed to be preoccupied with a fly, left over from the summer, buzzing against the window pane.

'I'm afraid there's nothing we can do.'

Topher smiled, sensing some joke. The man was having him on.

'The tumour has obstructed the pylorus and metastasised to the liver.'

'How long . . . ?' Topher began.

The surgeon shrugged. 'A couple of months at the outside.'

'How long will she be in intensive care?' Topher said irritably, as to some barrister who had wilfully misunderstood him.

'Only until her blood pressure settles. Probably by the time you've had a cup of coffee, she'll be back on the ward.'

'She's all right though?' Topher said.

3

'She's over the operation.'

Caroline had always been strong. She had never been in hospital other than to give birth to the children.

The surgeon looked at his watch. Topher accepted that his time was up. He had his own methods of indicating that an interview was at an end. He would put both hands on his desk and lean forward. 'Well,' he would say. 'Well.'

'I'm very sorry.'

Topher understood. The surgeon was a busy man. He was a busy man himself.

'I shall go and have a cup of coffee. As you suggest.'

When Penge, in her fake leopard coat, had flung her arms round her father's neck and sobbed and sobbed – she had always had exhibitionistic tendencies – Topher had comforted her, as he had when as a child she had fallen from her tricycle or come face to face with some imagined bogeyman in the night. Chelsea, as was her wont, had been more restrained. Caroline herself, after her discharge from hospital, had been unpredictable. She vacillated between falsifying the scales in the opposite direction from usual, to convince Topher that she was gaining weight (or at least maintaining it), and being realistic beyond endurance. He was to be sure to sell the house, she said in one of the latter phases, it was far too large for two, let alone for one. A small flat would suit him very nicely. And he was to dissuade Penge should she dream of throwing in her lot permanently with that highly unsuitable young man she was living with. And she was sorry to leave her affairs in such a mess, she had been meaning for years to go through her papers. And he was not to hesitate to re-marry. There was no question of disloyalty. He simply would not be able to cope on his own. He never had been able to. She even proposed possible successors, suggesting females with whom even *in extremis* Topher could not imagine having a relationship.

The discussions embarrassed him. He tried to change the subject. To the vexed and hypothetical topic of the convalescence; the roses which were still budding in the exceptionally mild December; possible delicacies in the way of nourishment he should suggest to Chelsea, who had moved back temporarily into her old room in order to look after her mother. Once only, unable to continue with the *façade* she had herself erected, Caroline had wept. Her despair discomforted Topher even more than did her bravado. She did not want to die. Before she got her free bus pass. Before she had grandchildren.

4

Before she had written the definitive book on British birds for which she had been collecting material for the past ten years. Why me? she asked with uncharacteristic naïveté, as if she had somehow behaved badly and had been singled out for punishment. It was not a simple question to answer. Topher did not believe in the prosperity of the righteous and the ultimate frustration of the wicked; that either the floods and earthquakes of the Old Testament or the present day scourge of Auto Immune Deficiency Syndrome was the result of Divine retribution, the judgement of God upon human sin. Fortunately his wife's soul searching did not last long, and the familiar stoical Caroline, with whom he was more at ease, reasserted herself.

'I suppose I shouldn't complain. Shakespeare died when he was fifty-two. Mozart was only thirty-five. And look at Siegfried Sassoon!'

On one dreadful afternoon, Topher shuddered when he thought of it, Caroline had suddenly screamed as loud as she was able: 'I do not want to die! I do not want to die!' She repeated the words over and over until she became quite hysterical. Unable to calm her, Topher had left the house and gone for a walk, her anguished voice in his ears.

Sometimes Caroline turned her face to the wall and would not speak at all. It was hard to keep up with her changes of mood. It was a confusing time. Chelsea kept him sane. She was an existentialist. After the first tears she ran the house — when she came back from producing her programmes at the BBC — and looked after her mother with philosophical efficiency.

Topher did not care for the 'when I'm gone' conversations. They made him uneasy. Adjustment to the situation needed time. Looking at Caroline, as her flesh dissolved and her bones assumed excessive prominence in her haunted face, there seemed to be precious little of it left. Much of it was spent playing what seemed to Topher was a ghoulish game of make-believe having to do with Caroline's diet. She could not stomach meat. The sight of fish made her ill. Vegetables would not go down and bread stuck in her throat. Chelsea did her best with mushes of ground rice and semolina, proprietary weight-gain mixes, and puréed soups, most of which ended up down the sink. The three of them put their heads together on a daily basis to discuss what might be managed. The fact that Caroline's digestive system had more or less packed up was not mentioned. As her cheeks hollowed, her abdomen swelled. Caroline put the latter down to wind. Topher averted his eyes from the shiny drum which had once been the tolerably flat planes of his wife's stomach. Even in her mid-fifties she had been a good-looking woman. Statuesque. It was what had first attracted him to her in the Union at Cambridge, when she had stood up to oppose his motion, culled from Trevelyan, that 'Education has produced a vast population able to read but unable to distinguish what is worth reading.' That Caroline's physique had been instrumental in advancing his career Topher had no doubt.

'I am Caroline Osgood,' she would introduce himself, drawing herself up to her full five foot eleven inches, 'wife of Topher Osgood the well-known criminologist.'

In the early days of their marriage, soon after Topher had been called to the Bar, where as the most junior pupil in his chambers he had twiddled his thumbs waiting for the odd crumb of a brief to come his way, Caroline's description of him had of course been a downright lie. She did not confine her declaration to social or professional gatherings. She broadcast his name and qualifications abroad in such unlikely places as the local fishmonger's and Harvey Nichols' hosiery department. Whether it was his wife's persistence or his own aptitude, Topher was never quite sure, but in what seemed no time at all he progressed from thumb twiddling to being one of the most feared and sought after prosecutors at the criminal Bar.

While advancing his career with disconcerting tenacity at every opportunity, Caroline did not altogether approve of it. She was invariably on the side of the defendant (whom she often mistakenly considered to be the underdog) and would have been happier had Topher confined himself to defending those she considered to be the hapless victims of circumstance. They had an ongoing argument in which Topher cited a conglomerate of murderers, rapists, arsonists and others whom Caroline, with her unique disregard of logic in all its forms, equated with the various species of threatened wildlife on which she was an expert. When, through Topher's instigation, some enemy of society was removed from the contemporary scene for periods coinciding with Her Majesty's pleasure, Caroline's lips would tighten with disapproval. Later, when it was her husband who did the sending down, the lip-tightening became more manifest.

They had been together for a long time. Interminable by present day standards, when any minor aberration, any unlooked for disharmony, any pinprick of marital discord, sent the protagonists rushing headlong for the divorce courts. It had not been roses all the way. God forbid. Topher had always been attractive to women. Caroline had said it was the irresistible combination of impeccable manners and

6

bedroom eyes. There had been the matter of Muriel Mills, a nubile law student, whom he had coached to supplement his income after Chelsea was born and Caroline had been engaged in the nursery. The tuition had necessitated a certain proximity. When Topher had accidentally touched Muriel's summer arm, a charge of electricity had passed between them and they had ended up in bed.

Topher had become so besotted with Muriel that he had contemplated throwing up wife, child, and career, and running off with her to the Great Barrier Reef, the ring of which sounded suitably romantic. If Caroline ever suspected that he had been unfaithful, nothing was said. Paradoxically, it was after the affair was over – Muriel had decided that she was not for the law but for Fine Arts and had left London for Florence – that Topher became overwhelmed with guilt and remorse. It was when he made retribution to Caroline in a number of uncharacteristic ways (including sending her a Valentine card which asserted his undying love about which she had never been in doubt) that she became suspicious. With his hand on his heart he was able to protest his innocence, although it was a long time before he could dismiss from his mind the image of Muriel, who discarded her inhibitions with her petticoats, from his more restrained and legitimate couplings.

If Caroline had ever been unfaithful, Topher had not been aware of it. There was a period when she had taken to playing squash – from which she returned with an unaccustomed glow which she attributed to the strenuous exercise – when the thought that his wife might have a lover had crossed his mind. Even when she returned one afternoon with the same unmistakeable glow, despite the fact that she had left her squash racquet in the umbrella stand in the hall, he did not remark upon it. Her addiction for the sport did not last and nothing was said about its demise.

Over the years there had been rough waters through which they had had to navigate the thankfully sturdy craft of the alliance forged in reckless youth; sticky patches during which each had threatened to leave the other (despite the fact that the actual mechanics of such a step had appeared so daunting) from which they had managed to extricate themselves more or less unscathed. Caroline was as headstrong as Topher was obstinate. Their polarity extended to patterns of sleep (Topher was the owl and Caroline the lark), travel (Topher had sat on deck reading about the Greek islands while Caroline explored them) and politics, in which Caroline's liberal opinions were countered by Topher's reactionary views.

There had been a point at which each of them had acknowledged the impossibility of making the other over in his image. The sandpaper of time had softened the sharp edges of the partnership. The disagreements of the latter years had been minor ones. Altercations over whose responsibility it was to renew the television licence, or whether they should take the draconian step of buying new and single beds (Caroline said Topher snored, and Topher accused Caroline of addressing the Cambridge Union in her sleep) had relegated such issues as the powers of the judiciary, and evolutionary theories, on which they held opposing views, to second place. Notwithstanding their differences (which had prevented the relationship from growing stale, had kept them on their toes) their love for each other had prevailed. It had sustained a marriage of which, like foreign travel, one only remembered the good bits. Now it was over. A fact brought home to Topher by the dearth of clean pyjamas.

It was a phenomenon which he had not encountered for thirty odd years – not even when Caroline had gone away to give birth to his daughters – and he was not at all sure how to deal with it.

There was no one upon whom he could call. Chelsea had gone home to her lover. The Polish help, who had little English and attended two mornings a week, only to clean the floors, was not privy to the secrets of the Osgood washing-machine. Topher had previously paid little attention to the contents of his drawers. If he gave the matter any thought at all, it was to imagine that he abandoned his soiled apparel only for it to appear again, clean and folded, by some kind of celestial intervention. Now he associated the miracle very definitely with Caroline. His wife had gone and so had his pyjamas. It was no use standing like an idiot, naked in his dressing-room. Something had to be done.

He opened the dirty-linen basket and surveyed its tightly packed contents with distaste. He would go to bed in his shirt and address the problem, together with the fact that he was down to his last tea-bag, before he went to court in the morning.

Chapter Two

Topher had never been in a supermarket. Apart from the newsagent's down the road, and Sweet and Maxwell where he bought his legal books, he rarely went shopping. Since the closing of John Barnes (where you had been able to buy everything from a pin to a Persian carpet), Caroline had sallied forth weekly to Waitrose, from whence she returned with a boot-load of filled cardboard boxes, to the contents of which Topher now wished he had paid more attention. Had it not been for the fact that he wanted to buy some more socks, he would have followed his late wife's example. He had been forced that morning to put on his white tennis pair, which went ill with his black jacket and striped trousers, and had decided that if he was to keep up his standards he must urgently replenish his hose. He had the suspicion that women did not go about these matters in an entirely practical way. They were conditioned, presumably by the manufacturers of soap powders, to washing socks too frequently when all that was required was more of them. It needed a man on the job.

He had been reading the letter from his sister, Tina, which reinforced her invitation issued at Caroline's funeral, to come and stay with her and Miles in Bradford (Bingley to be more precise), when the thought crossed his mind that while Waitrose most certainly sold tea-bags it did not, to the best of his knowledge carry socks. Folding Tina's letter, and mentally filing away her hospitable offer, he hit upon a visit to Marks and Spencer, which was on his way to Knightsbridge Crown Court, as the solution to his problem. All his needs could be satisfied in a minimum of time and under one roof. He sluiced his coffee cup and saucer beneath the tap, and dusted the toast crumbs from the table on to the floor. He felt rather pleased with himself.

He had to feel something. Pleased with himself. Or worried about something. Or immersed in the case in hand – today it was Arsenal and Everton supporters who had had a vicious go at each other on an underground station – to stop himself falling into the abyss of thinking about Caroline. He did think about Caroline. He allowed himself ten minutes a day after he had got into bed. He would lie against the pillows, adhering still to the left side, as if it were not quite right to infiltrate into territory which was not his own, stare at the cheval glass on the far side of the bedroom and recall her.

The difficulty he had been encountering was that, no matter how hard he tried, he was unable to picture Caroline other than in her last weeks. He had spoken to himself severely. Commanded himself to dwell upon Caroline on holiday, stalking the brent goose or the black-headed gull; Caroline as mother, manhandling the twin pram – Chelsea and Penge had been born within eleven mortifying months of each other – up the steep hill to the Heath; Caroline as author, burning the midnight oil over her *Birds of Passage* now translated into fifteen languages including Urdu; Caroline in the kitchen, straightening up flushed from the cooker with some succulent meat or familiar pudding between her oven-gloved hands; Caroline as lover, tender and intuitive; Caroline as friend, turning her attention from the winter flight of turnstone or widgeon to her husband, as he unloaded some legal quandary on to her broad shoulders.

Try as he would however, channel-hopping like mad through the stations of his mind, he was unable to tune into anything but Caroline's last illness. The recurring picture he received was of the day before she died. The last time she had spoken to him. Chelsea had gone down to the kitchen to make tea. Two previous cups, cold and white-scummed, stood untouched on the night table. Topher had thought Caroline was sleeping and had watched her gaunt face with a fragmented heart.

'Topher?'

It was no more than a whisper, a rush of air from the pillow. He wasn't quite sure whether his name had in fact been uttered at all.

'Topher?'

He crossed to the bed and sat on it, next to the thin stick that was

10

Caroline's arm. Again the rush of air. And on it something about it being Saturday. Words he could not quite catch. He inclined his head towards hers, stroking her hair.

'It's only Thursday, my love.'

'*Sad* . . .' Caroline said, making an effort.

'Sad?'

'Don't be,' she sighed.

But it was she who was sad. A tear escaped from the corner of one closed eye and trickled lazily, tracing a crooked path down her face.

'White walls,' she whispered suddenly. And then more quietly still as Chelsea came into the room with the tea, 'White walls.'

Topher looked at the stripe of the once biscuit-coloured wallpaper. Caroline had never liked white walls.

Chelsea put the tea down. 'I think she said "iced water".' She held a glass to her mother's lips but Caroline turned her head away.

'It sounded like white walls to me.'

But they never discovered whether it was 'white walls' or 'iced water' because Caroline did not speak again. Only opened her eyes, in which there seemed to be no message, no final communication, to look at Topher for the last time before she slipped into the coma from which she did not awake.

White walls. After so many years together, it was all he had to cling to.

There was nowhere to leave the car in the vicinity of Marks and Spencer. Topher had to be in court by nine forty-five at the latest and had no time to crawl round the block in search of a meter. Casting a furtive eye up and down the mews, he parked on a yellow line. Socks first. That shouldn't take long. In search of them he made his way through Pure New Wool Suits Made in Italy in the midst of which, even at this early hour, foreign visitors were deciding upon the length of a sleeve or the cut of a cloth.

'Excuse me, Miss.' Topher stopped a girl whose cream overall bore the Marks and Spencer logo, patterned in blue and red. She turned towards him and looked past his right ear.

'Alison!' she shrieked.

Topher looked round.

'Alison!' This time louder. 'Alison. AlISON. ALISON.' An ear-splitting crescendo. 'Can I borrer yer tape measure?'

Over the shoulder of the coloratura he noticed the sock section. He was making his way towards it when he realised that he had no idea

11

what size he wore. Socks, like lavatory paper and light bulbs, had been one of the minutiae he had left to Caroline. He hadn't realised that there had been so many of them. He decided to go for colour rather than composition, and vainly searched the fixtures. A girl (Alison?) was flicking the shelves with a feather duster.

'Do you have any socks in black?' Topher asked reasonably.

'Not if they ain't there.'

'Will you be getting any?'

The feather duster continued its dance.

'You can try next week and we'll know if they're coming in or if they ain't.'

No wonder the teachers were striking for more pay, Topher thought, if this was the material they had to deal with. He picked up a three-pair pack of grey socks as being the least discordant beneath his court attire. Unwilling further to distract the young lady, who clearly did not like to be diverted from her dusting, he infiltrated deeper into the store – wondering as he did so what manner of man wore boxer shorts bedizened with Mickey Mouses – searching for someone who would take his money. Two assistants, arms akimbo, seemingly concerned with neither tape measures nor feather dusters, stood in the aisle.

'Where do I pay?' Topher held his socks aloft.

'. . . it wasn't triplets she was 'avin' . . . it was twins . . .'

Lucky girl, Topher thought. Just then he spied the cash point, which was manned by what appeared to be a perky twelve year old wearing a dot of a diamond engagement ring.

He stood directly in front of her in an attempt to capture her dreamy eye.

'Queue this side, please!' The stentorian tones came surprisingly from one so slight.

Topher looked round for the other customers. There was no one to be seen. Not wishing to upset someone patently doing her job – albeit with an excess of zeal so early in the morning – he obligingly walked the length of the counter and faced smartly about.

'Woz it cash or woz it charge?'

Topher's money and his socks were summarily wrested from his grasp. He watched, mesmerised, as an instrument was slid along the bar-code, and a toccata and fugue played on the buttons of the till. The nymphet delved beneath the counter, from which she produced a slippery green carrier-bag into which she inserted the socks, tore off

12

the ejected receipt on which there seemed to be sufficient data for a degree in higher calculus, counted out change and thrust it into Topher's hand.

'There you go!'

Topher wondered where exactly. Clutching his purchase and feeling sympathy for the fiancé, whose future clearly would be no bed of roses, he asked the little madam, in the split second before she returned to space, if she would be so kind as to direct him to provisions.

The food department was brightly lit, like some fluorescent Hades. Prime cuts of meat, continental *pâtisserie*, exotic fruits and unfamiliar vegetables, filled the cornucopiae of the shelves. Picking up a basket Topher joined the tide of shoppers moving trance-like among the displays. He tried to dismiss the thought from his head that every year millions of children died of hunger-related causes, and that over one-fifth of the world's population was undernourished. That the situation was due to politics rather than economics he was well aware. He doubted whether the *pâtés* or the persimmons, the monkfish or the *moules*, which he by-passed in search of tea-bags, would do much to relieve it.

A woman, inconsiderately trailing a trolley at right angles to her body, obstructed his path to the food cabinets. If he didn't get out of the place soon he was going to be late for court. The case could not of course be heard in his absence but tardiness was against his principles. When the access was clear, he loaded his basket and hurried across to the tills before each of which several people waited. He wondered if he should find a sympathetic face and explain his predicament in the hope that he might be given priority. Deciding against it, he attached himself to the shortest line, realising too late that it was the one with the most loaded trolleys. He took it as a personal affront. As if, taking advantage of his ignorance in supermarket mores, he had been duped. He stood impatiently as the customer heading his particular queue requested Car Service. This entailed sufficient provisions for a siege being transferred, in slow motion, by a curly-haired youth, into various bags and boxes. The woman's place was taken by a pensioner, clumsily manoeuvring a shopping-bag on wheels in addition to her wire basket, who watched the flashing figures on the cash-register as her goods were rung up with the eyes of a well-trained hawk. Waiting until the grand total was arrived at, she delved into her shopping basket, removed her handbag, located her purse, and with some difficulty extracted twenty pounds. The cashier scrutinised the note, then waved it in the air above her head.

'Check twenty, Yvonne,' she demanded of her colleague on an adjacent till.

'What did you think of the trains last night?' was the unexpected response.

'Not much.' The money was consigned to a drawer. 'When I got there, there was a load of Sidcups.'

A shipment of wine and several dozen assorted items of cocktail savouries – someone must be having a party – was unloaded next. Two more to go. Topher thought that he shouldn't be more than a few minutes late. He wondered whether he ought perhaps to ditch the contents of his basket among the Buttered Mintoes and the Swiss Mountain Bars and forget the whole thing. He watched, appalled, as a cheque was written out with agonising slowness, a bank card produced from a pack which seemed to comprise every credit card known to man, and the two documents scrutinised by both the cashier, and an Inspector Clouzot of a supervisor, clearly trained to spot the counterfeitor. The transaction having proved successful, only a blonde goddess, wearing a fur coat over a track suit and tapping her foot with an impatience that matched his own, stood between Topher and the cashier. She put the 'Next Customer Please' sign in place on the conveyor belt, to separate Topher's goods from her own.

All went well, and his release seemed to be in sight, until it came to what he thought was a papaya. Unless it was a mango. The checkout girl did not seem too sure. She turned the misshapen object over and over in her hands, as if she were working out the sum of the sides of the square on its hypotenuse, and studied the price list in front of her. Holding the fruit aloft, preparatory, Topher thought, to hurling it into some imaginary goal, she let out a cry.

'D'yer mind findin' out 'ow much this is for us, Mandy?'

'Perhaps I could just . . .' Topher indicated the cash he had ready (no dilatory fumblings for His Honour Judge Osgood) before he realised he had spoken out of turn. There would be, could not be, any dispensations. A transaction in progress could not be interrupted, not without throwing the microchips, if not the entire store, disastrously out of kelter.

Mandy, he thought, whilst dribbling down the left wing with the papaya (or was it a mango?), must have gone for her coffee break, or at the very least a jog round the department.

'Ninety-five,' she announced on her eventual return, to the relief of all concerned. Action, which had been temporarily consigned to limbo, was resumed.

When it came to his turn, Topher was the very model of efficiency. He assisted the passage of his Cream of Tomato from conveyor belt to counter, receiving a glare for his pains. He tendered the exact money and smartly packed his provisions. Picking up his carrier, he resisted the temptation to look to those behind him for applause. There was nothing to it. If it were left to him he would re-organise the whole department, change the system. All it needed was a little common sense and some time and motion studies. He might write a letter to *The Times* about it, with the suggestion that a single queue, as it did in the more enlightened banks and post offices, should feed the first available cashier. Resolving on future occasions, the prospect of which he did not relish, to avoid positioning himself behind the elderly, the overloaded, or those with exotic fruit, he made his way to the escalator.

It was only when he was back at his car, beside which stood a black-stockinged traffic warden, that he realised he had left his socks at the food checkout.

'I am his Honour Judge Osgood.' He gave the warden the benefit of his smile which Caroline had referred to cynically as 'turning on the charm'.

'I don't care if you're the King of Lampedusa,' the warden said, slipping a ticket beneath his windscreen-wiper. 'You're on a yellow line.'

'I just popped in . . .' Topher indicated his shopping.

'Nine five to nine forty-five.'

'Good Lord, is that the time?' Topher removed the offending piece of paper in its plastic envelope and attempted to hand it back to the warden, who looked as if she should have been in a caring profession, or at the very least taking in washing in a laundrette.

'Couldn't you just . . .' He was about to tell her that his wife had recently died, but the words stuck in his throat.

'Not once they're written.' There was no animosity in her voice. She looked at him sorrowfully. 'You should know that.'

Chapter Three

'Good afternoon ladies and gentlemen. Welcome aboard the 14.50 King's Cross to Bradford. This train will be callin' at Doncaster, Wakefield Westgate and Leeds and is due to arrive in Bradford at 17.58. A *buffee* bar is available situated towards the centre of the train, for drinks, light refreshments, freshly made sangwiches, hot bacon rolls, alcoholic and non-alcoholic beverages . . .'

Topher had decided to accept Tina's invitation to go to Bingley. An incident had taken place before the Easter recess, a ridiculous occurrence which had unnerved him, had disturbed the equilibrium he thought he was managing to maintain so splendidly. He had to get away to somewhere he could think clearly. This no longer seemed possible in the house whose every echo whispered Caroline.

After three months he had got used to living on his own. Used, in the sense that was, of being able to tolerate it. He had not thought at first he would be able to. Before Caroline had died he had found isolation positively enjoyable. He had shut himself away in his study with *Heraclitus* or *The Odes of Horace*, while Caroline, in the bedroom, estimated the population of barnacle geese and choughs in the Inner Hebrides. He was a man not averse to his own company. He did not need people about him all the time. He could see now that there was a rider to his enjoyment of solitude. There had to be someone, another human being, in his case Caroline, waiting for one. The quality of his aloneness had changed. Hitherto he had been able to lose himself completely in the task in hand – his books or his music. Now, his concentration had a listening quality. He was conscious of the stillness in the house which would not be broken by the sound of his wife's footsteps. He had to keep an ear open, even when he was in the bath in the mornings. For the delivery of envelopes too large for the letterbox; for the clatter of the milk-float; once for the gas man, when Topher had stood obtusely, dripping on to the mat, trying to think where on earth the meter was located. Fortunately the fellow had led him down to the cellar and pointed it out, with his torch, between the Château Margaux and the Gewürtztraminer.

Topher had never had trouble in sleeping. He liked to read in bed. A thriller or detective story. Anything which took him away from the real world. Sometimes he read the Bible, in particular the Creation. He had, since his student days when he had been inspired by Descartes, come to terms with the existence of God. He had accepted that the universe was the product of one supreme, directing Intelligence. That it had not come into being either as the result of a Big Bang, or at the whim of some stick, stone or crocodile, or other deity of ancient cosmogeny. He acknowledged the genealogists assertions that Monera begat Amoeba, and Amoeba begat Synamoebae, and Synamoebae begat Ciliated Larva (and so on through Single-nostrilled Animals and Primeval Fish) until Man-like Apes begat Ape-like Men, and Ape-like Men begat Man. Until such time, however, as the scientists came up with a reasonable explanation of how man became endowed with speech, mind, soul and personality, until they could account satisfactorily for his grasp of religion, morality and ethics (or indeed of the birth of life itself), Topher was quite content to believe that the entire process was divinely inspired.

He still read at night. Without Caroline's presence, without the regular cadence of her breathing (they had been married for so long that sometimes he mistook it for his own), he found concentration hard. He would become aware of an emptiness in the bedroom which was filled not only with chairs and tables and bibelots acquired over a married lifetime but with memories. They imposed themselves between his eyes behind the half-glasses and the printed page. The most persistent and disturbing of these was the image of Caroline, with *Fisher*, or *Huxley*, or *Audubon* propped up on the bureau, amending some text or absorbed in her notes. At times Topher believed that she was actually in the room and had to restrain himself from getting out of bed in order to touch her. The prospect of encountering nothingness, as in some hideous game of Blind Man's

17

Buff, deterred him. He would apply himself with increased diligence to the reading matter at hand, only to be distracted by gurgling of the night-time pipes, a passing car, or his own obsessional ruminations.

There was no doubt that the house was now too big. Its reverberations had nothing to do with its size. Chelsea had suggested that he employ a housekeeper. She had offered to advertise for one. Topher could not tolerate the idea of a stranger sharing his roof, touching his things, breathing his air.

After the first Marks and Spencer débâcle during which he had lost both his cool and his socks, he had replenished his larder daily at the mammoth supermarket near his County Court. The effort of keeping house had, at first, appalled him. It was not so much the physical energy involved but the options which must be faced. His life was spent making decisions. Whom to send to prison, whom to evict, to whom to award the custody of a child. These resolutions were as nothing compared with having to make up his mind between the long grain and the pudding rice. It was Chelsea who suggested that he make lists of his household requirements with the result that now he was as often writing 'polyunsaturated marge', and 'washing-up liquid', as noting points of law to be incorporated in his summing up. He marvelled at what Caroline — besides bringing up the children, and lecturing, and writing and serving on committees — had done apparently so effortlessly, and certainly without complaint, for years.

Chelsea had often told him how far the judiciary was removed from the actual world. How little Topher knew of the man in the street, the man on the Clapham omnibus. In the past months the suspicion had dawned upon him that his daughter might be right. After much trial, and frequent error, his life was now running more or less smoothly. As he battled to maintain the house in some semblance of order, Arthur, who had for years looked after the large garden, had come to his rescue.

They were having their customary Saturday morning coffee in the kitchen. At the sight of the unwashed dishes, the accumulation of damp tea-towels, the drooping plants on the window-sill, Arthur — who kept his spade and his fork and his hoe polished as if they were silver — shook his head.

'I'll ask my Madge to come. You can't carry on like this.'

Sometimes Topher thought that he could not carry on at all. It wasn't so much the chores which bothered him. It was getting up in the morning to an unresponsive house, a tasteless day. Returning at night to a silence so tangible that sometimes he had the desire to shout in order to fragment it.

'Doesn't seem possible she's gone,' Arthur said, referring to Caroline, whom he had worshipped, and who had served him tea in the best china cups, like Royalty. 'She never said where she wanted the dahlias putting.'

He opened the bag at his feet.

'I fetched some wall-flowers. She liked wall-flowers.'

He looked despondently at the newspaper parcel. 'Hardly seem worth planting.'

Topher knew exactly what Arthur meant. It hardly seemed worth getting up in the morning, going to bed at night. Hardly seemed worth dressing, undressing, eating, sleeping, sitting in court, where it was sometimes with the greatest difficulty that he managed to keep his mind on the case before him. He rose from the table and fetched the whisky bottle from the top of the fridge. Arthur did not protest when Topher poured him a generous measure.

'Move, will you?'

Topher shook his head. The thought of estate agents and furniture vans filled him with horror.

The house in Hampstead, with its three floors and its gables, had been a wedding present from Caroline's mother, Lady Eskdale. Before moving to it, he and Caroline had lived in a rented shoe-box in Cheyne Walk, where Caroline had become pregnant.

'What on earth do we want such a big place for?' Topher had asked. Struggling at the Bar, he could not afford even to pay the rates. Caroline, who had inherited a considerable sum of money from her father who had died when she was a child, had taken care of everything. The house had given him stature, status. After Chelsea was born – they had christened her nostalgically after the manor in which she was conceived – Caroline had entertained anyone who could be of the slightest use in the advancement of her husband's career. Her parties, like these of Lady Eskdale, a between-the-wars hostess of some repute, became legend. Topher's name was much bandied around the Inns of Court. By the time Penge was born ('Hampstead' as an appellation being out of the question, they had stuck a pin in the map of Greater London) Topher was more or less established at the criminal Bar. Caroline turned her attentions to the proper rearing of her daughters.

She was not to blame for Chelsea's only brief flirtation with

Cambridge – Girton, following in her mother's footsteps – and her subsequent involvement in the media world where she had met her married man. Penge too had been recalcitrant. Insisting upon indulging her small talent for the stage, she had ended up living in a Hackney commune, with an extremely minor poet, while she waited for the ever elusive work. Caroline, grateful that her offspring were not into drugs or other excesses, accepted her daughters as they were. Their failure to conform to the pre-conceived notion he had of them, had made Topher less cheerful about their chosen lifestyles.

'See that programme on telly?' Arthur said, dunking his ginger-nut into the coffee.

When Caroline had been alive Topher had rarely watched the television. He did not care for the reiterations of the news bulletins, the canned laughter, the inane panel-games, the interviews and discussions with inarticulate 'spokespeople'. He found the medium inimical to conversation and that it kept him from his books. Recently he had found himself turning on the set for company.

'Which programme would that be?' Topher said, in answer to Arthur's question, although he knew perfectly well.

He had been scarcely able to believe his eyes when he had tuned in to a show inspired by the panic over the HIV virus. A middle-aged woman had stuck two fingers into a contraceptive to demonstrate to a studio audience how to put on what she referred to as a con*dom*. He had been saddened to discover that sex among the teenagers present (many of whom appeared to be scarcely more than children) was indulged in as regularly as visits to the local *pizzeria* and with about as much passion.

'With the French letters,' Arthur said. 'The boy was with us. Madge didn't know where to put herself.'

'*Fugaces labuntur anni,*' Topher said.

'Wassat?'

'"You wake up one morning and find you are old." I'm beginning to wonder if I belong any more in this world.'

'Some of them as was on telly won't be much longer for it, if you ask me,' Arthur said. 'Not with the way they're carrying on. I'd be scared stiff meself.' Arthur laughed at his unintentional joke.

'When one is young,' Topher said, 'one is inclined not to think of consequences.'

'That's what the boy said. "When you're pullin' a bird you got other things on your mind!"'

20

'Precisely.' Topher divided the remaining whisky between the glasses.

Looking round the train taking him to Bingley, he wished that he had bought a First Class ticket. The carriage was full. He was wedged into his seat between the window and an individual encased in an anorak which rustled irritatingly each time he moved, seemingly turned into a pillar of salt by page three of the *Sun*. Topher surveyed the plastic-topped table before him on which were the remains of a congealed bacon sandwich, a polystyrene cup of some ferocious-looking orange liquid, and an empty chewing-gum wrapper. Facing him, a ludicrously young mother who wore a crucifix over her tee-shirt but nothing beneath it, licked a dummy and stuck it into the mouth of her grossly overweight son. The child's tubbiness – he looked, Topher thought, like a miniature Michelin Man – was scarcely surprising given the number of potato crisps he had consumed between London and Doncaster. That the Michelin Man's name was Darren, Topher had learned before they had left King's Cross. The child had been held to the window and urged to wave goodbye to Nanny and Grandad who stood dotingly on the platform.

In order to spare himself from regarding either the dummy faced child or its gum-chewing mother, Topher turned his attention to the incident that had taken place at the Gordons and which had precipitated his flight to Bradford.

The Gordons and the Osgoods had moved in to the same street within a few weeks of each other and the two families had been friendly ever since. Marcus was a pyschiatrist, and April an interior designer (not decorator, she wouldn't have that). While Caroline had given birth to daughters, April had been delivered of four sons. It had been the fond hopes of their parents that there might be some intermarriage. The hopes had not materialised. The Gordon boys (three of whom were now scattered about the globe) seemed no more interested than did the Osgood girls in either permanent relationships or their parents' cosy expectations of them.

Since Caroline's death, Marcus had been Topher's lifeline. It was to Marcus that he confessed his anger that all about him less deserving men were holding their wives in their arms; his belief that life had been dispossessed of its meaning; his conviction that he wanted to die too. Other well-meaning people had pointed out to him the universality of his experience. The capacity of time to heal. The futility of self-indulgence. Only Marcus had appreciated that his despair was a

21

discourse to be understood, rather than a pathology to be corrected. That he stood before a mirror in which there was no reflection. That he had no self to indulge.

While he spent many evenings with Marcus, who was helping him to put together the shattered pieces of his life, Topher had avoided the Gordons as a couple. The sight of them both evoked memories of happy times together with their respective children which he was as yet unable to confront.

When Marcus had suggested that he come to one of April's dinner parties, Topher had been shocked.

'Only a few close friends,' Marcus said, aware of the hermit-like existence which Topher had recently been leading. 'You have to face up to it sometime.'

It was not so much the company that Topher wished to avoid. It was the sympathy which washed over people's faces when they heard of his bereavement, to which he had no idea how to respond. Women were the worst. They wanted to mother him, smother him.

'The longer you leave it, the harder it will become,' Marcus said. 'Look upon it as testing the water. If you want to go home early, April will quite understand.'

The appalling thing was that, despite what happened, Topher had not wanted to go home. It was this which had upset him. Which had precipitated his acceptance of the invitation to Bingley towards which the train was now accelerating.

Chapter Four

Topher had stopped on the way home from court to buy flowers for April. He rejected the daffodils which reminded him of happy times in the Scilly Isles with Caroline, looking for the grey-cheeked thrush. He found the irises unappealing. He had never considered blue an appropriate colour for flowers. The tulips were equally unattractive because of the egg-like configuration of their heads. He settled upon gerbera, imported Dutch blooms in pinks and orange, as sufficiently grand for the hearth in April's sitting-room where, in huge, hand-thrown vessels, she habitually massed her floral arrangements.

After so long on his own, the prospect of the evening had made him apprehensive. He felt like a small boy forced to go to a birthday party or as he had when, on his very first day in court in his newly acquired robes, he had been obliged to find his voice. By the time he rang the Gordons' bell, clutching the gerbera, he had stiffened his resolve with more than one nip from the new bottle of whisky on the top of the fridge.

The door was opened by John, down from Cambridge. From years of habit, as honorary uncle, Topher might have been tempted to embrace the youngest Gordon had he not been reminded of the passage of time by the boy's recently acquired beard. This luxuriant growth was a topic of conversation soon to be eagerly seized upon to dispel the awkwardness engendered by Topher's presence in the drawing-room. The assembled guests had been suitably primed. Their smiles of welcome (after which they contemplated the Chinese carpet or their shoes) had obviously been vetted for the least sign of commiseration.

Marcus effected the introductions: Robert Holdfast, a fellow psychiatrist, whom Topher knew well, whose wife Barbara was a psychotherapist; Inez (with an unpronounceable surname which she had inherited from the last of her three husbands) who was April's business partner; Peter Gordon, a cousin of Marcus' from Edinburgh, in London for a conference; and Sally Maddox, short and dumpy – a condition exacerbated by the brown, shapeless two-piece she was wearing – a fiction writer of whom Topher had not heard. Clearly anxious that any ice be broken, they exclaimed over the flowers which Topher had brought and which April was now cradling.

Inez, putting her nose into the scentless gerbera, said: 'Divine!' in an accent you could cut with a knife.

Barbara Holdfast remarked how well the colours looked against the sack-cloth curtains, and Sally Maddox volunteered how hopeless she was both with flowers and with green plants which habitually died on her (a warning glance from April). This remark seemed to exhaust the subject, whereupon April left the room in search of a vase. There was a brief hiatus filled by Marcus, together with the glass which he put into Topher's hand.

'Lamberhurst,' he said. 'Made outside Tunbridge Wells. I'd like to know what you think of it.'

Topher was not disposed to think anything. He wanted to go home to his pot noodles and *Don Giovanni*.

Robert held his glass by the foot, and the wine in his mouth for a moment.

'A Rheinhessen? Or a Rheinpfalz?'

'Not bad, Bob.' Marcus topped him up by way of reward. 'To let you into a secret, it actually comes from Muller Thurgau grapes. It makes a reasonably provocative apéritif, don't you think?'

Topher had nothing constructive to offer. He thought that Marcus had left the wine for too long in the fridge. He said: 'Very pleasant.' And then repeated it. 'Very pleasant.' Which seemed to knock the Lamberhurst on the head.

There was a long silence, broken desperately by Peter from Edinburgh who addressed his nephew.

'How long have you had those whiskers?'

Before John could answer, his father broke in with: 'Too lazy to shave.'

24

'It hardly seems reasonable,' John said affably, 'to waste one hundred and fifty days of your life removing hair from your face.'

'It's part of the image . . .' Marcus tweaked his son's beard with ill concealed pride '. . . like going to India in a Land Rover.'

Glancing surreptitiously at his watch, Topher realised that he had an entire evening to get through. He should not have come.

At dinner April sat him on her right, next to Sally Maddox. He was glad to have been spared Inez who always came on so strong that one felt compelled to flirt with her. Peter Gordon, sprung temporarily from his wife and children, had the honour of her attentions. From the expression on his face, as he held her chair for her, it did not look as if coping with Inez was going to be too much of a chore. John (who would have put his mother's table out) had not been invited to join them.

Taking in the *mise en scène* over which April had, as usual, taken considerable pains, Topher realised both how hungry he was and that he had not eaten at a properly set table since Caroline's death. He had of course dined both with Chelsea and Penge, neither of whom subscribed to the theory that '*le plaisir de la table commence par celui des yeux*'. They both derided the complexities of bourgeois cutlery and were not in the least concerned with formal seating arrangements. Dinner at Wapping consisted of Chelsea aimlessly wandering in and out of the warehouse kitchen (divided by an Edwardian birdcage from the living-area), unwrapping whatever she had bought at the delicatessen on her way home from the BBC. By the time they actually sat down at the table, on which Chelsea, almost as an afterthought had slung some knives and forks, Topher had lost his appetite. A breathtaking view of London's docklands, together with the mournful sounds of the tug-boats, did little to compensate for the cold or re-heated dishes (frequently still with the price on) which were Chelsea's idea of a meal. Penge, in her commune, took nutrition more seriously. Her wholefood concoctions seemed to be composed largely of pulses, however, which gave Topher indigestion.

April's polished table, the colours of the floral centrepiece matching those of the Limoges china, compensated for the Lamberhurst. Topher felt himself responding to the visual stimuli and hoped that Sally Maddox could not hear the rumbling of his stomach. Caroline had been an excellent cook but, unlike April, not artistic. Her tastes had been simple. No sprigs of parsley, no radish roses, no slices of kiwi fruit. She was not beguiled by *nouvelle cuisine* with its warm salads (in her book a contradiction in terms) and preposterous conglomerations of seasonal vegetables. If her guests didn't like the spinach or sprouts that she gave them, that was their problem. She would serve them a generous plate of smoked salmon, a perfect chicken (roasted with a bundle of rosemary), and a little cheese. There would be linen napkins, and wine, in big plain glasses, to complement the food. Caroline never made a fuss. April's menu would, Topher knew, be more ambitious. She did not begrudge spending half a day on a sauce and had been known personally to eviscerate mallards.

'Oh good, pudding!' Peter Gordon said, making them all laugh. 'I get depressed when there are no dessert spoons.'

'Not much chance of that here,' Barbara Holdfast said. 'There will be an *embarras de* puddings, if I know April. Probably at least three.'

The first course came on an oval silver platter: An arrangement of sliced hard-boiled eggs on a bed of *frisée*, topped by Mediterranean vegetables. The dish, with its outsize serving spoon, was passed round the table. It was followed by a basket of rolls. Helping himself to three curls of butter, Peter put a hand to his stomach which lapped comfortably over his belt.

'I'm supposed to be dieting. Don't tell my wife!'

In the silence which followed, everyone avoided looking at Topher.

Marcus leaped up to fetch the decanter from the sideboard. It was while he was circumventing the table, filling the glasses, that the incident occurred.

Topher held the dish, with its lattice of red and yellow peppers, while Sally Maddox helped herself. Then Sally Maddox held the dish for him. He was just wondering how much of the *hors d'oeuvre* one could reasonably take without appearing greedy, and whether there would be sufficient to go round, when she said softly: 'Marcus told me you have recently lost your wife.'

Topher felt a constriction in his throat which prevented him from replying.

'You must be very sad.'

Topher nodded. It was rarely that one's feelings in the matter of bereavement were acknowledged. The subject was either studiously avoided or tactics employed which were designed both to take one's mind off the event and save the questioner from embarrassment.

Topher replaced the serving spoon on the platter which he held aloft. He passed it on to April who was looking anxiously round the table. It was as he relinquished the cumbersome oval of silver, that he

26

felt a hand slide beneath the napkin on his lap, investigate his private parts through his trousers and briefly, but unmistakably, clutch his balls. In the nick of time April rescued the dish from his grasp. Topher turned to Sally Maddox, who was calmly buttering her roll.

Marcus filled his wineglass. 'Château La Courolle. From the Montagne St Emilion area. Quite a decent little chap if you allow him to relax for half an hour.'

Eyeing the Château La Courolle with suspicion, Topher thought that he had perhaps been affected by something in the Lamberhurst. You could not really trust an English wine made from German grapes grown in the wrong climate. Perhaps he had had an hallucination brought about by pollutants. Additives such as dried blood, ferrocyanide and gelatine had all been recently detected in certain wines. He stole a glance again at Sally Maddox in her brown, with her brown hair scraped back into a falling down arrangement at the back of her head. She was tasting a forkful of yellow peppers. When she'd finished her mouthful she turned towards him. He was almost too abashed to look at her. Her glance was open, friendly, as if she had nothing to hide. Perhaps he had, after all, been imagining things.

Sally Maddox put a hand on his arm and leaned towards him conspiratorially. Topher shrank back. He dreaded to think what was coming.

'I wonder,' her whisper was intimate, 'if I might trouble you for the salt.'

He had no recollection of his plate being taken – perhaps he had even handed it to April himself – or of the next course being served. He found that he was addressing a portion of oriental chicken on a bed of saffron rice. The conversation was gyrating about his head.

They were discussing the Common Market's agricultural policy, with which Peter Gordon, an investment banker, seemed to be involved.

At some other time perhaps, Topher, aware of his obligations to sing for his supper, would have contributed to the discussion. As it was he was too stunned. He hoped that his host and hostess would put his lack of concern for the butter mountain down to his general loss of interest in the world about him, a direct result of his recent misfortune.

It was not the fact that he had been groped by Sally Maddox that bothered him – he had rejected the idea of hallucinations – but that the result of this affront to his person was still uncomfortably evident.

It was unbelievable. Such a thing had never happened to him. Certainly not at a dinner party. He tried to keep track of the small-talk while he sorted out the conflicting sensations assaulting his brain, which were a direct result of the assault upon his person.

His first reaction was one of shame, as if he had betrayed Caroline. As if he had defiled her memory when she had only been dead three months. His second thought was one of surprise at his own prompt response. His first thought about his second thought was to tell himself not to be so dishonest, so hypocritical. There seemed, as he had discovered over the past weeks, to be a direct association between grief and desire. He had been meaning to discuss it with Marcus.

Nothing had been further from his mind than sex during the weeks of Caroline's illness. The morning after her death he had woken in his lonely bed with an unambiguous desire for it. The longing had not been for his wife but for relief. The fact that his flesh was outside his control did not please him. He was a controlled man, one of Her Majesty's judges, and it distressed him to think that, while he was directly responsible for the lives of others, he was not in command of himself. Apart from with Muriel Mills, he had not been unfaithful to Caroline. It upset him to think that, while eating his saffron rice, he was being disloyal to her memory.

Returning his attentions to the table, Topher discovered to his horror that the subject now under discussion was 'genitalia and sexual selection in the animal kingdom'. He wondered whether it had been arrived at subliminally, as a result of the ordeal to which he had been subjected a few moments before. He grew both increasingly ill at ease and conscious of the presence of the unpredictable lady on his right, as Marcus informed the table that, while some flies rejoiced in penises which were larger than the rest of their bodies, the male spider – like the male seahorse – did not possess a penis at all.

Applying himself to his pudding – Barbara Holdfast had been right, there was a *tarte au citron*, a passion fruit sorbet and a redcurrant mousse – Topher listened, with morbid fascination, whilst willing the discussion to take a less sensitive turn.

Marcus was just getting into his stride. One theory for the evolution of complex genitalia in the animal kingdom, he said, was that male and female structures had a lock and key relationship. This ensured that, for purely mechanical reasons, individuals could only mate with a partner of their own kind. He was expounding on the sex-life of the moth, whose organ carried an elaborate file and scraper that rubbed together to produce a vibratory stimulus heard by the female through her genitalia, when April said: 'Really, Marcus, you can't expect us to believe that *that's* where moths keep their ears!'

Against the general hilarity which greeted her remark, April enquired if anyone would care for some more of the sorbet before she put it back in the freezer. While she was in the kitchen, Topher, glad that Marcus had been deflected from the mating habits of animals by his desire for a second helping of passion fruit, turned to his outrageous companion.

'Marcus says you're a writer.'

Sally Maddox raised a hand. Topher flinched. Surely she wasn't going to assault him again in front of the whole table which had gone suddenly quiet. To his relief the hand was merely to silence him.

'I work every morning for three hours, in accordance with Trollope's prescription, and the ideas just come.'

She had answered the question before Topher had voiced it.

'It's a writer's catechism. Doesn't the law have one?'

'When I was at the Bar I was required to explain how it was that I could defend one fellow against another, even if it was the second who was in the right. These days I get asked for my qualifications to sit in judgement. There are none, of course, and I don't. My task is simply "to interpret law and not make or give law".'

'Psychiatrists are confused with mind readers,' Marcus chipped in from the sideboard where he stood with a bottle of Rémy Martin in his hand. 'People either clam up completely, or expect me to know what they're thinking. I sometimes wish I were a shoe salesman.'

'I am confronted with a scrap of material,' Inez said, 'from which I am expected to suggest which colour should be "picked out". Colours should *meeeld* . . .' She made a cadenza of the word. 'They should have to do with the perssonality of the house.' She leaned close to Peter and put her hand on his arm. 'Tell us about investment bankers, darlink?'

'Get-rich-quick tips. I wish I knew some!'

'Writers always get the shitty end of the stick.' Sally Maddox shocked Topher for the second time. 'People sink their teeth in to you and never let you go. They think they have only to know what sort of paper you use, and whether you write with a pen or a pencil, to be able to do it themselves.'

'Do what themselves?'

April retrieved the fag end of the conversation as she came in carrying the coffee pot. 'Don't tell me we're back to moths again!'

Chapter Five

Looking out of the window of the train as the sheep and pastures of the English landscape flashed rhythmically by, Topher thought that that had all been three weeks ago. In the time which had since elapsed, the memory, like a recurring fugal subject, had rarely been far from his mind. He had been so disturbed by the indignity which he had suffered at the hands of Sally Maddox that, when he went to bed that night, he had had to take one of Caroline's sleeping pills. The effect of the drug had not worn off when he set out for court next morning. He had switched on the radio in the car to keep himself awake. The statement that the *seckertary* of state had just announced the trade figures which the *goverment reckernised* were a reflection of wider market forces, provided just the irritant he needed.

Penge called him a pedant. He supposed he was. He could not tolerate the current misuse of English, a direct result of an educational system which had produced a generation unable to parse and, *a priori*, to construct the simplest sentence. He appreciated that the days when Greek or Latin verses flowed from the lips of national leaders were long past. Now, cut off from their own language and literature, even those in high office perpetrated grammatical bloomers which would have once disgraced a schoolboy. Pronouns were misused, metaphors mixed, and participles left to hang. Solecisms, such as those he had just heard, together with *contempory, ecksetara, grievious*, and *mischievious* (none of them to be found in the English dictionary) were commonplace.

He had tried to convey to his younger daughter that he was not opposed to linguistic change. In his own lifetime he had seen the transmogrification of such words as *gay* and *swing* and *shoot* and *snort*, not to mention the introduction of the dreadful *Ms* which sounded more like the drone of a bumble bee than a form of address. It was ignorance he railed against, a direct result of the neglect of classical studies which closed the doors to so much of European language, literature and culture. Common abberrations betrayed a disregard of root and source by many of those – including his own daughter – who might have been expected to know better. While Topher shuddered at Penge's misapplication of prepositions – 'bored of' and 'on the week-end' – she countered with the archaic frills and superfluous curlicues employed in his court. Why did barristers (counsel) kick off with the obsequious 'If Your Honour pleases' rather than a cheery 'Good morning, Judge'? Why were they bound to *make submissions* rather than present arguments? Why did they defer to opponents as *learned friends* when they were about to put the boot in? Why, Penge wanted to know, apart from the *aforesaids, heretofores* and *thenceforths*, was the judge himself addressed 'with the greatest respect' when what followed indicated that in the opinion of the speaker he had not understood the first thing about the case?

Topher tried to keep count of the number of inaccuracies he was able to detect in the course of a single news bulletin, but his mind kept returning to April's dinner table and to Sally Maddox. What remained of the evening following her abuse of him passed in a blur only partly induced by the Rémy Martin, a second glass of which he had accepted as the treatment of choice for the shock he had sustained.

When the farewells were said, Sally Maddox had kissed him on both cheeks with the demureness of an ice-maiden. He seriously wondered once again if he had imagined the whole episode.

Arriving at his County Court he felt his gall rise at the sight of a van parked partially across the space reserved especially for him. He realised, not for the first time since his widowhood, that he would have to watch himself. He was operating on an extremely short fuse.

He nodded curtly to Registrar Wilmslow whom he met on the stairs, and grunted when his usher, a widow who rejoiced in the name of Mrs Sweetlove said: 'Good Morning, Your Honour,' as she set down his apple juice together with his neatly folded copy of *The Times*.

'There's a van in my space, Mrs Sweetlove!' Topher said, although it was not strictly accurate.

'I'll look into it right away, Your Honour,' Mrs Sweetlove replied in her 'nanny' voice, not at all put out by his petulance. He had noticed a change in attitude in everyone since his wife had died and he wasn't at all sure that he liked it. People humoured him – Registrar Wilmslow and Registrar O'Donnell, the clerks of the court, Miss Fletcher and Miss Roderick – no matter how displeased he was with them. And Mrs Sweetlove, her eyes brimming with understanding, for whom he was now able to do no wrong. He did not care for their solicitude, their overt sympathy. He would rather they had treated him as if nothing had happened. He would not then have been reminded at every moment of the day of the unoccupied house to which he must return, the aching chasm in the region of his heart.

He glanced at *The Times* Law Reports and the current *Law Society Gazette* for a possible mention of his name. Finding that he was not really paying them a great deal of attention, he hoped that it was not a sign of age. Despite Plato's contention that a good judge must not be a young man but an old one, Topher had no intention of staying on the Bench until he was as senile as some he could mention, who should long ago have accepted their pensions and been put out to grass.

He opened the cupboard in which he kept his robes and stood before the long mirror inside the door. 'Years as they pass plunder us of one thing after another.' Horace, as usual, had put his finger on it. Topher's hair, retreating only a little from his high forehead, was still only lightly, and not unattractively, feathered with grey. The dimple in his chin which had, on Caroline's own admission, been her undoing, was still in evidence. He stood over six foot in his socks and carried no superfluous weight. A cursory glance, in not too strong a light, could he supposed have placed him at the tail end of the fifties instead of at the very beginning of the sixties. Sally Maddox . . . No he must definitely not. He removed his jacket, put it on the hanger provided by Mrs Sweetlove, and took off his tie. With the disappearance of suitable laundries he had been reduced to paper collars. Madge had undertaken the starching of his white bands. Pulling in his stomach he noticed, for the first time, the tell-tale bags of misery beneath his eyes. He shrugged on the black gown of his office, tied the purple sash, and set what, according to Penge, was the symbol of legal pomposity, his horse-hair wig, firmly on his head.

On the stroke of ten Mrs Sweetlove knocked on the door to enquire if he was ready.

Following her figure, neat as usual, from the curls the colour of autumn leaves to the high-heeled black sandals (on what must once have been elegant, but were now somewhat varicosed legs), Topher felt the customary surge of adrenalin as she opened the door that led to the dais.

He had never got used to it. Not even after twenty years. The deferential silence. The sight of counsel prostrating themselves. The rising of the court, which then waited until it pleased him to be seated. The high and indisputable drama of the moment was, he imagined, shared only by the conductor mounting his podium, Her Majesty the throne. It was the daily fix which liberated an exquisite energy, sharpened the faculties, focussed the mind and, for the time being at any rate, banished Sally Maddox with her brown eyes and her brown dress, from Topher's thoughts.

The first case, a possession order, was brought by counsel whose frizzy hair erupted haphazardly from beneath her wig and was only partially restrained by a tired black ribbon. Sloppy demeanour in court, whether of barristers or solicitors, vexed Topher more than did incompetence. The girl reminded him of Penge. There was absolutely no reason why Penge should not have followed some proper profession, instead of messing around with the stage and ending up in a Hackney commune. The only acting part she ever seemed to land was that of an old peasant, on a proscenium empty except for a table holding three earthenware jugs, in an auditorium strewn with dirty washing. What dreams he had had for his daughters who had both been seduced by the curious restlessness endemic to the age.

Chelsea, unable to face three years at Cambridge (having almost bust a gut to get herself accepted) had bummed around the world for two years with a monosyllabic pop star with designer stubble and cowboy boots. Topher had to take her word for the fact that beneath his shoulder-length hair lay a scintillating brain. The pop singer's parting gift to Chelsea, when they 'split', had been an introduction to the inner echelons of the BBC. There, on the rebound, she had fallen hopelessly for the producer of *This Week's News* who had been her lover – although Topher was not at all certain he was the only one – ever since. When she had brought David Cornish home, Caroline was so impressed with him that she had immediately begun to make plans for the wedding. It was as much a shock to Chelsea as it was to her mother to discover that there was a mentally unstable wife (as well as two children) whom her paramour could not leave. It was difficult to say who was more disappointed. Even Topher, who privately considered no prospective son-in-law adequate, had been able to find no fault with David. With the one proviso, he made Chelsea very happy. The arrangment was neither neat nor tidy but it was the best they could all do.

Penge, since her performance as a Flowerpot Man in the kindergarten play at the age of five, had always wanted to be an actress. With the success of her dramatic rendering of *How Horatius Held the Bridge*, wearing a frilly pink party dress, her fate had been sealed. She had finished school, torn up her UCCA forms, and applied to RADA. Unable to dissuade her, Topher had reluctantly agreed to pay for her training. Since her graduation, and the acquisition of her Equity card, Penge's life had been a series of theatrical ups and downs matched only by her affairs of the heart. Before the minor poet there had been a zoo keeper, a hospital porter (Penge had had her appendix removed) and a trombone player. There had been others who either had not lasted sufficiently long, or had been too disreputable to bring home. The minor poet was harmless. Which was about the most charitable thing one could say about him.

Topher looked into the blue eyes of the tadpole of a barrister who stood before him. She belonged to a generation which not only addressed its superiors by their Christian names, but came to work looking as if it had just rolled out of bed. She was representing a landlord. Mr Biswas, who was trying to evict his tenant, one Mr Archibald. Topher waited patiently as Mr Biswas, clutching the Koran like a terrified rabbit, stumbled through the oath. His counsel riffled frantically through her brief in the manner which Topher had learned to associate with the fact that she had never clapped eyes on it before. She addressed her client.

'Are you the er owner of er . . . number . . . 39 Clarendon Road, N18?'

While Mr Biswas considered his answer Topher leaned over the Bench to address the clerk of the court.

'May we know counsel's name?'

'Miss Devanney, Your Honour.'

Mr Biswas' reply to Topher's question was inaudible. He held a hand to his ear in the manner which Caroline always said made him look like a very old man.

'Kindly address your replies to His Honour,' Miss Devanney said, indicating the Bench.

Mr Biswas, blinked through his pebble glasses and nodded uncomprehendingly.

'Face in this direction, speak up, and address your remarks to me,' Topher said loudly.

'Are you the owner of number 39 Clarendon Road, N18?' Miss Devanney was more sure of herself this time.

Mr Biswas smiled at Topher.

'Please?'

Topher sighed. It was going to be one of those mornings. These days it didn't take much to provoke him. He had a mild headache with which he had woken, due he supposed to the excesses of the previous night. The boring sensation above his right eye was exacerbated by the pressure of his wig. He listened, making notes as he did so, while the grizzled haired Mr Archibald (in the two mismatched halves of his suit) related, with eye rolling histrionics, how he had been minding his own business in the privacy of his room, when he had been summoned by his landlady, *Mrs* Biswas, to her parlour. On entering he had to his amazement been served not with the nice cup of tea he had anticipated, but with a 'notice to quit'.

Poor Mr Archibald had nowhere else to live. All he asked for was time to find another place. Granted all the time in the world, Topher knew, given Mr Archibald's age and his lack of employment, it would not be easy. But Mr Biswas wanted him out. He had served him with the proper notice. Topher gave Mr Archibald two weeks to find alternative accommodation. Mr Archibald looked crestfallen, Mr Biswas unbearably smug. Miss Devanney gathered up her papers, which were as messy and all over the place as she was herself, and bowed to Topher. Acknowledging her, he drew a line beneath *Biswas and Archibald* and noticed, to his horror, that he had written *Sally Maddox* in the margin of his red notebook.

The next case was an application by the local authority for possession of a flat unlawfully occupied by two sixteen year olds, Sarah Scott and Sandra Bishop, one with green hair and the other with pink. Aware that but for the grace of God it could have been his own daughters who stood before him, Topher disabused the girls of their right to occupy the premises. When he gave them an opportunity to speak, Sarah Scott pointed out that she didn't see why the council couldn't give them a flat when it was dishing out homes 'right, left, and centre to the Pakis', and Sandra Bishop added that they had come down to London from Newcastle and had nowhere else to live. Topher told them that much as he appreciated their situation, homeless people could simply not be allowed to move into, and retain, other people's property. The law of the land must be upheld. He explained that he was not a housing officer and that he had no control over lettings (which were a matter for the council) and advised them as a last resort to apply to their local Citizen's Advice Bureau. His suggestion, intended to be helpful, was received with derision.

The morning stretched before him. He listened to the petitions of authority against those who defied it. To accounts of breaches of contract and domestic violence. Although conscious that the scales of justice were often weighted in favour of the few against the many, he did his very best to adjudicate fairly between those in power and those who felt themselves to be exploited. Despite himself, he found that he snapped at counsel for feeding him piecemeal with scraps of paper instead of providing him with a proper bundle of documents, chastised the clerk of the court for not obeying his instructions sufficiently smartly, and rebuked a surprised solicitor who was wandering around the court whilst the oath was being taken. When Mrs Sweetlove smiled sympathetically at him as she handed up a bulging folder, he glared at her too. He didn't want her sympathy. Nor Sally Maddox's. Nor that of any other bloody woman. He wanted Caroline. Sometimes he pretended that she was not dead and almost managed to convince himself.

When the court rose for lunch, Mrs Sweetlove led him into his room where, as if it were to be a five course banquet, she set the table for his tub of cottage cheese.

'I've had the vehicle removed, Your Honour.' She smoothed the creases from the tablecloth.

'The vehicle?'

'From your parking space.'

Topher had quite forgotten about the van. He wished that Mrs Sweetlove would end her messing about and be gone.

'A bit better today,' she said, fetching what she referred to as 'the cruet' from the cupboard.

When Topher didn't answer she said equably: 'The weather.'

Mrs Sweetlove was not averse to carrying on conversations with herself.

She stood back to survey her handiwork. To see if there was anything she had forgotten.

'I remember this time last year . . .'

'That will be all, Mrs Sweetlove.' Topher hung up his robes and buttoned a navy-blue cardigan over his shirt. 'I can manage nicely now.'

'Very well, Your Honour. I'll leave you in peace and quiet.'

Topher doubted if his usher knew the meaning of the phrase or if, when Sweetlove had been alive, there had been much peace and quiet in the Sweetlove household.

Over lunch he read the papers for a breach of contract case which he was to hear in the afternoon. At four o'clock he went home, which was of course a euphemism suggesting the fixed residence of a family or household, the place of one's dwelling and nurturing. He made his way, more precisely, to his house, which over the past months had taken an oath of silence.

Opening the front door on to the forsaken hall, the table piled with junk mail but innocent of the seasonal flowers (cultivated or wild) which had always greeted him when Caroline was alive, he was glad to hear the ring of the telephone. He took the call in his study, sure that it must be Chelsea or Penge.

It was Sally Maddox.

Chapter Six

Rural England had given way to cabbage-filled allotments at the backs of houses all seemingly fashioned from the same drab plasticine. In another five minutes the train was due in Bradford. Preparations for arrival were already being made. Opposite Topher the rubber limbs of Darren were being inserted by his mother into a yellow snow-suit. From the monologue which accompanied this feat (which clearly required both skill and dexterity) he deduced that the child, having bidden farewell to one set of grandparents at King's Cross, was being taken to see their northern counterparts. Each time the child's arm was directed to the sleeve of the garment – survivor by all appearances of a million drubbings in the washing-machine – he made a grab for the empty crisp packet on the table. Darren's mother smiled conspiratorially at Topher. Topher, as if having in mind the acquisition of one of the grim properties that lined the railway track, looked pointedly out of the window.

The last person he had expected to telephone him was Sally Maddox. He couldn't think how she would have the gall. But there she was. As if less than twenty-four hours previously she had not laid her hand upon the most intimate region of his anatomy.

'Christopher?'

It was a lifetime since anyone had called him that. Topher recognised her voice at once.

'Isn't it a wonderful day?'

Shades of Mrs Sweetlove.

'I don't suppose you've even noticed. What are you doing on Saturday?'

She didn't wait for him to answer.

'I'd like you to come for tea.'

It was not a question.

'I live in Kentish Town.'

He had no intention of accepting the invitation. He could not imagine why he had written down the address on the back of *Counsel*.

Apart from April's dinner party, Topher hadn't been anywhere socially since his bereavement. Not even to close friends. He had certainly no intention of visiting Sally Maddox in Kentish Town where – if past form was anything to go by – he might not only be given tea but violated.

He had discussed Sally's behaviour with Marcus, who clearly believed that Topher's mind, affected as he himself suggested by either the Lamberhurst or the passing of his wife, had been playing tricks on him.

'I assure you,' Topher said, casting his mind back both to the incident and his reaction to it, 'that I did not imagine it.'

April was unable to shed much light on the situation. Sally Maddox was an old schoolfriend. She had, until recently, lived in the country.

'She has been married, and she was hopeless at hockey. We re-met at Swiss Cottage Library. Apart from having read her books I know very little about her.'

'What does she write?' Topher suspected that beneath the deceptive brown exterior beat a Mills and Boon heart.

'Novels,' April said. 'Of great sensitivity and imagination. You must have dreamed the whole thing. Perhaps it was the yellow peppers.'

He did not go to tea with Sally Maddox. She telephoned every few days to renew the invitation. She also wrote to him. On postcards from the Tate Gallery (*Woman in a Tub*, which was, Topher suspected, a reasonable facsimile of herself in the nude) and the Rijksmuseum.

The fact that he was beginning to look forward to Sally's calls troubled him. He confessed as much to Marcus.

'One part of the mind frequently judges the behaviour of another.' Marcus said. 'It's nothing to worry about.'

But Topher did worry. And decided to get out of London for a few days. He contacted his twin sister in Bingley, and as soon as court rose for the Easter vacation made his preparations.

The suitcases were in the attic among memorabilia of his married life. Skis, and dusty picnic baskets taking him back to outings when it seemed always to have been raining; a carriage pram which Caroline had, with her usual optimism, saved for her grandchildren (it would create a mild sensation in Wapping); surplus gifts from Caroline's bazaars and jumble sales; warped tennis racquets of the out-dated wooden variety; lamps without shades and shades without lamps; a lacrosse boot; skates; grocery boxes of files – 'O' levels and 'A' levels – which the girls had abandoned but must not be destroyed.

Penge had come round when, with his open suitcases, he was standing bemused before his wardrobe. She had slung a few shirts and ties and pullovers into the case he had brought down. On top of them she put his shoes. She did not take after her mother in attention to detail.

'It will do you good,' she said, referring to his proposed trip. Topher realised that what his younger daughter meant was that it would do her good. That she would not have to worry about him. With Caroline's death he had become a liability.

Penge was dressed in black – trousers, oversize shirt, black kerchief over her hair and down to her forehead – which emphasised her fragile beauty. They were not mourning clothes. She wandered round the bedroom lightly touching the things that were her mother's. Her collection of paper-weights, her Indian pin-cushion, her bird-watching diary. Penge's eyes met Topher's wondering how long everything was to remain just as Caroline had left it. Penge picked up a postcard – an El Greco from the Museum of Fine Arts in Budapest – of the Holy Family with Saint Elisabeth in which Mary offered a luminous breast to the Christ Child. On it, Sally Maddox had written enigmatically, 'Our father's house really does have many mansions.'

'Who's this from?'

'A friend.'

There was an alabaster statuette – a little girl, holding a teddy-bear – on the window-sill, an artefact of the twenties. It had belonged to Lady Eskdale, who had died before Penge was born. Penge held it out, an unspoken comment on the postcard.

'May I have this?'

'Of course.'

41

Penge, as the youngest, had been closest to her mother. Topher put his arm round her.

'Are you all right, Daddy?'

'As well as can be expected. You?'

'The same.'

Tears welled in the eyes of both father and daughter. Penge's overflowed on to Topher's shoulder.

'Bloody hell,' she said, 'I have to go.'

'Are you working?' Topher asked, back on safe ground.

'Not actually at the moment but there's a very good chance.' She blew her nose into an inadequate pink tissue. 'I met this guy who's putting on this Lorca. They're auditioning next week.'

Topher could not understand how it was that she was able to continue fooling herself. It was not the moment to tell her. The train, as if it would be thankful to reach its destination, trundled wearily through the outskirts of the station. Darren, now incarcerated securely in his snowsuit, stared at Topher. Wondering whether Tina had come to meet him, Topher stared back. Although they were twins, Chris*tine* having preceeded Chris*topher* into the world by fifteen minutes (a fact which in their early years Tina had never allowed him to forget), Topher and his sister were unalike. As a child, knowing no fear, he had made the more timid Tina's life a misery. He had pushed her into the deep end of the swimming pool where she had almost drowned – leaving her with a lifelong fear of the water – put spiders in her bed at home, and jelly-fish down her back on holidays where he was the self-crowned king of the sandcastles. Notwithstanding his youthful ill-treatment of his sister, he was extremely fond of her, as she was of him. He had been disappointed both by her decision to marry at the age of eighteen, and her subsequent removal to 'foreign parts', just when he had been looking forward to renewing her acquaintance after his years away at school. The separation had become more than geographical as they met less and less frequently. They had been briefly reunited by the deaths of their parents, but the drift apart had been exacerbated by the passing of time.

Next to Topher, the man in the anorak was folding his newspaper into an impossibly small rectangle. He stowed it into his pocket, leaning against Topher as he did so and crowding him even further into his corner. The guard, in his red-trimmed uniform, swayed through the carriage, glancing proprietorially from right to left.

Topher stood up to get his coat. The train lurched. Darren's mother smiled at him.

He looked along the platform, with which they were now level, but he could not pick out Tina, whom he had last seen at Caroline's cremation. He realised that he was looking for a slim red-head, and readjusted his mental sights.

At the barrier a plump, outdoor-looking woman, with short grey hair, waited anxiously. Her eyes were the same hypnotic blue as Topher's. Tina's embrace expressed the empathy the two had always felt.

In the car they caught up with the news. From the back seat a black labrador licked Topher's ear.

'It's Miles' sixtieth birthday on Saturday,' Tina said. 'We're having a party. Is that all right?'

Topher sought to reassure her.

'Of course it is.'

'How have you been?'

Before Topher could answer, Tina put her hand on his arm. In view of her erratic driving he would rather she had kept it on the steering wheel.

'It was a stupid question.'

Miles and Tina lived in a prosperous suburb. The West Yorkshire lawns, embraced by carriage drives, were green and manicured. In front of the house, the dog, anxious to get out, leaped across Topher.

'Laddie!' Tina said, as he went to lift his leg against the chestnut tree.

'Bloody dogs!' Topher was not enamoured of the species.

Tina switched off the engine and ruffled Topher's hair as she had done when it was as red as her own had once been.

'You haven't changed.'

Neither of them had. One didn't. You could not mess about with genes.

The evidence of tender loving care in Tina's house, brought home to Topher the recent signs of neglect in his own home. Tina had made the curtains in the bedroom to which she showed him. She had covered the cushions on the window-seat against which Evelyn's dolls still leaned.

Topher opened the suitcase Penge had packed and gave Tina the Belgian chocolates he had brought, remembering her weakness.

'You shouldn't encourage me.' Tina hugged him, then stood back with her hands on his shoulders. 'Stay as long as you like. Feel free. Miles will be in soon. I'm going to see to dinner. Why don't you have a rest?'

Topher did not want, suddenly, to be left alone in this room which did not belong to him.

'I'd rather come and talk to you.'

'Fine. I'll make you a cup of tea.'

She saw Topher's face fall.

'There's some Scotch in the sitting-room. You know the way. Help yourself when you're ready.'

When she had gone, Topher questioned the wisdom of his decision to come to Bingley. He disliked staying with people. Apart from the strange beds and unfamiliar bathrooms, it imposed restrictions and inhibitions. He looked round at the cushion covers and the dolls and wished he was at home in his study where each evening in sought solace amongst his books. Shakespeare with his facility to illuminate the darkest secrets of the human soul; Cicero who believed (but did not manage to convince Topher) that nature, having so wisely distributed to all other periods of life their peculiar and proper enjoyments, had not neglected to endow the last act of the human drama with similar advantages; Horace with his Alcaic metres. Sometimes he feared he was in danger of becoming a recluse.

Tina's sitting-room looked out onto the garden. It was redolent with Tina's colours, yellow and blue, reflected in the furnishings. A half-completed tapestry lay on the sofa. Tina's reading glasses were on the coffee table on top of the novel she was reading: *An End to Dying*. Recognising the quotation from Montaigne, 'Death is but an end to dying,' Topher picked up the book, turning it over. Sally Maddox's face, the untidy hair falling over it in wisps, stared at him from the jacket. He put the book under his arm and found the whisky bottle.

Tina was preparing dinner. The dog followed her with adoration as she crossed and recrossed the kitchen. Topher noticed with surprise that his sister's movements were no longer those of a young woman. He remembered that dining with Tina, who had little idea of time or timing, was inclined to be traumatic. There was none of Caroline's efficiency or April's panache. 'Calamity Jane' had been their private name, his and Caroline's, for Tina for whom invariably the toast burned, the meringues wept, and the *soufflés* failed to rise. Topher could have coped with all that, were it not for the fact that at the moment he thought he would die – either of frustration or starvation

44

– if the meal were not served, Tina would rush out into the garden and pick the spinach. Topher had only the vaguest idea of vegetable patches but hopefully, he thought, it was too early for spinach.

Tina was opening all the drawers in the kitchen units one after the other and peering into them as if she were taking the inventory.

'Scissors . . .'

'Can I help?'

'. . . I doubt it.'

The scissors were on the table, partly buried by a tea-cloth. Topher handed them to her. Followed by Laddie she snipped herbs from a pot on the window-sill.

Topher showed her the book.

'Is this any good?'

'I've only just started it.'

He flipped through the pages.

'What's she like?'

'Sally Maddox? I read everything I can lay my hands on. There's always a waiting list at the library. There are so few people these days one cares to read.'

'May I borrow it?'

Tina looked at him doubtfully over the tomatoes she was extracting from a paper bag.

'I think Miles put some reading matter in your room.'

'I've met Sally Maddox.'

She was not only pursuing him but had followed him to Yorkshire.

'She must be a lovely person.'

Topher would not have used exactly those words to describe what he knew of the author of *An End to Dying*.

Tina tore the basil leaves into tiny pieces. 'I hate buying them. Help yourself.'

Topher assumed that since Tina grew her own, the first remark related to the tomatoes and the second to the book. He picked up the whisky bottle.

'Hang on,' Tina said, 'I'll find you a glass.'

Topher opened a cupboard.

'*I'm* supposed to be looking after *you*.'

'Tina, I'm not ill.'

His sister put a heavy tumbler on the table.

'It's a garage one. We use them in the kitchen.'

Tina, notwithstanding her abortive comings and goings, long

45

moments when, engaged in her narrative, she forgot what she was doing, brought Topher up to date with her children and grandchildren. By the time Miles came home (Laddie jumping excitedly to attention several minutes before he put his key into the door) the meal had, miraculously, been assembled.

Although Topher had little in common with Miles he was extremely fond of him. As his brother-in-law came into the kitchen (followed by Laddie who welcomed his master with a series of little jumps and hand-lickings), his first words were for his wife.

'Hallo, sweetheart.'

The warmth of their embrace, after so many years, made Topher feel both superfluous and sad.

Miles wore a heather-green suit made, Topher guessed, from cloth woven in his own mills. When he'd released Tina he turned to Topher. The pressure of the welcoming arm he put round his brother-in-law's shoulders indicated the depth of the feelings he was unable to put into words.

'Well,' he said, 'how's His Nibs?'

Sitting between the two of them, eating Tina's steak-and-kidney pie – while she rose from the table to fetch the salt and the wooden salad-servers and the rolls which she had put into the oven and forgotten about (and which were only slightly charred) and the extra gravy – Topher felt even more isolated than he had at Marcus' and April's.

'I hear they're thinking of making Your Worships work a bit harder.' Miles (who had been upstairs to put his slippers on) said, over the cognac in the sitting-room. Tina, who had refused offers of help, was attending to the dishwasher in the kitchen.

'I wouldn't say no,' Miles went on, 'to knocking off at four. With eight weeks off in the summer *and* an index-linked pension at the end of it.'

'There was a time when judges never sat more than *three* hours a day. They employed the rest of their time in refection.'

'Refection?' Miles raised his eyebrows.

'Eating and drinking. In mitigation I must say that the work we do is highly concentrated. It's very exacting. It's questionable whether a judge could actually absorb more if he did sit a longer day.'

'I daresay it must be a bit of a strain, being a living oracle,' Miles said, not unkindly. 'But what about the delays? What about the age it takes to get a case heard? If I ran my business along those lines, I'd be bankrupt in no time.'

'I'm not saying that there isn't room for improvement.'

Topher explained some of the proposals which had recently been made to enhance the functioning of civil justice.

Over coffee (Tina going back to the kitchen for the sugar, then the spoons) they discussed what Miles said was the British Establishment's unshakable belief in its own infallibility, and the perennial problem of unemployment in West Yorkshire. Tina picked up her tapestry. Miles sucked at his pipe and read the newspapers. He quoted little snippets aloud for Tina's benefit. When it was time, as if it was a ritual, he turned on the television news. Topher was glad when he could decently excuse himself from the domestic scene, without appearing rude, and retire to Evelyn's room.

He had just removed his shoes and his tie when Tina tapped at the door.

'You forgot this.' She put *An End to Dying* into her brother's hand.

Chapter Seven

Topher lay in Evelyn's bed. The first night in Bingley, fearful that he would suffocate, he had slept only fitfully beneath the duvet, which threatened to obstruct his breathing but left his feet exposed to the elements. The feather-filled monstrosity had led him, in one of his few unconscious moments, to relive Caroline's cremation, in a re-enactment in which he was both onlooker and corpse.

The day of the funeral had been sunny, but cold enough to make Topher glad, in a way, that his wife was being cremated and that he did not have to leave her beneath the sod. Her wishes had been specific. She had made Topher promise. That her mortal remains would be consigned to the flames. Her ashes scattered amongst the birds she so loved. Preferring regular cemeteries and gravestones, where you knew what was what (who was where, Chelsea said), Topher had, with reluctance, agreed to do as Caroline had asked. His wife's was the first cremation he had witnessed.

The chapel had been filled with flowers, as it had been with mourners. Although the immediate family was not large, Caroline had had many friends. Topher had chosen the music. He smiled wryly as he remembered that Caroline had been tone deaf. Verdi's *Requiem* for her departing and Beethoven's *Ode to Joy* for what he hoped, but did not believe, was the world to come. There had been a moving address by Caroline's brother. The stillness of the congregation, while Mathew Eskdale's carefully chosen words were being delivered, testified to the fact that his sister had played a significant part in the lives of those who had come to pay their last respects. It had been like an earthly version of the Last Judgement. True worth was tested and revealed for all to see. As he listened to the proceedings, Topher had tried to take his mind off the coffin (adorned with the single rose he had placed upon it) in which he had had his final sight of Caroline. Her ravaged face had been serene in death and he had been unable to convince himself that she lay other than in an untroubled sleep. He did not want her to be burned, incinerated like so much rubbish disposed of by Arthur in the garden. He did not think he would be able to tolerate her annihilation. He had put his arms round the rigid Chelsea and the tearful Penge, who stood on either side of him in the front row of the chapel, for support. The moment when, with a small grinding sound, the doors flanking the bier were opened and the coffin began its mechanical slide, had recurred often and vividly in his dreams.

On his first night at Tina's it was his own remains which had, in his slumbering fantasy, been substituted for Caroline's. As he fought to avoid his descent into the inferno, he had woken relieved to discover that it was the quilt from which he had struggled to escape rather than a wooden box. He was glad that he had come to Bingley. To get away not only from the torment of his home and the attentions of Sally Maddox, but from his preoccupations. The week had gone by quickly. One of its more positive aspects had been the opportunity to renew his acquaintance with his sister. Outnumbered at home by Caroline and his militant daughters, it had been comforting to discover that the tentacles of feminism had not yet reached this particular backwater of Yorkshire. His sister was the archetypal woman. *Kirche, Kinder, Küche*. Except that Tina didn't go to church. On her shoulders she took the burden of house, dog, husband, children and grandchildren – roughly in that order – and looked at Topher with uncomprehending eyes when he suggested that, just occasionally, any or all of them might be left to fend for themselves.

Evelyn and Jane seemed similarly deaf to the seminal reverberations of the women's movement. He had accompanied Tina on visits to their houses which were replicas of her own. Both the young women were dressed neatly, like their mother, in recognisable sweaters and skirts, rather than in the bundles of rags affected at similar ages by Chelsea, and even now by Penge. The welcome his two nieces gave their uncle was warm. Topher shuddered to think what might confront Tina where she to present herself unexpectedly at the

Wapping warehouse or the Hackney commune. Evelyn, married to a dentist, had twin babies in the Osgood tradition. She served her visitors coffee, not in mugs but in china cups and saucers, set on a tray, with a teaspoon for each person. Afterwards she took Topher proudly out to the garden to show him her greenhouse. Jane – whose husband, John, was working his way up the ladder in his father-in-law's business – had one five-year-old daughter whom Tom had fetched from nursery school. Both Evelyn and Jane enquired warmly after their London cousins, but tactfully avoided any reference to their late Aunt Caroline. There was an old-fashioned simplicity to life in Bingley, where Tina still paid weekly visits to the local hairdresser and the shopkeepers called Topher 'love'. The highlight of the visit had been Miles' birthday party at which Topher had met Lucille.

He had come downstairs on the Saturday morning to find preparations in hand for what Miles – who had sensibly escaped after breakfast to the golf course – referred to as a 'slap-up do'.

Feeling superfluous, and anxious to get out of the way of Paula (of Paula's Pantry according to the van in the drive) who had taken over the kitchen, Topher took Laddie, with whom he had come to some kind of mutual agreement, if not understanding, for a long walk. As Laddie bounded after the skylarks and meadow pippits, startling them into flight, it was inevitable that Caroline, never far from Topher's thoughts, addressed him from the grave. Not that she had one of course. A fact about which he was none too happy. He would have preferred some specific spot, some stone engraved with her *curriculum vitae* which he could see and touch from time to time, rather than the open spaces of Hampstead Heath where, in a macabre ceremony he preferred not to recall, he had scattered her ashes in accordance with her wishes. Alone on the Yorkshire moors, wearing Miles' waxed jacket against the howling wind, he heard his wife's voice as clearly, as conversationally, as if she strode beside him. She told him that, just because birds were able to fly, he was not for a moment to imagine that they were free to go where they pleased. They were creatures of habit, and restricted to a particular area by the need for food and shelter. Caroline's ecological studies and her easy familiarity with the countryside had contributed to her skill as bird watcher. In the area they were in now, Topher thought (as Laddie in his element covered twice the ground he did himself), the birds would be those endemic to grass moorland; merlin and golden plover, wheatear and dunlin, red grouse and partridge. Unless perhaps they belonged to heath or bracken. He was not quite sure. Busy with his own thoughts he had never paid all that much attention to the diatribes which accompanied their walks, as Caroline, by his side, rattled on. Well, she wouldn't rattle on any more.

He called Laddie who was bounding away into the distance, disappearing almost over the horizon, leaving him alone on the vast expanse of West Yorkshire terrain. Stumbling over a pothole he swore an unaccustomed oath. He had a sudden longing for the rubbish strewn streets of London with their familiar smell of diesel, where you were not in danger of ricking your ankle every minute.

'Oh God, Caroline!' he cried aloud to the panorama. 'Why did you have to die?'

In an attempt to keep himself out of Tina's way while preparations for the evening were in progress, Topher took himself to a pub for lunch.

By the time he got home with the inexhaustible Laddie, much of the sitting-room furniture had been carried out to the garage and the house had been transformed. The formality of the arrangements – gilt chairs and the expanse of parquet flooring where the rugs had been removed – reminded Topher of the parties Caroline had once given, another world ago, in the Piano Room for Chelsea and Penge. A party in Bingley, it seemed, was exactly that. In London, as far as he could make out, the term now seemed to cover any gathering in which more than two people and a bottle were involved. Invitations, anticipating replies, were unheard of (as were even the most cursory gestures of gratitude) and more than one of these get-togethers might be, and habitually were, visited in the course of an evening. In view of the lack of specific declarations of intent, it puzzled Topher how people knew where that particular night's action was to take place. Invariably they found their way to it. Tina had sent out jokey invitations (on which were depicted fizzing champagne glasses and coloured balloons) with enclosed reply cards.

She knocked on Topher's door as he lay resting on the bed with *An End to Dying*. Following Sally Maddox's assault upon him, he had been expecting a novel in the modern idiom in which areas of the body were described in anatomical detail (reserved hitherto for medical textbooks) and the sex act awarded a diversity which defied the most liberal imagination. Instead he had found a well structured story in which the passion of the protagonists had been handled with both delicacy and wit.

51

Tina was wearing a blue silk dressing-gown brought back by Miles from one of his many trips to Hong Kong.

'May I come in?' she said when she was already in the room.

Topher put down the book and removed his reading-glasses.

'I'm afraid I didn't bring a suit,' he said. 'I had no idea . . .'

'I didn't tell you.' Tina sat on the bed. 'I thought you might not have come.'

'Caroline always packed for both of us. Penge just . . .'

'You'll be fine in your sports jacket. Everyone's looking forward to meeting my brother the judge.'

'The pain *fort et dur*,' Topher said, recalling the Gordon's dinner party. 'I can't stand everyone feeling sorry for me and not knowing where to look.'

Tina took his hand.

'I shan't say anything about time being a healer.'

'*Haec olim meminisse iuvabit*. Time heals all wounds.'

'One just has to accept changes.'

'I knew there would be no platitudes from you.'

'One must be realistic. I think you're doing jolly well. I just wish you lived nearer so that I could keep an eye on you. How are you getting on with the Sally Maddox?'

'I'm impressed.'

'I thought you would be. Tell her how much I admire her, when you see her . . .'

'I don't suppose I shall be doing that.'

'. . . and to keep writing.'

Dressing for the party Topher realised that he was being deliberately slow. He brushed his teeth in the manner prescribed by the dental hygienist (a squeaky-clean young lady with an unbelievably wholesome mouth) and attended to his nails with the same meticulousness which had often driven Caroline to distraction. In Evelyn's bathroom – the tub adorned with the grandchildren's ducks and fishes – he stood shaving until his face was sore, and listened to the sound of the doorbell and the exchange of greetings from the hall. Back in the bedroom he selected a shirt and tie (without reassurance from Caroline as to their suitability) and polished his shoes with a dirty handkerchief and his glasses with a clean one. He straightened the duvet, putting Sally Maddox on the night table, from where he thought for a fraction of a second that she winked at him, and practised his smile in Evelyn's mirror which pronounced it false. He needed a drink. That was the main problem. But in order to get it he must go downstairs. He buttoned his sports jacket over his stomach and lifting his chin made for the door.

At the bottom of the stairs, before he could reach the bar, he was waylaid.

'You must be the judge! We've heard ever so much about you from Tina, it's a pleasure to meet you.'

'Very proud of her brother, is Tina.'

'My nephew is a lawyer in London. I don't suppose you've come across him?'

'Come to see how the other half live, have you?'

'Tina told us about your wife passing away. We'd like to offer our condolences.'

'Play golf, do you?'

'When your sister throws a party, you know it will be the best in Bingley.'

'We've known Miles and Tina and the girls of course . . . How long is it now, Cyril?'

'Tina must love having you up here. She won't want to let you go.'

'I had an *Anty* in Hampstead. *Fern* . . . something or was it *Rose*? I don't suppose . . . no you wouldn't really. Anyroad she moved to Canford Cliffs a while back.'

Topher declined the champagne proffered on a silver tray by Paula, and made his way to the trestle-table manned by her husband, a bull-necked barman in a white coat.

He asked for whisky. Ahead of him a pin-thin woman in a yellow dress, with a diamond like a small cauliflower on her vermilion-tipped hand, was being served. When she turned round, holding a glass of wine, which was clearly not her first, it was impossible to ignore the fact that the dress, made of some shiny material and sequinned at the wrists, was slit almost to her navel.

'You must be Topher. We've all been dying to meet you. I'm Lucille. I expect you've been warned about me. I'm looking for a husband to add to my collection.'

'How many have you had?'

'Including my own?'

Topher accepted his whisky from the barman. Lucille held her glass to his.

'It's too boring. Tina — we play bridge — told me your wife had died. Let's sit down and you can tell me about her.'

They made their way to a pair of gilt chairs set at right angles to each other in a corner. Topher found himself in the bizarre situation of sitting next to a total stranger, trying to keep his eyes from her cleavage, while he explored in some depth his relationship with Caroline. He couldn't think what had come over him. Against the hubbub of the room, assisted by the whisky, he treated the streaked-blonde Lucille, whose one gold-braceleted ankle swung nonchalantly against the other, to an only slightly expurgated version of their life together.

'I honestly don't know why I'm telling you all this.'

'I can't keep a thing to myself . . .'

Topher had been on the Bench long enough to know that she was lying.

'. . . I don't believe a word of it anyway.'

'No?'

'You've made it sound like a moonlit trip down the Grand Canal in a gondola. Anybody who's ever been married could tell you that, ninety-nine times out of a hundred, it's hell on wheels.'

'That being the case, why do you want another husband?'

'Look at the alternatives, love! It's not exactly a load of laughs being on your own.'

Thinking about it later, Topher thought that she was wrong and that his marriage to Caroline *had* been like a moonlit trip down the Grand Canal in a gondola. He was unable to say as much to Lucille, however, because just at that moment silence was called for and Miles' dentist son-in-law took the floor.

Listening to the speech eulogising Miles, Topher felt suddenly as isolated as he had on the Yorkshire moors. Lucille had left him to make her unsteady way to the bar. He stood up with everyone else and was surprised when the words of 'For He's a Jolly Good Fellow' came from his own lips as if from the mouth of a stranger.

Miles responded to the kind things said about him by his son-in-law. With patent sincerity he declared that any happiness he might feel on this day was due entirely to Tina. It was Tina who had given him his dear daughters, Evelyn and Jane—who in turn had presented him with his three grandchildren—Tina who had cared for him in sickness and in health, not to mention the times when he came home bad-tempered from the golf course (pause for laughter), Tina who was his sun and his moon and his stars. Looking round the room Topher met the cynical glance of Lucille as she drained her glass and turned back to the bar.

By the time supper was served Topher was pleasantly drunk. He did not in the least mind explaining to the group of Miles' friends, in to the bosom of which he had carried his salmon *coulibiac* and his garlic bread, the difference between the Crown Court and the County Court, and the fact that it was a High Court – and not a Circuit – judge who went on circuit.

Lucille collared him as he stood at the dessert table. The waitress asked if he would care for some sherry trifle. Lucille enquired whether he would like to go to bed with her. He said yes to the sherry trifle, and no to Lucille. He spent the rest of the evening defending the current sentencing procedure to a charming, but cynical, solicitor who felt strongly that too many lenient sentences were doled out by judges fearful of their chances of promotion.

When all the guests and Paula, together with her Pantry, had departed, Miles and Tina, carried out a post-mortem among the presents which had been left in the morning-room. Molly Collins wasn't looking at all well; Walter and Rachel Bosworth hadn't been heard to say a civil word to each other all night; Harriet Middlebrook had over-indulged in the sherry trifle and had had to be taken home, and Frank from the golf club had been found in an alcoholic stupor in the best bedroom, flat out amongst the coats.

As his sister and brother-in-law sat on the floor and exclaimed over the books on gardening, and the photograph frames, and the boxes of golf-balls and the initialled handkerchiefs, Topher excused himself. The sight of their faces as they wished him goodnight, testified to at least one moonlit trip down the Grand Canal. Lucille, in her yellow dress, with her cynicism, had been understating the case.

Chapter Eight

There were three postcards waiting for him from Sally Maddox. Manet's *Déjeuner sur L'Herbe*: 'Rang but no reply? Are you all right?' *Odalisque with Tambourine* (Matisse): 'Presume you are away. Why didn't you tell me?' and Picasso's plump-thighed *Grand Baigneuse*, with a postmark from Ireland where Sally Maddox had gone to research her new novel. She didn't say when she would be coming back. Topher felt rejected by her departure just when he had made up his mind to discuss *An End to Dying* with her.

Tina had driven Topher to the station and seen him into his First Class seat. He was taking no chances on another Darren.

'I can't thank you enough,' Topher said. 'I feel quite human again.'

'It's getting away from The Smoke. It's a wonder you aren't all asphyxiated down there. Come and see us again. Miles loved having you around. We don't need any notice.'

Topher drew his twin sister to him.

'Don't be alone, love,' Tina said.

With his mind on Sally Maddox and clutching her postcards, he had taken his suitcase upstairs and stopped at the threshold of his bedroom. Something was different. It took him a few moments to realise what it was. Caroline's things had gone. Her *Guide to Bird Seasons* and her diary, her bird sketches and binoculars. Putting down the suitcase, Topher went slowly towards her wardrobe knowing what he would find. It wasn't only the garments which were missing, the coats and cardigans which he would have been hard put to describe. Trying to be helpful, Chelsea and Penge had disposed not only of Caroline's personal effects, but the last tangible vestiges Topher had of her. Dresses and blouses, imbued with her aura, which during the past months he had been known to hold to his face for comfort. Closing the cupboard with the gentle solemnity of an undertaker, Topher felt more bereaved than he had at the cremation. The coda of Caroline's passing was more poignant than the actual song.

He was startled by the telephone bell and guessed that it was Sally Maddox back from Ireland. It was Chelsea. Hoping he didn't mind about the clothes. It had to be done. Oxfam had been delighted. Penge was in Germany, auditioning for a small part in a television play. How was Bingley?

Abhoring the vacuum, Topher hung a few of his suits in Caroline's cupboard to ease the congestion in his own. Feeling like a traitor, he put them back again. Only to transfer them a few minutes later with a stern admonishment to himself that he must now make a positive effort to come to grips with a life in which he was categorically on his own.

By the time the new Law Sitting started there had been no word from Sally Maddox. He had grown accustomed to her postcards, of which he now had quite a collection, and was disappointed at their abrupt cessation. The mail, which he picked up eagerly from the mat every day, turned out to be nothing more than the daily ration of unsolicited letters, bills, and the odd note of condolence from the further reaches of his acquaintance to open up the wound.

He spent one morning in Bond Street where he bought a Hermès scarf for Tina and a ship's decanter from Asprey's – a belated birthday present – for Miles. What remained of the Easter recess he passed closeted with his solicitor while they thrashed out the details of Caroline's estate; catching up with his reading; walking – he missed Laddie and thought semi-seriously about getting a dog; debating the wisdom of dry-cleaning the loose-covers in the drawing-room with Madge; talking to Marcus; and taking his daughters out for dinner. Penge (who had not got the German TV part) insisted on a wholefood restaurant where they sat on hard chairs and ate from blue-glazed pottery bowls. Chelsea, who talked about little but her David, opted for the plusher comforts of the Gay Hussar.

The first weeks of the new term he was sitting at Southwark. His splendid room in the Crown Court was a far cry from the utilitarian quarters of his County Court which were themselves luxurious compared with some of the disreputable facilities to be found on the north-eastern circuit. The English judiciary was not well catered for. A visiting colleague on an American Judges Convention had been amazed to discover that, unlike his USA counterpart, the British judge was not only expected to work in some of the most antiquated accommodation in Europe, but was provided by Her Majesty with neither personal library, secretary, nor legal assistant. Topher had to write his own letters and his judgements. He had to make do with the services of his *éminence grise* at his County Court, and Mr Squeers at Southwark. Squeers evoked a Dickens character in manner and appearance as well as name. Thankfully he made no attempt to mother Topher as did Mrs Sweetlove.

As he walked with his rolled umbrella and his brief-case from the underground station, past the London Dungeons and the Cathedral, Topher thought how relieved he was to have something to fill the unoccupied corners of his mind. Although the criminal hearings – where apart from taking detailed notes he had to keep quiet most of the time – were less distracting than the civil cases, he was glad to be back at work.

Outside the courts, contractors, busy with the remodelling of Hay's Wharf, were mixing cement. Picking his way over the planks, Topher opened the door at the rear of the red-brick building. A security man, whom he had never seen before, sprang, like a uniformed Jack-in-the-box, out of his cubicle.

'Judge Osgood,' Topher said.

He could just as well have said Yasser Arafat.

The security man touched his hat.

Topher took the lift up to the third floor and walked along the corridor so thickly carpeted that it never failed to remind him of a superior hotel. Through the picture-window of his room he had a clear view across the Thames of the new Lloyds building and the Port of London Authority. A carton of apple juice, a bottle of mineral water, and the luncheon menu waited for him on his desk. He removed the copy of *Private Eye* from his brief-case, hung up his umbrella, and rang the bell for Squeers.

Squeers, pudding-faced and obsequious in his black gown, wrung his hands and trusted that His Honour had had an enjoyable recess. He then imparted the unwelcome news that the Crown Prosecution Service had failed to produce a police officer whose statement was a *sine qua non* of the first case.

'Where *is* the police offcer?' Topher asked.

'According to the clerk of the court, Your Honour,' Squeers said, reminding Topher of nothing so much as a horse as he pawed the carpet with his feet, 'counsel for the prosecution instructed the CPS last night that they must produce the witness at 9 o'clock this morning . . .'

'It is now five minutes to ten!'

'. . . unfortunately the CPS instructed Sergeant Bullock to come to court at 10.30.'

Topher picked up the telephone on his desk.

'This is Judge Osgood in Court Six. I want to speak to the person in charge of the Crown Prosecution Service. What do you mean, there's no one available? There must be *someone*. Well, get Miss Walsh up here immediately!'

While he waited impatiently for Miss Walsh, Topher studied the menu. In Southwark, luncheon was served formally in the Judges' Dining-Room. Judge Doughty-Smith, flanked by his sycophants, always took the high chair. Topher put neat ticks beside mushroom soup, fried fillet of plaice and chips, steamed swedes, and plum duff with custard, and handed the menu to Squeers.

Miss Walsh, from the Crown Prosecution Service, knocked timidly at the door and came apprehensively into the room. She said she was unable to produce the missing police officer for the very good reason that it was her first day in the job and she knew nothing whatever about the case. When she had gone, looking as if she was about to burst into tears, Topher made a telephone complaint about the gross inefficiency and negligence of the Crown Prosecution Service. He dismissed the impotent Squeers with instructions to apologise to the jury, and settled down with *Private Eye* while he waited upon the pleasure of Sergeant Bullock.

He was reading a snippet about a fellow judge who had been stopped by the police on his way home in his Volvo at three o'clock in the afternoon, found to have blood alcohol levels two-and-a-half times over the legal limit, and fined and banned from driving, when Squeers sidled once more into the room. Sergeant Bullock had arrived.

'I suppose we shall now have to wait while he makes his statement,' Topher said impatiently, hoping that by keeping his nose clean he would never find his way into *Private Eye*.

'I've told counsel that the judge in Court Six is about to blow his top,' Squeers said.

59

Topher, who was about to do no such thing, let the exaggeration pass. He looked out of the window at the grey rigging of *HMS Belfast* which was moored beneath it.

'Tell the jury we won't be long.'

It was eleven o'clock before Squeers preceded Topher, in his scarlet sash, into Court Six and called imperiously for silence. In his nasal monotone, on a single breath, he opened the proceedings.

'AllmannerofpersonswhohaveanythingtodobeforetheQueen'sJusticesdrawnearandgiveyourattendance. God Save The Queen.'

The case concerned the alleged attempt by the accused to steal a lady's handbag from a public house in Covent Garden. Harry Andrews, in his defence, said that he had taken a mini-cab from his home in Acton, to the pub in Covent Garden, in order to meet a girl, who was to give him some clothes to take to a friend in Ashford Remand Centre. When the girl did not show, he had stayed in the bar for only two minutes before returning to the mini-cab. Before he could reach it he was – to his complete astonishment – not only arrested, but assaulted, by Sergeants Bullock and Quinn. They nicked him for 'doin' 'andbags', a misdemeanour for which he had, on his own admission, been sent down on two previous occasions.

The girl, who also lived in Acton, declared on oath that she had arranged to meet Andrews in Covent Garden (rather than pop round the corner with the clothes) because she thought it 'would be nice'. She failed to turn up for the rendezvous because she was watching television and 'forgot'.

Sergeant Bullock described in ponderous detail how he had observed Andrews take up his position against a pillar in the Public Bar. How he had placed a hold-all (covered by his raincoat) on the floor next to a lady's handbag. How he had been about to draw the handbag into the hold-all, when he spotted the police officer (whom he recognised) and hurriedly left the premises.

Andrews' own description of the incident was decidedly more graphic.

'. . . what 'appened then. 'e pushed me against the wall, right? Grabbed me bag out of me 'and, right? "Bollocks," 'e said, "there's nuffin' innit." Wiv that, 'e grabbed me scarf and started to strangle me. "I know you," 'e said, "I've nicked you before, for car 'andles."'

Andrews' additional complaint, that he had also been roughed up by the police – "it on the right eye and me arm twisted' – for smoking in his cell at Wormwood Scrubs, held up the case considerably. A statement, taken from the prison doctor, concerning his injuries, was agreed, and instructing the jury to return promptly at two o'clock, Topher adjourned the case for lunch.

By the time he arrived on the second floor, wearing a black silk mess jacket over his bands, most of the other judges (a few of whom he knew well, some by sight, and others not at all) were assembled. He collected a tomato juice (he did not like to drink in the middle of the day) and helped himself to a handful of dry-roasted peanuts. He nodded to Roger Sopforth, an active campaigner against jury challenges, and 'Killer' Kershaw, renowned for the severity of his sentences, and gravitated towards the window where grey gulls glided gracefully out of the grey sky towards the *Belfast*. Arthur Critchley, who had been up for his circuit judgeship at the same time as Topher, appraised Topher's drink then looked at his own glass.

'Wish I could keep off the stuff.' He followed Topher's gaze towards the swooping gulls.

'Your wife, is it not, Osgood, who's the authority on birds? I recall readin' . . .'

Topher recalled freezing winters watching the white-fronts at Slimbridge. Bewick's swans on the Ouse Washes. Bean geese in an unmentionable part of Norfolk. Brent at Wells-next-the-sea.

Critchley was waiting for an answer.

Topher nodded.

'My wife died.'

'Good Lord,' Critchley said, 'I say, I *am* sorry. I had no idea. Put my foot in it.' He raised his empty glass. 'Can I get you another?'

'Not for me, thank you.'

Topher watched Critchley's retreating back.

At luncheon, at the long table presided over by Doughty-Smith, he found himself sitting next to the only female in the room. She introduced herself, as she picked up the roll on her side-plate, as Jo Henderson, a stipendiary magistrate.

'Topher Osgood.' He passed her the saucer with its foil wrapped squares. 'Would you care for some butter?'

Topher had always considered lady magistrates (from whom he didn't exclude the professionally trained 'stipes') all to be cast from the same mould. Jo Henderson with her boyish black hair, her

61

black dress buttoned seductively at the rear and set off, quite charmingly he thought, by her white bib, made him revise his opinions.

'I do like it at Southwark.' She fixed Topher with a pair of large green eyes and leaned away from him as the waitress set a dull-looking salad, topped with a dollop of mayonnaise, before her. 'It's so civilised. Sadly this is my last day here. Next week I shall be sitting in a Sunday school, and will have to robe in full view of the court.'

'I would like it here too – ' Topher inclined towards her, receiving the full blast of her perfume, while his plate of mushroom soup was positioned ' – were it not for the diabolical inefficiency of the Crown Prosecution Service.'

He recounted the morning's *contretemps* which had tried his time and patience, not to mention the time and patience of the jury. Overhearing his comments, Their Honours on the right of him, and opposite him, and even further along the table, joined the discussion. The concensus seemed to be that if the Civil Servants who manned the CPS were adequately remunerated they might be more attentive to their task.

'If we had to work forty years before we saw our pensions,' Doughty-Smith said, looking down upon the company from his high-backed chair, 'we mightn't be so enthusiastic about manning the department either.'

He removed a smoked-mackerel bone from his mouth and leaned across the fruit bowl.

'Splendid letter in *The Times* this morning, Sopforth. When I was called to the Bar no one would have even dreamed of exercising the right to challenge the members of a jury. The situation is getting quite out of hand.'

'If I had my way,' His Honour Judge Sopforth said, 'I'd do away with peremptory challenges altogether. A jury, after all, is supposed to be twelve good men and women chosen *at random*. Once you begin to argue about who is qualified and who is not, you diminish the random quality.'

His Honour Judge Godber rolled bread-crumbs into grey pellets. 'The whole business of challenging anyone who looks in the least well turned out – or even marginally intelligent – is based on the misconception that important human truths come only from the mouths of the socially deprived.'

'Surely *one* peremptory challenge would cover the remote chance that someone might have a grudge against the defendant?'

The speaker was His Honour Judge Barley-Brown who was known not only to read the *Guardian* but to ally himself with the Social Democrat Party.

Further discussion of the challenging system was prevented by the arrival of the main course, to which the company, with a proper concern for priorities, turned their attention.

The advent of the pudding separated the men from the boys. As Topher tucked into his plum duff, Jo Henderson, who had helped herself to three grapes and was peeling them, looked at his plate and said: 'Bet you don't get that at home!'

Topher thought of the individual puddings, composed largely of chemicals, which he spooned each night from their plastic pots.

'No.'

Tired of pity, he refused to expand further. He glanced at Jo Henderson's elegant pink-tipped hand on the fourth finger of which was a gold wedding band. She was too quick for him.

'I'm a widow.'

Surprised into confession by her honesty, Topher said: 'So am I.'

Jo Henderson had been a solicitor. Her husband, a judge, had drowned in a yachting accident at Cowes. Topher remembered reading about the tragic incident in the newspaper. He recalled that the wife, trying to save her husband, had almost drowned herself.

It was after Henry's death, Jo said, that she had decided to become a stipendiary magistrate. It kept her out of mischief. Looking at her, Topher had his doubts.

The fruit bowl did its rounds. Over what passed for coffee, Jo Henderson surprised Topher with the news that she had a son in his twenties. He was down from Oxford and desperate to find work in television. Topher suggested that Chelsea might be able to help. Taking a card from her handbag, Jo Henderson gave it to Topher. She lived in Lowndes Square.

'It might be better if your son contacted Chelsea direct . . .' Topher searched his pockets for a piece of paper.

Jo took out a slim black *aide-memoire*.

Handing her his gold pen, Topher gave her the telephone number of Lime Grove studios and Chelsea's extension. He looked at his watch. The lunch had gone quickly.

'I have to be getting back to my chappie who has been accused of attempting to "nick 'andbags".'

'Was he nicking handbags?'

Topher chuckled and pushed back his chair from the table.

'Without the shadow of a doubt.'

Chapter Nine

Harry Andrews was found not guilty of attempting to steal a lady's handbag from the public house in Covent Garden. The verdict was unanimous. Topher could only surmise that the jury had been swayed by the allegations of police brutality made by the defendant. By and large, officers of the law were honest. When they were convinced, however, that a defendant was guilty (no matter how trivial the offence), they were quite capable of bending the rules.

Judging by the police officer's expression as Harry Andrews left the dock, Topher felt sure that it would be only a matter of time (and a little leg-work on Sergeant Bullock's part) before the two of them met again.

He had been sitting at Southwark for a month when he was woken one morning by the doorbell from a deep sleep in which he had been dreaming of Sally Maddox. Sally, draped in marble, had usurped Pauline Borghese from her couch in the Villa Borghese and was holding out her stone arms to him.

Opening the front door to an unfamiliar postman, Topher wondered if the dream had been significant and whether there would be word from the still silent Sally.

'Recorded delivery. Parking fine.'

'Not me,' Topher said smugly.

'Osgood?'

Taking the stub of pencil, Topher signed where requested. He guessed that a mistake had been made. Chelsea was always taking chances in her Renault 5.

The name of the street where the alleged offence had taken place meant nothing to him. The registration number of the offending car was his own. He cast his mind back to the expedition to Marks and Spencer from which he had returned minus his socks. He had always prided himself on the efficiency with which he dealt with his correspondence. He couldn't think how the ticket, issued by the traffic warden, whom he now recalled quite clearly, had been overlooked. He wondered what he had done with it. It was certainly not in the car.

Padding across the parquet in his bare feet, he looked for his winter overcoat in the closet at the back of the hall. Caroline's wellingtons, her parka, and her ancient leather gardening jacket had been missed by Chelsea and Penge. There had been times lately when Topher did not think of Caroline. When the intimacies of their life together seemed to belong to an earlier civilisation. At moments such as the present one, he was assailed by a trenchant recollection of things past. The leather jacket, an unusual extravagance for Caroline, took him back – an archeologist with a forgotten shard – to Paris, and the wedding anniversary (he could no longer remember which one) for which it had been bought. It had been pelting when they left London and they had worn their raincoats. It wasn't until they were flying over the English channel that Caroline discovered she had left her new jacket on the bed. The incident had coloured the week-end. Caroline would not be mollified. The celebration had been only a qualified success. Topher had done his best to understand her disappointment, to reassure her that she looked fetching in her macintosh. She refused to be placated and they had, he remembered, almost come to blows in the Jeu de Paume.

Perhaps there had been a kernel of truth in the words of Lucille from Bingley. Marriage, even to Caroline, had not *always* been a moonlit trip down the Grand Canal in a gondola. Searching through the pockets of his winter overcoat, he thought that even at its very worst, when the waters had been turbulent, and the moon decidedly skulking behind a cloud, matrimony was, without question, preferable to the arcane existence he was now leading. Extracting from his pocket nothing but a half-eaten packet of Polo mints, a soiled handkerchief, and a fistful of silver which he kept for the evening newspaper, he put the oversight of the parking ticket down to his equilibrium having been so savagely shaken by Caroline's death.

The day at Southwark was uneventful. The novelty of *HMS Belfast* beneath his window was beginning to wear off. Squeers, with his obsequiousness, was getting on his nerves.

In order to defer the onset of the prolonged evening at home, he had taken, after court, to going to his club. No sooner had he arrived, however, than he was assailed by a profound disinclination to enter into conversation with anyone who might address him.

He had adopted several ploys to fill the arid hours at the nether end of the day. Sometimes he thought that they would never pass. He had tried the commercial theatre. It not only frequently disappointed, but entailed the tedium of finding somewhere to park, a descent into the bowels of the Soho earth, and the necessity of bobbing up and down from one's seat every few minutes to allow latecomers to pass. The National Theatre was more rewarding, but when the mailing list arrived he found himself unable to commit himself to far-off dates and times and preferred parts of the auditorium, and let the whole exercise go by default. The programmes were stacked up on top of the fridge beneath the whisky bottle.

He had tried the films, both alone and with Penge, but the cinema seemed to address a culture with which he did not associate himself. Music, as therapy, had come out tops. He preferred to listen in the comfort of his own home.

A reading of the poetry of Alexander Sergeyevich Pushkin, on Radio Three, heard by chance when he was timing his boil-in-the-bag kipper, had recently given him a new interest. With Latin as his first love he had no knowledge of, and thought he had no interest in, the Russian language. Listening to *The Covetous Knight*, read in the original, followed immediately by the English version, made him realise what he might be missing. Through his battles with Horace, he had always been aware of the pitfalls of translation. He decided, nonetheless, to dispose of an hour each evening, with the aid of a dictionary and a grammar, getting to grips with Pushkin. When he succeeded in reading the lyrical *Pyeryedo mnoy yavilas ty*, 'Before me didst appear thou', he almost danced for joy. As the evenings progressed he became convinced that no British horse ever galloped as poetically as did Peter the Great's – *kak budto groma grokhotanye* – and that no love-lorn English maiden's heartache could match her Russian counterpart's *tryepyetanye*.

He was struggling with *Autumn*, when the telephone disrupted him.

Hearing the unfamiliar voice of a woman, his first thought was that Sally Maddox had returned from Ireland.

'Sally?'

'This is Jo . . .'

He was about to tell the caller that she had a wrong number.

'Jo Henderson. We met at Southwark.'

'Of course. I'm so sorry. I was expecting . . . How did you . . . ?'

'Squeers gave me your number. I went off with your pen.'

A Gold Cross. Initialled. A present from Caroline. He had thought it lost.

'I found it in my handbag. What would you like me to do?'

While Topher was considering the matter she said: 'Look . . .'

She meant listen, Topher thought.

'. . . why don't you come over here for a drink?'

There was no reason at all why not. Topher did not need to consult his diary. A day a week ahead was fixed. Six o'clock at Lowndes Square.

'By the way,' Jo Henderson said, 'how long did you give your fellow for nicking handbags?'

Topher remembered his assurance that Harry Andrews would be condemned 'without a shadow of doubt'.

'The jury found him "not guilty".'

Hearing a laugh from the other end of the phone, he realised that there had not been too much laughter lately in his life.

He had just settled down again with Pushkin when the telephone rang for the second time.

'Hallo?'

'Hallo.'

A woman's voice. He was not going to make a fool of himself again.

'Christopher?'

There was only one person who called him Christopher.

'This is Sally. Sally Maddox. I did ring from Ireland but your cleaning lady told me you were in Yorkshire. Then I got bogged down with work. Are you alone?'

'Apart from Pushkin.'

'Is that your cat?'

Topher disillusioned her. Sally Maddox asked him how he had been keeping. She sounded as if she cared. The author of *An End to Dying* seemed less threatening than the Sally Maddox who had groped him at the Gordons'. He found himself accepting, even with some enthusiasm, her renewed invitation for tea in Kentish Town. His diary began to look less boring. When Sally's call was followed by that

68

of Tina, on the line from Bingley, he was able to reassure his sister, in all honesty, that he was very well thank you, and that he had plenty to occupy him.

It wasn't until after lunch on Saturday that he realised he had lost Sally Maddox's address. He remembered making a note of it after the dinner party, but he couldn't for the life of him think where it was. He dialled April's number, then remembered that she and Marcus had gone up to Oxford to visit John. The telephone book revealed an S. Maddox in SW19, a Stuart Maddox in E5, Maddox *Salon de Lingerie* in W1, but no Maddox, Sally, in Kentish Town. He had been looking forward to his visit. He had stopped at Books Etc. in Fleet Street, on his way to the Law Courts, to buy a copy of *An End to Dying* with the intention of asking Sally Maddox to sign it. Waiting for his change, and for the novel to be wrapped, his attention was caught by John Gould's *The Bird Man*. He picked up the book and turned over the laminated pages, but was unable to focus on the plumed partridge, the white-fronted falcon, the toco toucan with its great orange beak, because his eyes were filled with tears.

Surrounded by the ordered chaos in his study (into which Madge was forbidden to venture with her hoover), Topher tried to recall what he had done with Sally Maddox's address. He had always been a hoarder but had been delivered from his own excesses by the fact that Caroline liked to throw everything away. The sea of papers with which he was now surrounded was not entirely his fault. He could scarcely be blamed for the deluge of junk mail beneath which he was in danger of sinking. With every post, unsolicited printed matter – from within the folds of which fell further printed matter – came through the letter box. Each day he was persuaded of the futility of his existence without a Welsh miner's lamp, simulated pearls, an embossing press for stationery, or a polyester *djellabah*. He was exhorted to send away for mini-computers of the most daunting complexity, sides of oak-smoked salmon and flea collars for the dog. The credit card companies were only partly responsible for this effluent. Personal Lucky Numbers, attached to catalogues of household goods or thermal underwear, advised Topher that he might already have won thousands of pounds. Names of previous winners – Piddlesden and Wigglesworth – living in places one had never heard of, did little to reassure.

As if all this were not enough, there was the recent addition of gratuitous property magazines, offering houses with indoor swimming pools and 'his' and 'hers' jacuzzis, and a confetti of visiting cards promising 24 Hour Messenger Services, Radio-controlled Taxi-cabs, and rogue plumbers. Somewhere beneath this accumulation lay Sally Maddox's address.

Topher began, half-heartedly, to throw some of the detritus into the waste-paper basket. He then decided that it might be more useful to sit down and think the matter out. It had been the day after April's dinner party when his assailant had phoned him. He had been sitting in his own court. Mrs Sweetlove. Possession orders. Mr Biswas and Mr Archibald. Two girls with coloured hair. A breach of contract, after which he had gone straight home to an empty house. A deserted hall in which he had remarked the lack of flowers. The welcome sound of the telephone bell. He had been expecting Chelsea or Penge. . . . He got up from his chair and crossing to the bookcase picked up a back number of *Counsel*. 'Advertising and the Bar: The Debate Begins'. 'Bar's Withdrawal of Credit Scheme – How and why it will work . . .' He closed the journal and on the back cover, in an almost illegible hand, as if he were not really interested in recording it, was Sally Maddox's address.

Chapter Ten

Topher stood beside the dustbins on a doorstep in Jeffrey's Street clutching an *An End to Dying* and a bottle of tawny sherry, which reminded him of Sally Maddox herself. Stooping to read the labels on the entryphone, most of which seemed to have faded into illegibility, he had his hand in his pocket for his half-glasses when Sally Maddox threw open the peeling door.

'I thought you'd got lost.'

'I mislaid the address.'

Topher stepped into the hall and into Sally Maddox's outstretched arms. She drew him to her generous bosom against which he stood awkwardly, not knowing quite what to do. Deciding upon inertia as being in the best interests of self-preservation, he waited for her to release him, then followed her down the stairs to what he half-imagined, on the strength of their first meeting, would be some den of vice.

He was not unused to bed-sits. Chelsea and Penge had lived in a few in their time. Somehow it was an arrangement he had not associated with grown-up people. Far from the bordello he had expected, Sally Maddox's room seemed mostly to be furnished with books. There was a plain wooden table on which was her typewriter, a double bed (covered by a spread of crisp white lace which reminded Topher of his grandmother), a sofa, and an armchair. The simplicity of it all made Topher wonder suddenly what he needed such a large house for, when it seemed that life's needs could be adequately catered for in the space of a few hundred square feet. Any uncertainty he might have had about accepting the invitation to Kentish Town was soon dispelled. He was spared even from volunteering the sherry.

'Is that for me?'

Topher handed over the bottle. There was no dissimulating with Sally. Once again, this time with Topher's acquiescence, she flung her arms round his neck.

He put *An End to Dying* on the table next to the coffee tin filled with pens.

'I don't read many novels . . .'

'"Things that never happened to people you don't know."'

'I brought it for you to sign. I thought it extremely moving.'

'Thank you.' She accepted the compliment with grace.

'Was it well received?'

'I assume you mean by the critics? I don't take too much notice. I'm a reviewer myself. I know how easy it is to demolish, in a sentence, a novel it has taken someone two years to write. It's your readers you have to worry about. They are more discerning, bless them. I shan't be a minute. Make yourself at home.'

Sally disappeared behind a curtain from where Topher, who had been anticipating the call of sirens, could hear the rattle of teacups. He wandered over to the books. The titles, in no particular order, proclaimed the catholic tastes of their owner.

'Milk or lemon?' The voice floated from behind the curtain.

Topher presumed that Sally Maddox was referring to the tea and asked for milk.

When she reappeared, with a loaded tray, he moved to take it from her. She put it on the low table in front of the sofa.

'I'm used to doing things for myself. I *was* married. A good man but it didn't work out. We still see each other. There are scones, with or without currants, and crumpets. Home-made jam from Killarney. How does one get to be a judge?'

'By accident really.' Topher sat down and accepted a plate. 'One starts out, as a young man, desperately wanting to be an advocate. When one reaches one's peak, one finds oneself faced with two alternatives. The first is to become progressively disillusioned as the up and coming young barristers pass one by. The other is the soft option of twenty years on the Bench – leading the life of Riley – while one waits for one's index-linked pension based on half-pay. I had no ideas when I started out of becoming a judge. It's really not much of a choice.'

72

Sally put sugar into her tea and offered the bowl to Topher.
He shook his head.

'My first appearance on the Bench came quite by chance. A member of my chambers, who had been made a Recorder, asked me if I'd mind sitting as his assistant. His previous chap had been rushed into hospital with some surgical emergency. I went on from there. There were no special qualifications to become a judge in those days. It didn't seem to occur to anyone that middle-aged men, starting a new job, might need some sort of training. You learned, like brick-laying or paper-hanging, by watching others do it.'

'And you send people to prison?'

'Of course.'

'Does it do any good?'

'Putting people inside protects the people outside. Sometimes it's necessary to deprive an offender of his liberty for quite a long stretch in the interests of public safety.'

'"One learns patience in a prison."'

'*The House of the Dead?*'

'I thought lawyers only read law books. Do you lie awake at night, thinking that you might have given the wrong sentence?'

Topher helped himself to a crumpet oozing with what, he was certain, was not polyunsaturated margarine.

'The time to worry is before you make a decision, not after it. Sentencing is a serious matter. Imprisonment is a waste of the human spirit. Every day of it must be justified.'

Sally Maddox passed him the jam.

'What about capital punishment?'

'What about it?'

'Do you believe in it?'

There was no spoon. Topher put his knife into the jam.

'Let's say I believe all life to be sacred.'

'You're religious then?'

'I just happen to think that there is some good in every human being.'

'Even murderers?'

'Most murderers are insane. They wouldn't qualify for capital punishment anyway.'

'Doesn't the threat of being topped act as a deterrent?'

'It can't intimidate a man who does not know he is going to commit murder. The statistics indicate that there is no connection whatsoever between the death penalty and the incidence of crime. It seems more reasonable to me, that those who have shown themselves unfit to be in contact with the rest of society should be removed from it for the remainder of their lives.'

'Until they sink into mindless senility?'

'If necessary.'

'But you wouldn't reinstate the death penalty?'

Sally was nothing if not persistent. Topher put his empty cup into her outstretched hand.

'Step back into the dark ages? Certainly not.'

He heard her breathe a sigh of relief, and felt as if he had passed an examination.

'Writers have to know everything. We use every crumb. I shall probably put you into a book.'

'I'm flattered.'

'I might even ask if I can come to your court.'

'With the greatest of pleasure.'

'You can get your own back now. Ask me anything you like.'

'There is something I'd like to know.'

Watching her tuck into her umpteenth scone – sure that it wasn't wise, she really was extremely plump – Topher thought how harmless Sally Maddox appeared, dressed today not in brown but some sort of loose dress covered with scarlet poppies. The material looked as if it could quite easily have been made into curtains. Fortified by the crumpets, he decided to solve the mystery of her attack upon him at the Gordons' table.

Topher put his empty cup and saucer down on his plate, and replaced the plate on the tray. 'What I've been meaning to ask you . . .'

Whether it was because he was unsure how to phrase the question, or whether he feared Sally's reply, he was not quite certain. At the last moment his courage failed him. 'What I wanted to ask you is . . . how do you write a book?'

' "Begin at the beginning; carry on till you come to the end; then stop." '

'*Alice in Wonderland* used to upset Chelsea, for some reason. Particularly the White Rabbit. Do you write every day, or do you wait for inspiration?'

'I wait for inspiration. But I make sure that it arrives at nine o'clock every morning! Seriously though, Christopher, it's a job like any other. I have to keep myself, remember?'

74

'Since you've given me *carte blanche*,' Topher said, 'tell me where you get your ideas.'

'You only have to live for one day with your eyes and ears open and you have more ideas than you know what to do with. "The jog of fancy's elbow", Henry James called it. When your subject matter is the relationship of one human being to another, until we're all blown into kingdom come, there can be no shortage of material.'

'Do you plan the whole book out before you start?'

'There are those who do. I know where my characters are going but not how they are going to get there. I start them off then allow them to take over. I have a rough idea of the *shape* . . . a bit like an architect having to carry the entire plan of the finished building in his head. Writing never gets any easier. You start out determined to write *Hamlet, Beethoven's 5th, The Brothers Karamazov* . . . and end up with *Little Noddy*.'

'In *An End to Dying*,' Topher said, 'I particularly liked the way you coped with the . . . physical relationships.'

As soon as the words were out of his mouth he wondered what had possessed him.

'Sex is a special interest of mine,' Sally Maddox said.

Topher avoided her eyes.

'I'm glad you noticed.'

'*En passant*.' Topher tried to extricate himself from the hole he had dug.

'Reading about sex is like being forced to look at holiday snaps. It's extremely boring to watch other people doing something you'd rather be doing yourself.'

Topher let the comment pass.

Sally warmed to her theme. 'Any decent writer can say all he wants to say without resorting to "gross details of lascivious images". What passion there is in Emma Bovary hurtling round Paris in a closed *fiacre* with Leon, in Rhett Butler sweeping Scarlet O'Hara into his arms and up the stairs at Tara, in the exchanges between Zhivago and Lara. Tell me about your wife.'

Topher was thrown by the abrupt change of subject. The unexpected imperative. It was still not easy to discuss Caroline. Not without disgracing himself. He knew that he should. That it was therapeutic. Marcus had told him as much. Diffidently, stumbling over his words at first, he made a blundering attempt. He told Sally about Caroline's love affair with the natural world, about her infatuation with birds.

How, when he came home from court in the afternoon, no matter what the weather, they would walk on the Heath, Caroline searching for chaffinches or starlings. He told her about the contributions Caroline had made to ornithological classification, about the papers she had written, and the book she was − had been − writing.

He must have talked for a long time. When he stopped, the basement was in semi-darkness. Sally got up from the armchair to put on the lamps. From a cupboard she brought a bottle of wine and two glasses and set them beside the tea tray. Topher looked at his watch. He had never known time pass so quickly. He was about to say he really must be going. Sally put a glass of wine in his hand and sat down beside him on the sofa.

'Now,' she said, and her voice was firm, insistent. 'Tell me about your wife.'

Topher sipped his wine. Sally waited. He knew that she didn't want to hear how Caroline had tracked down the green woodpecker or the female shrike.

'I watch people's faces in repose,' Sally said. 'I know who is putting on a brave front.'

Topher knew that it was not possible to describe the rapport which had existed between himself and Caroline. That he could not put into words the love, which neither *philos*, nor *agape*, could adequately describe, which had bound them together.

He had emptied his glass and it had been refilled before he said: 'I never really told Caroline how much I loved her.'

'Didn't she know?'

'Perhaps she did, perhaps she didn't. I never said it. Not even when she was dying. In my family the words were not used. I did say them. But it was too late . . .'

On the day that he had disposed of Caroline's ashes, Topher had felt that he was as near as he had ever come to manslaughter. He had been putting it off and putting it off. At first he had blamed his procrastination on the weather. It had been raining. Then it had been snowing. For some reason, as if it were a picnic he was planning, he was waiting for a fine day. He had kept the wooden casket in Caroline's bureau in the bedroom, in the little cupboard next to the secret drawers. Aware that his action was morbid, he discussed it with neither his daughters nor with Marcus, knowing what they would say. He never touched the box. Only looked at it.

When he found himself sitting in court thinking about the moment when he would go home to it – as if Caroline herself were waiting in the house to welcome him – he knew that the time had come to dispose of its contents.

He left it until the week-end. On Saturday morning Marcus had rung him to ask whether he would like a game of chess. Topher had prevaricated. Not long afterwards Chelsea had called to enquire what he was up to.

'I'm going for a walk on the Heath.'

'Alone?'

Topher thought about it. He was unable to bring himself to tell her that he would have the company of her mother on the way up Fitzjohn's Avenue, but that he would be alone – and lonely – on his return.

'Not exactly.' It was the best answer he could think of.

'What do you mean?'

'It's hard to explain.'

'Do you want me to come over?'

'Good Lord, no.'

'I mean, are you all right?'

He had reassured Chelsea with more composure than he felt, and dressed carefully. For Caroline. In her favourite suit. He put on the tie she had brought him from the States where she had gone to watch seabirds. When he had looked for something in which to carry her remains, and found himself wondering whether Caroline would prefer the dark green of a Harrod's bag, or the paler shade used by Fortnum and Mason (where she bought the Bath Olivers), he realised that the entire manoeuvre had assumed an air of farce. No one, as far as he knew, saw him leave the house. As he crossed Arkwright Road a passing policeman led him, as if he had indeed committed some felony, to quicken his step. He stopped at the Whitestone Pond. In his mind he heard one of the girls call, 'Mummy, Mummy,' as her frail craft capsized in the water. He turned to look at Caroline, who was not by his side but in the bag – Fortnum and Mason – he clutched beneath his arm. He thought that he could not go through with it. Pulling himself together, he left the frozen pond and walked quickly to the spot where he and Caroline had taken their daily walks.

It had not been easy. He had had to remind himself that he had a promise to keep. It was a hard thing to do. To open the casket and touch the pale grey powder. He looked over his shoulder. There was no one about. Not even a jogger. It was too early in the morning for walkers. Too cold for the birds. Staring at the contents of the box he wondered, did one hurl them into the air like confetti, or allow them to slip in thin rivers through one's fingers onto the ground as if one was feeding bone-meal to the roses? Should he tip them out all at once, or prolong the agony? He took off his gloves and stuffed them into his pocket. He plunged his hand into the ashes and with an underarm movement, as if he were playing bowls, scattered the light dust onto the unyielding earth, into the air, on to the toe-caps of his shoes. When the box was empty, he turned it upside down and shook it, before hurling it into the trees.

'I love you,' he yelled, falling to his knees on the white powder. 'Oh God, I love you!'

Sally Maddox was the first person he had told.

When he had finished speaking, wondering where he had found the strength, she covered his hand with hers. He did not protest. He realised how much he had missed the warmth of human contact, someone to touch as of right.

'She knew,' was all Sally said.

And when Topher did not reply: 'Didn't she?'

Topher looked at her. He wondered why her face was so distant, so distorted, before he realised that he had been crying.

'Say it,' Sally said. 'You'll feel better.'

Topher took out his handkerchief and blew his nose.

'Yes,' he said firmly. 'She knew.'

Sally left him alone while she removed the tea-tray. After a while Topher carried the empty crumpet plate, which she had forgotten, into the miniscule kitchen. She took the plate from him and laughed, lightening the mood.

'There's no room in here for two!'

He went back into the other room and didn't protest when Sally called out that she was cooking some spaghetti. He was feeling hungry, although he had no idea of the time. They opened another bottle of wine and balanced their supper on their knees.

'How's Pushkin?' Sally asked.

Topher recited: '"Do not sing to me again/You songs of Georgia/They bring to memory/Another life, a distant shore . . .,"' from *The Poison Tree*. He repeated the verse, haltingly, in his newly acquired

Russian. Sally reciprocated with Verlaine: '"*Ah! Quand refleuriront les roses de Septembre?*"'

It was after midnight when, leaving the car in Jeffrey's Street, Topher walked home.

Chapter Eleven

Topher was woken abruptly by what he thought was the sound of his gavel calling for silence in court (which bore an uncanny resemblance to Sally Maddox's basement flat) but was in fact the slamming of his own front door.

Both his daughters had keys. The sound of a bicycle being man-handled into the hall told him that this was Penge.

She tip-toed into the bedroom, lighting it with her yellow smock which ballooned over black harem trousers.

'Are you awake?' Her whisper was of the stage variety.

'I am now.'

'I've been ringing and ringing.' (Lady Macbeth.) 'The telephone must be out of order.'

'I switched the bell off.' Topher squinted at the clock. It was 10.30. 'It is Sunday.'

'Chelsea tried to get you yesterday.' The voice was accusing. 'She tried all afternoon.'

'I was out for tea.'

'Until after midnight?'

Topher did not think it necessary to account for himself.

'We were worried about you.'

There was indignation as well as concern in Penge's over-reaction. Casting his mind back to the wide-awake small hours he and Caroline had spent listening for the sounds of Chelsea or Penge returning from a night out, Topher concealed a smile beneath the bedclothes.

'I appreciate your concern.'

Penge sat on his feet, only slightly mollified.

'Where were you?'

'At Sally Maddox's.'

Turning to the bedside table to show Penge *An End to Dying*, he realised that he had left the book in Jeffrey's Street. He did not need Marcus to interpret the significance of his action.

'Who's Sally Maddox?'

'Just a friend.'

He was surprised to hear in his own voice the defensive tones he had hitherto associated with the young. He saw Penge's lips tighten, as his and Caroline's must so often have done, when the girls had lived at home. He did not elaborate, any more than they had elaborated.

'As long as you're all right.'

Penge's opinion of his exploit was obvious from her tone.

'What did Chelsea want?'

'They're having a drink at the Beeb on Thursday. After her programme ends for the summer. Six o'clock. She thought you might like to go.'

'I'd be delighted.' Topher was touched that Chelsea had thought to include him in the celebrations. Then he remembered. He was promised in Lowndes Square.

'On second thoughts,' he said, 'I have a previous engagement.'

'Sally Maddox?'

Topher shook his head. Penge appeared relieved. He thought it neither politic or necessary to tell her about Jo Henderson. Penge moved herself from his feet and opened the curtains. Clutching them, with one hand raised in what Topher recognised was her Hedda Gabler pose, she looked out into the street. Her face, touched by the pale sunlight, seemed troubled. Topher wondered if she had really called because she was worried about him, or if she had something on her mind. He guessed it was her love life which was not running smoothly.

'How's Chad?'

The name was assumed. The minor poet had been christened Gary by unimaginative parents.

'Fine.'

Penge was in monosyllabic mode. It was clear that whatever irked her would have to be forcibly extracted. Topher was considering the best approach when she surprised him by saying: 'Do you miss Mummy?'

Wallowing in his own self-pity, Topher wondered whether he had perhaps given insufficient thought to his motherless offspring. Penge did not wait for his answer.

'I find myself wanting to ask her opinion . . . tell her something . . . I have my hand on the telephone . . .'

'I know exactly how you feel.'

'I keep thinking she's away on one of her trips. Morecambe Bay. Or Sandwich. I can't believe she's dead.'

'There is her jewellery in the bank,' Topher said. 'I put it away when she was ill. I must get it out for you and Chelsea.'

He could not think what had possessed him to say it. He knew that it was not Caroline's collection of Victorian rings and bangles that Penge was after.

'Thanks.'

She had withdrawn again into herself.

The minutes passed.

'Sure you and Chad. . . ?' Topher said.

'I told you. Everything's OK.'

'Are you managing?'

He meant money.

Penge nodded.

'I'd better be going.'

'Won't you join me for breakfast?'

She shook her head.

Topher put on his dressing-gown and helped her out with her bicycle. The tyres left dirty marks on Madge's polished floor. Penge kissed him.

'Take care,' Topher said.

'You too.'

He watched her, her yellow top billowing, cycle off down the empty street. The newspapers were on the step. He picked them up and went into the kitchen. Taking two eggs and a packet of bacon out of the refrigerator and setting the frying-pan on the gas, he realised that he was not sorry that Penge had refused his invitation. After the first chaotic months of his widowhood his life seemed to have settled itself into some sort of routine. He would, he acknowledged, never be anything of a cook. He was temperamentally unsuited to the 'sweating' of vegetables or the making of *roux*, all of which – according to those of Caroline's cookery books he had consulted in his idle moments — seemed to be integral to the good table.

Breaking the eggs into a cup (with an expertise which he had learned from a man in a striped apron on the television), Topher slid them into the pan, together with a rasher of bacon, and pondered on his change of status. Before the Second World War he remembered, when he had been growing up, roles had been clearly defined. Women had raised children and run the homes. Men had worked. *Tilting the pan he splashed the fat which had run from the bacon over the eggs.* A more complex pattern had now developed. Parents had ceded their responsibilities to the Welfare State. Women worked. Couples divorced and re-married in what seemed like a contemporary version of musical chairs (or more accurately beds). There were more single parents. More one person households. Schools, once the preserve of children, were taken over, as night fell, with enthusiastic adults seeking new skills. *The eggs were sitting up nicely. He added pepper to the yolks (salt came afterwards according the man in the striped apron).* In many households, men were no longer the breadwinners. While their wives brought home the bacon . . . *It was amazing how it always shrank to half the size* . . . they stayed at home. There was no statistical evidence to evaluate the actual extent of their involvement in the home. *The whites of the eggs were crisping nicely. He turned the gas down.* Notwithstanding the loud noises made by the feminists, equal sharing — *he scooped up the contents of the frying-pan deftly with the spatula* — was still a concept honoured more in the breach than in the observance, more an ideal rather than a reality. Taking his plate to the table, Topher reflected with satisfaction, that tradition, said by some to be dying, was not only taking an unconscionably long time about it, but, thankfully, was nowhere near dead.

The telephone rang as he was finishing his breakfast. He had been half-expecting Sally to phone about the forgotten book.

'Sally?'

'This is Lucille . . .'

He cast his mind back to Bingley, and Miles' birthday party. He remembered perfectly. A cleavage. And a yellow dress. Long red nails. Lucille.

'I'm coming to London. I thought we might do a show.'

Topher considered the matter.

'I suppose you've seen *Cats*? I've a friend, well, a friend of a friend, who can get tickets.'

'I haven't actually.'

'I thought *everybody* in London had. I thought I'd try for the week after next. I'm coming down for the dentist and to see a couple of girl-friends. Most of my pals are in London. Is there any particular night?'

Topher hadn't said that he would go.

'No particular night.'

'That's smashing then. I often think of you. How have you been keeping?'

'Very well. Very well indeed.'

'What's the weather like? It's bucketing up here. I'm still in bed. I don't bother getting up on a Sunday. I have everything on a tray and watch the television. There's a James Bond this afternoon. The one with Ursula Andress where she walks out of the water with her blouse clinging to her nipples . . . Are you still there?'

'I'm still here,' Topher said.

'You don't go to church do you?'

'No,' Topher said.

'I wasn't sure. I expect you're very busy so I won't keep you. I'll let you know when I get the tickets. I'll be staying at the Mount Royal. They know me there.'

As Topher put the phone down he felt slightly shaken by the fact that for the first time in his life he had been invited to the theatre by a woman, and that he had – if only by default–accepted the invitation. The horrendous thought suddenly occured to him that, with Caroline's death, he had become a 'catch'. He left the remains of his eggs to congeal on the plate and hurried to get dressed. He needed to talk to Marcus. Sally telephoned as he was leaving the house.

'You left your book. I've got to be in Hampstead on Thursday, about sixish. I'll bring it round.'

'I shan't be in.' He realised that he would much rather see Sally than go to Lowndes Square.

'If the invitation to come to court with you still stands, I could come on Monday and bring the book with me.'

'I can't promise that it will be anything very interesting.'

'I just want to see how judges judge.'

Topher arranged to pick up Sally at nine-fifteen. He made a mental note to solve the riddle of her attack upon his person on their next meeting. The longer he left it, the harder it was going to be.

'Thank you for yesterday,' he said. 'I'm sorry if I out-stayed my welcome. I didn't realise . . .'

'It was a good evening. We must do it again.'

Marcus set two whiskies down on the table in the Saloon Bar of the Bull and Bush.

'What am I to do?' Topher said. 'Women keep ringing me up.'

Marcus helped himself to a potato chip. 'You are a man of learning and of property, not bad-looking and patently in need of care. Many men would feel flattered.'

'I do. The world seems suddenly to be peopled with available females. How is it that I never noticed them before?' Topher applied himself to his whisky. 'I feel ashamed of myself.'

'For *talking* to them?'

Topher was silent. His recent sexual fantasies had not only encompassed Sally Maddox, and Lucille from Bingley, and Jo Henderson (who had accommodated his gold pen), but horror of horrors, Mrs Sweetlove.

'I feel that Caroline is looking over my shoulder. Not to mention Chelsea and Penge.'

Marcus, in his Sunday sweater, waited for him to continue. Topher could not go on. He sometimes had the feeling that were it not for the necessity to earn his living he should, out of respect for his late wife, stay alone in the house remembering her.

'The desires are natural enough,' Marcus said. 'The trouble is that they are in conflict with what you see as acceptable behaviour. You feel that you have let Caroline down. I would say that you are suffering from a nasty dose of what is known in the trade as guilt.'

'What am I to do about it?'

Marcus considered the problem.

'Guilt can have a tremendous effect on people's lives. Without it I'd be out of business. It is, however, extremely damaging. It gives rise to pain, and shame, and a whole host of other disabilities.'

'Go on.' The fact that Topher had voiced his misgivings had made him feel lighter of heart already.

Marcus picked up the empty glasses.

'Let me.' Topher took them from him. 'In lieu of your fee.'

When Topher returned from the bar, Marcus raised his glass.

'Cheers.'

'Cheers,' Topher said.

'People who don't feel any guilt behave selfishly and dishonestly,'

Marcus said. 'They have absolutely no sense of right and wrong.' His gaze wandered to a group of young people who had just come into the bar. 'What I'm trying to point out . . .' His eye was taken by a scarlet mini-skirt. 'What I'm trying to point out, is that one should neither be ashamed of one's guilt, nor try to avoid it altogether. One must simply learn to control it, in an attempt to restrict the damage it can do.'

'How does one do that?'

'Firstly, its necessary to differentiate between the relevant and the irrelevant. Secondly, we have to put the guilt into proportion and perspective. Finally, we have to build up our defences in order to cope with it.'

Topher tipped the remains of the potato chips first into his hand and then into his mouth. He wiped the crumbs from his lips with his handkerchief.

'Do you really think I'm capable of sorting that lot out?'

'You must ask yourself if your guilt stems from the fact that you have actually done something wrong, or that your behaviour is inconsistent with your unrealistic expectations.'

'I have always had a punishing conscience.'

'Like many successful people you have used it as a positive, rather than a negative, force. Do you think it was by chance that you became a judge?'

'Certainly,' Topher said. 'I just happened to be around at the appropriate moment.'

Marcus made no comment but continued: 'As for putting the matter into proportion and perspective, you have to accept firstly that you have not *done* anything and secondly, that Caroline's dying wish was that you should not be on your own.'

'I can't help the way I feel.'

'Of course you can't. That is where your defences come in.' He looked at Topher's empty glass. 'One for the road?'

Topher put his hand over the glass. 'BREATHALYSED JUDGE OVER LIMIT. I don't think it would look too good in the *Ham & High*.'

'Possibly not,' Marcus agreed.

'You were speaking about defences.'

'You have certain rights as an individual. It's important not to forget that those rights exist. Because Caroline has died – and God knows I loved that woman as much as anybody – does not mean that you have to spend the rest of your life being miserable. That's the last thing she would have wanted. You have a *right* not only to enjoy yourself, but to expect others to respect your rights. You have a *right* to make decisions without thinking of everyone around you.'

' "Easy to say, difficult to do".'

'It will come.'

'Allowing Lucille to get tickets for *Cats* felt like knocking another nail – metaphorically speaking – into Caroline's coffin.'

'Perhaps it would help you to feel less badly about yourself if I tell you that people who suffer most from feelings of guilt generally have a lot going for them. Don't underrate yourself, Topher. Spend a little time looking at your good points instead of concentrating on your faults.'

'On an intellectual level all that you say makes a great deal of sense. Sadly it doesn't make two-pennyworth of difference – ' Topher put a hand to the front of his pullover – 'here.'

'Think of yourself as an observer. What would you say to some chap in the dock who had lost his wife, but had confessed to the heinous crimes of having tea with a woman, going for a drink with another, agreeing to see *Cats*, and having the odd sexual fantasy by way of good measure?'

'Good luck to him.'

Marcus stood up. 'They say that charity begins at home. I think that in your case it should be compassion. Be fair to yourself Topher. You don't *have* to spend Sunday afternoon alone, punishing yourself with Pushkin. My professional advice is that you give that conscience of yours a break. Come and have some of April's *lasagne*.'

Chapter Twelve

Driving to Lowndes Square Topher considered his conversation with Marcus. In the course of it he had learned that guilt was more commonly engendered by self-criticism than it was by foul deeds. The blame he was always ready to attribute to himself for wrong-doings real or imagined, stemmed, according to Marcus, from his relationship with his parents who had loved him not too little but too much. He and Tina had been conceived (in the days before children were spawned in petrie dishes) when their mother had given up all hope of fertility. The twins were so precious to their parents, and were reared so fondly, that their childish misdemeanours often went unpunished. Listening to stories of abuse, both verbal and physical, from his peers at school, had led Topher to rejoice in his own good fortune. The odd clip round the ear, however, or reproof from his mother or father – whose one wish was to protect him and Tina from the evils of the world – might, apparently, have created less emotional havoc than did their excess of devotion. The latter had left Topher with the feeling that it would be impossible for him ever to repay his parents' kindness, that he would remain forever in their debt.

Throughout his adolescence it was clearly anticipated that Topher would live up to his father's high expectations of him. That he would not let him down. His father had died before Topher had proved himself, long before he had been sworn in as a judge. Only Tina had been present to hear the words of affirmation he had repeated before the Lord Chancellor in his oak-panelled room, after which His

Lordship had spent a few affable moments chatting to them both. Although neither of his parents had lived long enough to see him at the pinnacle of his career, he had, in the early days, felt as uneasily aware of his father's presence at his elbow as he was now of his late wife's.

'I am only going to fetch my pen,' he told himself firmly, turning the car out of Hyde Park at the Epstein sculpture known irreverently in the Osgood family as 'bottoms'.

As he passed the lighted shop windows, already exhibiting brief swimsuits on headless models, he told himself that he had every *right* to be going out; that Caroline would be only too pleased that he was not staying at home with Pushkin. It was to no avail. By the time he had parked the car in Lowndes Square, and asked the uniformed porter of Jo Henderson's block for number sixteen, he was possessed by the uncomfortable and familiar sensation that he should not really be there.

'Lady Henderson?' the porter inquired.

Lady Henderson. Topher nodded and followed the man to the lift. 'Press the top button, Sir, and I'll tell Her Ladyship you're on your way.'

The lift opened directly into Jo Henderson's apartment. She was standing by the door to greet him. As if they were old friends, and as naturally, she kissed him on both cheeks.

Topher could not help contrasting the apartment with Sally Maddox's basement. Interior design was a language in which furniture, fabrics, and accessories, were the words. So April said. Clients who put their trust in herself and Inez could be sure, at the very least, of getting their grammar right. Where Sally Maddox's flat had been decorated in the main with books, Jo Henderson's was furnished with chairs and tables of doubtless impeccable provenance, hung with paintings individually illuminated, and awash with *objets d'art*. Standing in front of the marble chimney-piece – on which a pair of silver knights on horseback guarded a Second Empire clock – Jo Henderson had the appearance of an *objet d'art* herself. She was wearing a slim black skirt with a tight, long-sleeved jacket of pink silk fastened with large round *diamanté* buttons. There seemed to be a great deal of gold round her slim wrists. On her finger was a substantial emerald ring.

'The porter said *Lady* Henderson . . .'

'Henry was a High Court judge.' She picked up a silver photograph frame and showed Topher a picture of her late husband in his full-bottomed wig.

'I'm so sorry,' Topher said, the boot for once being on the other foot.

Jo replaced the photograph, fussing with its exact position on the *boulle* side-cabinet. She opened her mouth to speak and Topher thought that she was going to talk about the husband who had drowned but she said: 'What can I get you to drink?'

From the range of bottles on display she poured whisky into heavy goblets for Topher and herself. He was running a finger reflectively over the curved blue head of a china bird which regarded him cheekily from a small table.

'It's a chaffinch.' Jo gave him his drink.

'I know.'

He had not intended to talk about Caroline. Despite his good intentions he found himself exhuming her for Jo.

When he had finished telling her about Caroline and her birds, Jo said ambiguously: 'To imagine one can love only one person is like expecting a single candle to burn for ever. I booked a table at Le Mazarin. Is that all right?'

Topher contemplated the proposition and its alternative. Solitary fish-cakes (albeit salmon), despatched at the kitchen table, and Pushkin. He cracked his knuckles, as he often did on the Bench – despite the best endeavours of Mrs Sweetlove to cure him of the habit – before making a decision.

'That sounds splendid.' He wondered if he could safely put the fish-cakes back into the freezer. Because he could think of no further comment to make, he repeated it. 'Absolutely splendid!' They drove in Topher's car to Pimlico. Aware of Jo Henderson's perfume, and her slim knees, he attempted to keep his eyes on the road.

They made a great fuss of Jo in the restaurant. '*Bonsoir*, Lady 'enderson', and ''ow are you today?' and escorted her to a reserved table.

'Where do you usually dine?' Jo asked Topher, when they had been seated.

'At home.'

She raised a plucked eyebrow.

'I cook for myself. Well, it's not exactly cooking . . .' he thought of the fish-cakes with their precise instructions. '. . . thirty-five minutes in a pre-heated oven'.

Jo Henderson picked up her menu.

'I can see,' she said, 'that I shall have to take you in hand.'

Studying the overblown descriptions of the dishes on offer, Topher's eye fell upon the *salades tièdes* for which Caroline had had such scant regard. His determination to confine her to the back burner of his memory failed him once again.

Jo was speaking. His mind on Caroline, Topher had to ask her to repeat what she was saying.

'The *soupe au cresson* is divine.'

It would at least not be derived from a tin.

There were two large whiskies on the table. Topher had not noticed them appear.

His companion lifted her glass.

'To all the lonely people.'

Sitting directly opposite her, in close proximity to her smile, Topher noticed that she had very good teeth which looked as if they had been recently polished. The fronds of her lashes, long and black, each one seeming to be separate, accented the remarkable translucence of her eyes. When you had to describe eyes for the purposes of fiction, Sally Maddox had said, it's amazing how few colours there are to choose from. Jo Henderson's eyes were green, but there was in them a certain superficiality. It was easier to imagine skating over their surface than drowning in them.

Topher ordered the watercress soup, followed by veal, and Jo, warm chicken livers to start with, then fillet of fresh salmon in a sorrel sauce. She waved away the basket of seed-covered rolls and from the wine list settled upon a Château Neuf du Pape '81.

'My son gave up the idea of BBC, by the way. He met a girl from Guadalajara and dropped out.'

'He'll drop back in again,' Topher said, without much conviction.

The conversation turned to legal matters. Over the soup and the chicken livers they discussed the repercussions of delays in the due process of law. Topher's complaint was that, after a long period, the memories of witnesses, unreliable at the best of times, were apt to deteriorate still further. Jo was more concerned with the sleepless nights suffered unnecessarily by the defendants, the pressure on remand accommodation, and the general lack of confidence in the system and those who administered it. Topher had his own theory how the matter might be resolved. It was that judges should sit in the evenings to hear cases which did not require jurors or lay witnesses.

'Why has no one thought of that before?'

'The suggestion has not exactly been received with enthusiasm. The judges would, of course, have to be paid. But it's a question of getting one's priorities right. The present situation is intolerable.'

Further discussion was prevented by the arrival of the main course. Topher had been so engrossed in riding his hobby horse that he had not noticed that the restaurant had filled up. It was now reverberating with a cacophony of multilingual voices punctuated by geysers of laughter. He picked up his knife and fork and regarded the still-life on his plate. A round of veal, sitting on a pasta nest, was set amid a circular vegetable mousse, three tiny carrots, a few miniature *mange-touts* and some dill fronds. Across the table Jo's salmon in its sauce was similarly arranged. Topher wondered whether an attempt to emulate the artistry with his chippolatas and baked beans might not improve the gustatory results.

'What do you do at week-ends?' Jo interrupted his thoughts.

Pushing a recalcitrant strand of pasta into his mouth, Topher considered. On Saturdays, ostensibly, he helped Arthur in the garden. Caroline's garden, in which she had planted pyracantha and berberis, elder and hawthorn, holly and cotoneaster, and set a peanut cylinder for her birds. A great deal of the morning seemed to be taken up sitting at the kitchen table putting the country to rights. On Saturday afternoons he read. Sometimes he fell asleep to the accompaniment of whatever was on offer on Radio 3. In the evening — if he were not visiting Chelsea, or the Gordons, or occasionally the cinema — the afternoon's programme was repeated. On Sunday mornings he walked on the Heath with Marcus and later caught up with any legal work and personal correspondence. The evening was the mixture as before.

'Nothing in particular.'

The reply to Jo's question made him sound dreadfully dull.

'You must come down to the country. I've a place in Berkshire. Between Stockcross and Woodspeen, if you know the area. Overlooking the Lambourn Valley and the Downs. Do you ride?'

'I'm afraid I don't.' He had spent too much time stalking old barns for owls and swallows, pacing wet fields after rooks and magpies. He was not a country person.

To his horror Jo had taken out her diary.

'What about the week-end after next?'

Topher removed his own diary from his pocket and, holding the virgin pages close to his nose, tried to invent some pressing engagement. He had never been much good at lies. Not even the socially acceptable variety.

'My sister . . .' he clutched at Tina for help. 'Bingley . . . Could I possibly let you know?'

Topher was not surprised when Jo refused dessert. While he was concentrating on his *bavarois*, which seemed to have come out of the same mould as the vegetable mousse, and was set in a raspberry sea latticed with cream waves, he looked up to find her green eyes contemplating him speculatively.

'Are you aware,' she said, 'that you are an extremely attractive man?'

What was it Marcus had said? 'You are a man of learning and property, not bad-looking and patently in need of care.'

Jo saved him the trouble of replying. Leaning towards him she lowered her voice and said, 'There's a gorgeous young woman over there who hasn't taken her eyes off you all evening.'

Curious to discover who it was who found him so fascinating, Topher turned round in the direction Jo had indicated. He found himself staring straight into the accusing eyes of Chelsea. She was dining at an alcove table with David Cornish.

'That young woman,' he turned to Jo, 'happens to be my daughter.'

On the way out of the restaurant Topher greeted Chelsea. He introduced her and David to Jo. After the hand-shaking there was an awkward pause. It was filled by David, who said what a pity it was that Topher had not been able to join them at the BBC party. Whilst David was speaking, Topher was conscious that Chelsea was appraising his companion from the top of her sleek head to her elegantly shod foot. He had not the least doubt that she found her, in every respect, wanting.

On the way back to Lowndes Square, Topher told Jo about Chelsea and David and the stalemate of their relationship.

'Your daughter's a fool, if you don't mind me saying so,' Jo said. 'If the man hasn't the guts to leave his wife, she should find somebody else.'

'I suppose she thinks the half of David she has is better than nothing.'

'Poppycock! She's wasting the best years of her life on someone who's incapable, or afraid, of making a commitment to her. She needs to be told. I shall take her out to lunch.'

Topher did not tell her that Chelsea would not take kindly to interference. Where he and Caroline had failed, it was distinctly unlikely that an outsider to whom Chelsea (if her attitude in the restaurant was anything to go by) was evidently hostile, would succeed.

In Lowndes Square Topher escorted Jo to the street door of the flats, and thanked her for the evening.

'You'll come up for a drink.' It was not exactly a question. The porter, who had been dozing behind the desk, leaped up as if he had been doing no such thing and put on his cap smartly.

'Good evening, Lady Henderson. Good evening, Sir.'

'This is His Honour Judge Osgood,' Jo said. 'You'll know him another time.'

'A pleasure, Your Honour.' The porter held the gate of the lift. Topher doubted if there would be another time.

Upstairs he agreed to just one small drink. He poured it for them both and sat down on the sofa. Jo put a record on – Dizzy Gillespie – and sat extremely close to him. Topher, who had drunk more than he should in the restaurant, attempted through a pleasant haze to keep his wits about him. The situation in which he now found himself reminded him of an old movie. He imagined that he was Cary Grant, or Spencer Tracy, and tried to remember his lines.

Before he had a chance to consider them, Jo had put down her drink and undone the *diamanté* buttons of her jacket. Topher guessed that both Cary Grant and Spencer Tracy would have been amazed to discover that she wore nothing at all beneath it. She had the breasts of a young girl.

Topher stood up and muttered that he must be going. It was Jo's turn to be amazed.

'I don't understand.' She looked puzzled. 'Why did you come up?'

Topher considered his reply. He did not wish to appear boorish. 'You forgot to give me my pen.'

Chapter Thirteen

Each time Topher got into his car he was reminded of Jo Henderson. He was aware of her perfume, which clung tenaciously to the upholstery, as he drove towards Kentish Town to pick up Sally Maddox. Since the evening at Le Mazarin, with its extraordinary finale, he had been sorely troubled. What bothered him was his lack of perception, the fact that the wires had so obviously been crossed. 'You'll come up for a drink?' How was he supposed to know that since his day – admittedly a very long time ago now – the words had acquired another meaning. The misunderstanding was not the only thing about the evening which bothered him. Try as he would he was unable to get the picture of the proffered breasts out of his mind. They were most attractive. Like nothing so much as firm, long-stalked pears. Caroline's breasts, she was a big woman, had been soft and pendulous. Jo Henderson had been amused rather than angry at his refusal of her favours. To Topher's disappointment she had promptly buttoned her jacket and crossed to the *bureau plat* from which she retrieved the pen.

'You'll let me know about coming to the country?' she said, as matter of factly as if nothing at all had happened.

'Of course. And thank you again for this evening,' Topher said awkwardly.

'It's been a great pleasure.'

For the second time Jo kissed him on both cheeks.

Thoroughly confused, he got into the lift.

In the days that intervened he had, in his mind, returned to the scene. He had performed it several times over, altering the *dénouement* at will. More often than not, in its replay, he had accepted the tacit invitation and (Cary Grant and Spencer Tracy rolled into one) fallen into Jo Henderson's arms and, by extension, into her bed. That he had not done so in reality was due to his upbringing which had left him with the firm conviction that morality and happiness went hand in hand. In his youth a period of courtship – often protracted to unbelievable lengths by today's standards – invariably preceeded sexual relationships. He had been to bed (he could not, even in his head, entertain the contemporary idiom) with several girls before his marriage to Caroline. He had not however slept with his wife until after the wedding. Hitherto, he had associated the shift in mores solely with his daughters. Having been groped by Sally Maddox, an event now overshadowed by the exposure of Jo Henderson's breasts, he should have been alerted to the fact that the change in his status entailed more than mastering the idiosyncrasies of the spin-dryer and learning how to approach a Cabbage and Mushroom Bake.

Wanting to be in court early to cast his eyes over the papers before the first case, he arrived in Jeffrey's Street fifteen minutes before the agreed time. In answer to his ring Sally's voice came through the Entryphone.

'Christopher? You said nine-*fifteen*! I shan't be long. Come in and have some coffee.'

Unnerved by his experience at Lowndes Square, he wondered if the seemingly innocent invitation could possibly have a similar connotation. In view of the early hour he decided to take the risk.

To his relief Sally Maddox was fully clothed, although her hair, surprisingly long and lustrous, was round her shoulders. She was wearing the dress with the poppies.

'Will this do?' She held out the skirt.

'That's fine,' he said. And then, the words coming out involuntarily, 'I liked you in that brown thing.'

'I haven't got a "brown thing". I look ghastly in brown.'

'The one you wore at April's.' He could have bitten his tongue out.

To his relief Sally laughed.

'That was purple.'

Topher remembered that he was colour-blind. Caroline had always told him so.

He drank his coffee while Sally finished her *toilette* in the bathroom from where she carried on a conversation.

'How's Pushkin?'

Topher recited some verses, the Russian now flowing more easily from his tongue: '*O rose maiden,/you fetter me;/But I am no more ashamed/ To be fettered by you/Than is the nightingale king/Of woodland singers, ashamed/To live close-bound to the rose,/Tenderly singing songs for her/In the obscure voluptuous night.*'

He decided against translating.

In the car Sally wrinkled her nose.

'*Arpège,*' Topher said. Caroline had worn it. It was the only perfume he knew by name. 'Chelsea uses buckets of it.'

'Not on your Nelly,' Sally said. 'It's Halston. You can smell it a mile off.'

To cover the confusion of his lie, and deciding to take the bull by the horns, he said: 'Talking of the Gordons . . .' Although they had in fact not been. Sally waited expectantly. Topher swallowed.

'Why did you do what you did?'

'What did I do?'

'It was while the *hors d'oeuvre* was going round.' Topher, suddenly feeling very warm, prayed he would not be called upon to continue. 'I was just about to pass the dish to April . . .'

'Oh, you mean this?'

To his horror, Topher felt Sally's firm hand again between his thighs. He removed his own hand from the steering wheel.

'Sally, please!'

'You looked so utterly miserable. I was only trying to cheer you up. You *do* take things seriously, Christopher.'

'Sometimes . . .' he said, driving with one hand only on the wheel by way of precaution, and thinking of Jo Henderson, 'I'm inclined to think I don't take them seriously enough.'

Mrs Sweetlove who was, Topher had noticed lately, taking more trouble with her appearance (today she was sporting white earrings like miniature door-knobs, white spectacle frames, and a lacy white jumper, with a little bow at the neck, beneath her gown) was waiting, with his apple-juice, in his room.

'This is Miss Maddox,' Topher introduced Sally. 'I want you to look after her for me. Find her a seat in court. She will be staying for lunch.'

Mrs Sweetlove looked at Sally as if she had at that moment been overtaken by the pangs of severe indigestion.

97

'Very well, Your Honour.'

Topher turned his attention to his guest.

'These are my chambers. It is here that I change into my robes.'

Sally Maddox took a micro cassette-recorder from the depths of her capacious hand-bag.

'Is it all right if I use this in court?'

'Not unless you want me to send you to prison. Under section 9 of the Contempt of Court Act 1981, it is a contempt to tape-record proceedings. Put it away, for goodness' sake. I'll tell you something about the case.'

The case, adjourned from the previous week, concerned a development company which, under the terms of the Rent Act of 1977, was trying to get possession of a mansion flat in Maida Vale. The flat was let to a wine-importer who had lived in it for twenty-one years. The development company, having bought the entire block for conversion, had offered the wine-importer and his family alternative accommodation in North Finchley.

At Friday's hearing it had been established that the alternative accommodation was not *exactly* in North Finchley but in a sleazy backwater of Friern Barnet, and that the premises had yet to be converted.

The development company based its case on the fact that the wine-importer was not only the owner of a large, listed house in Oxfordshire, but that his alleged 'family' (two grown-up daughters) had, in fact, long since left home.

'I have to hear an *ex parte* first,' Topher told Sally adjusting his robes. 'A case of wife beating.'

'That sounds much more my cup of tea.'

'I'm afraid that must be heard in chambers. It shouldn't take very long. You can stay here if you like.'

'I thought these were your chambers?'

'Ah, the *court* as chambers. That is to say, *privately*.'

'In that case I shall wander around, if I may.'

Half-an-hour later, having disposed of the *ex parte*, Topher watched Sally Maddox, escorted by Mrs Sweetlove, take her seat in the front row of the public gallery. She took out her notebook and, to his horror, looked directly up at him and winked.

Topher's embarrassment at the gesture led to Mrs Sweetlove's having to make frantic signs at him during his *resumé* of the possession case, to draw his attention to the fact that he was not wearing his wig, which he had removed for the *ex parte*. He retrieved it from the Bench, and raised a laugh in the court by apologising, with a twinkle in his eye, for his oversight.

From the witness box, the wine-importer appealed to Topher for the right to remain in the Maida Vale flat, on the grounds that a central London address was essential for his business activities, that he needed to be within walking distance of his aged and ailing parents, and that the alternative premises were unsuitable.

Questioning his client about the said business activities, the wine-importer's counsel referred *ad nauseam* to the fact that wine purchased abroad, *wholesale*, must reside in bonded warehouses before it was distributed to shops in Central London, from which it was sold *retail*. Topher intervened to point out that he was fully aware of the difference between wholesale and retail, and there was no need to labour the point. Changing the subject, and hoisting his gown on to his shoulder with a gesture born of long years at the Bar, defending counsel went on to describe, in some detail, his client's mother's diabetes.

'It is quite obvious, Your Honour, that this elderly lady is house-bound . . .'

'That is an inference I cannot accept.' Topher prided himself on his knowledge of medicine, most of which he had picked up from Marcus. Having made his point he made the mistake of looking towards Sally Maddox. She was shaking her clasped fist jubilantly, as if it were a football match she was watching and Topher had scored a goal.

When it was his turn, counsel for the prosecution attempted to prove that only a small percentage of the wine-importer's clients were in fact located in central London; that when he was in England the defendant resided, more often than not, in Oxfordshire; that as far as the 'family' claimed by him was concerned, one daughter was married – and well able to afford a place of her own – and the other was in India, where she had been for six months, sitting at the feet of her guru.

Counsel for the defence, in his summing-up, respectfully drew Topher's attention to Schedule 16, Section 98 of the Green Book on his desk, and urged him to take a broad common sense view of the case bearing in mind the defendant's present proximity to his work, that the alternative premises did not as yet exist, that even if they had existed they would be too small, and the fact that there was a world of difference between urban and suburban living.

99

Counsel for the prosecution referred Topher to McDonald and Daley, 1969, in which an artist, in possession of what Topher understood to be three brooms, was offered two.

'*Brooms?*' Topher said.

'*Rooms!* Your Honour.'

Raising his voice so that he could be heard more clearly, he pointed out for Topher's benefit the difference between 'suitable' and 'reasonable' accommodation. He suggested that it was in the public interest for the Maida Vale flat to be made available to some unfortunate family who did not even have one, let alone two homes. Topher, with one eye on the lunchtime clock, courteously thanked the representative of the property company for the detailed plans he had provided for the rehousing of the defendant. The needs of the tenant must however be taken into account. The alternative premises were totally unsuitable in location, totally inferior in character, totally inferior with regard to size, and totally inferior bearing in mind proximity to the defendant's work. The fact that he had two homes was largely irrelevant, but the age and poor health of his parents must be taken seriously into consideration. Bearing in mind all three factors the plaintiff's case could be said to disintegrate like a pack of cards. He could see no alternative but to dismiss it.

Counsel for the defendant, looking decidedly pleased with himself, jumped up to ask for costs, and from the corner of his eye Topher saw Sally Maddox put her notebook and pencil away.

Over lunch in his room, during which Mrs Sweetlove appeared an inordinate number of times to enquire if there was anything further His Honour wanted, Sally Maddox said: 'My problem is that I can always see both sides of everything. I started off feeling sorry for the development company then, when the wine-importer's wife said that the flat in Maida Vale had been the 'nerve centre of the family' and their home for twenty odd years, I felt sorry for *her*. I'd be hopeless as a judge.'

Topher passed her a tub of apricot yoghurt.

'The case has to be decided on questions of law – taking into account the precedents – and fact. One has to interpret such terms as needs, in the legal sense, and to be aware of the precise difference between reasonable and suitable. Emotions, fortunately, do not enter into it.'

Mrs Sweetlove tapped and entered.

'Will your guest be requiring coffee, Your Honour?' She addressed Topher pointedly as if Sally Maddox did not exist.

When she had gone, Topher said: 'I saw you writing. Did you get what you wanted?'

'Strangely enough,' Sally fished for the lumps of apricot in the yoghurt, 'one of the more interesting moments was outside the court. I eavesdropped on a couple of barristers. I thought I might catch some pearls of legal wisdom.'

'And?'

'They were discussing car telephones. Apparently one is not only charged for outgoing calls, but incoming calls have to be paid for too. Henry James would have been fascinated.'

'What has Henry James to do with car telephones?'

'The "jog of fancy's elbow". Do you have any books about judges?'

'Several. We'll stop at the house on the way home if you like.'

The invitation had been issued lightly. It had not occurred to Topher that to take Sally Maddox home was to invite her to tread on his dreams. Unlocking the front door and stepping back to allow her, in her scarlet poppies, to enter the house he felt the silent accusation of its greeting.

He left Sally in his study before the books on the judiciary and went into the kitchen to make some tea. As he was filling the kettle he heard the telephone ring.

'Shall I take it?' Sally called from the study.

'Please.'

He plugged in the kettle and depressed the automatic switch.

'She says her name is Lucille.' There was incredulity in Sally's voice. 'This Saturday is sold out but she can get tickets for the following week. Is that all right?'

Topher remembered that he had agreed to go to *Cats*. Also that the following week-end he was promised to Jo Henderson in Berkshire.

He removed two tea-bags from the caddy and dismissed the swift image of Jo Henderson's *déshabillé* from his mind.

'Tell Lucille the week-end after next will be fine.'

As he filled the tea-pot the telephone rang again.

'Someone called Tina?' Sally, her eyebrows raised, stood in the doorway.

Topher put down the kettle.

'That's my sister.'

'Pull the other one!' Sally said.

Chapter Fourteen

'Who's Lucille?' Sally Maddox, her scarlet poppies brightening up the kitchen, helped herself to the last of Topher's chocolate-chip cookies.

Topher did not answer immediately. He wondered if his hesitation to reply to Sally's question stemmed from the fact that he was ashamed that he had actually agreed to go and see *Cats*, or from a natural disinclination to discuss with her the details of his private life. Before he had a chance to resolve the problem, he heard himself tell Sally about Miles' birthday party and about Lucille. He also told her about Jo Henderson and the evening at Le Mazarin. To spare his own blushes he applied a blue pencil to the penultimate scene.

When he had finished speaking, the tea was cold. Sally got up to refill the kettle. As she passed behind Topher's chair she ruffled his hair and, for a moment, held his head against the scarlet poppies. He could feel both the warmth of her flesh and the comforting leaps of her heart.

'All these lady friends, and there are you sitting up there in your wig,' she said, releasing him, 'as if butter wouldn't melt in your mouth.'

'I assure you it wouldn't.' Topher straightened his hair and passed her the teapot.

'After tea,' Sally changed the subject, 'will you show me the house?'

They started with the Piano Room. Topher looked at the polished oak boards, the carved wooden cowl over the fireplace, the ebony

concert grand which Caroline had brought to the marriage. He saw
black ties, long dresses, hired help circulating with silver trays of
canapés. The image faded. It was replaced with a children's party, in
which Chelsea and Penge sat in a semi-circle of their friends on the
floor, before a conjuror who produced china eggs from the air and
ribbons of coloured handkerchiefs from the tightly closed fists of
astounded volunteers. He saw Christmases with brightly lit trees.
Caroline's Bring-and-Buy sales (tables piled high with *bric-à-brac*)
from which he would run a mile. Discos – the music from which could
be heard as far as Marcus and April's – in which the men wore 'Doctor
Martens', and the girls all looked as if they could do with a good
scrub. He saw the silver wedding celebrations at which Penge (in
electric-blue crêpe, with a matching headband low over her forehead)
had recited an adulatory ode, composed by herself and Chelsea, to her
parents. The girls' nuptials, which he and Caroline had pictured as
taking place in the Piano Room, had not materialised.

Sally Maddox, on the threshold of the room now redolent only of
disuse, made no comment. Topher was grateful. He closed the door,
turning the key on his recollections. They made their way upstairs.

Seeing his home through other eyes, Topher was conscious of the
threadbare patches of carpet, of the heavy furniture and dated décor.
In the two functional bathrooms there were no twin washbasins, no
gold taps, no marble surrounds. April had been itching to get her
hands on the house for years. He left the bedroom until last. His
throat tightened as he opened the door for Sally Maddox. She touched
the bed, and Caroline's bureau, lightly – as if her fingers were
recording the chenille bedspread, the inlaid mahogany – then crossed
the room and looked out at the plane trees which lined the street.

'Shall you move?'

'The girls want me to.'

'The house *is* rather large.'

'There are things in it which one couldn't put into a packing-case.'

'You're wrong, Christopher. They're in your head. They will
always be there.'

Downstairs, in the little used sitting-room which overlooked the
garden, Sally looked at the photographs of Chelsea and Penge. She
studied them for a long time.

'I had a child,' she said.

Topher was surprised.

Sally sat in the armchair, which had been Caroline's, clutching a photograph of Penge in her school uniform. It had been taken when Penge was ten.

'We lived in Holland Park. We had a big house then. Oliver published art books. Coffee-table. Thomas went to St. Paul's. Oliver used take Tom to school every day on his way to the office. Tom was never ready. He took after me. Oliver was obsessional. Tom drove him to distraction. Oliver used to threaten him. If he wasn't waiting with his cap, and his satchel, and his foot-ball boots – or whatever it happened to be – at quarter to eight, Oliver said he'd have to go to school on the train.

'One morning Oliver carried out his threat. He was in the car. Tom was still in the bedroom looking for his French verb book. It was five to eight. Oliver hooted, and Tom banged on the window to say he wouldn't be a moment. Oliver didn't hear him. Perhaps he did. I don't know. He drove off. To teach Tom a lesson. I helped Tom look for his book. It was under his pillow – he'd been learning *connaître* before he went to sleep. He was furious with Oliver. 'Now I'll be late, Mummy,' he said. 'It's not fair!' Those were the last words. 'It's not fair.' He ran across Notting Hill to the station. He was knocked down by a bus . . .'

She stopped and looked at Topher.

'. . . he was eleven years old.'

'Oh, my God,' Topher said.

'He would be twenty-one now. Sometimes, to console myself, I think that he might have been into drugs, or that I'd be worrying about AIDS. That perhaps his death was some kind of divine salvation. I don't believe it. I try not to think about it more than I can help but occasionally . . .

'After Tom died, Oliver and I split up. Not immediately. Things were never the same. Oliver went completely to pieces. He started drinking. Then he took to religion of various kinds, some of them completely cracked. After that it was analysis. It didn't seem to do him much good. The publishing went to pot. He never stopped blaming himself for Tom's death, although of course it wasn't his fault. I couldn't look at him without accusing him in my head. As if he had actually murdered Tom with his own hands. When we realised that we were slowly destroying each other we decided to call it a day. I went to live in the country where I wouldn't see those red buses, in reality as well as in my dreams. Oliver went to Ireland. He has a farm. Outside Killarney. And a woman he lives with. I went to visit him when I was there.'

104

'Does April know?' Topher thought it strange that she hadn't mentioned anything about a child.

Sally shook her head.

'There are not many people whom I tell.'

She stood up and replaced the photograph of Penge on the table from which she had taken it.

'There's not really much point.'

Topher watched her compose her face. As if she was putting the memory of Tom away where it belonged.

'You must be lonely.'

'It's better for a writer to be alone. The thoughts come. I enjoy solitude, the way some people enjoy being in a crowd. Being by myself gives me an enormous sense of being alive. I loved Oliver, but my internal certainty – I think all artists have it – made him uncomfortable. He wanted me to *need* his approbation, his agreement, his consolation. Like most men *he* needed constant attention. He had to know what I was doing, where I was going – and how long I would be – had I seen the corkscrew, and wasn't dinner ready. Sometimes he made me feel like a dilatory housekeeper. I'm not exactly a feminist. I'm not even very sure what it means. But I do think that marriage is not very fair on women. We are *still* always expected to accommodate men. If I ever had a lasting relationship with anyone again, it would have to be on very special terms.'

Topher said nothing. He could think of nothing to say.

'Let's sit in your study,' Sally said abruptly, as if she had talked enough about herself.

Looking round the bay-windowed room at the front of the house, she said, 'This is how I pictured you. When April introduced us, at the dinner party. You looked as if you were sorry you'd come. As if you wanted nothing so much as to go home. Home, I imagined, was like this.' She waved an arm at the bookshelves, the leather armchair with its footstool, the record player, the complete set of Law Reports, the stacked journals, the desk which had belonged to Topher's father.

'This is *you*, Christopher. The rest of the house is Caroline.'

She took the copy of *An End to Dying* from her handbag.

'I almost forgot.'

Topher opened the book to see what she had written in it.

'But if the while I think on thee, dear friend/All losses are restor'd and sorrows end.'

'*Two Gentlemen of Verona*,' Topher leaned forward and kissed Sally on her cheek, smelling her fragrance.

Putting *An End to Dying* on a shelf he said: 'What shall I read next?'

'It's extremely embarrassing to have to recommend one's work. Almost as bad as admitting to writing it. Sometimes I wish I were a harpist, or a vet. Having owned up to being a writer, people want to know your name. When you tell them, there's a tangible silence. Then they ask should they know you? Or insist that you tell them what you have written. You have to go through the humiliating process of reciting the titles. Said aloud they sound so inane that you can't think how you ever came to choose them.'

She looked round the room. 'You don't look like a novel reader, Christopher.'

'I'm not. I'd like to know more about you.'

'And you think that you will find out by reading my books?'

'Won't I?'

Sally Maddox thought for a moment. 'Possibly. Perhaps you will be disappointed. If I *have* to recommend one it would be my first, before the disillusionment, the cynicism set in. Read *Unto the Rainbow*.'

'"To smooth the ice, or add another hue/Unto the rainbow. . . ."'

'What I like about you Christopher is that I don't have to dot the "i's" and cross the "t's". The book's out of print.'

'I'll get it from the library.'

'You don't have to do that. I'll lend it to you. I must be off. I've taken up enough of your day. I'm going to say hallo to April.'

'I hope you got what you wanted.'

Sally patted her handbag in which was her notebook. 'It was most useful.'

'I'll walk down the road with you.'

At the Gordons' gate, Sally said: 'I can't offer to take you to *Cats*, or to a poncy French restaurant, but there's the Quarterly Dinner at the PEN club next month. Will you be my guest?'

'I'd like that very much.'

'If you don't hear from me for a bit it's because I'm in the grip of the muse.'

Topher felt a sense of disappointment.

'I tend to shut myself away when I'm starting a new book.'

Topher, used now to the kissing game, was about to plant a chaste peck on Sally's cheek by way of farewell, when she flung her arms round his neck and fastened her mouth on his as if she were a honey-seeking bee. The experience was not unpleasant. He hoped that April was not looking out of the window.

Back in his house he cleared away the tea things. He was spending the evening with Chelsea and David. There was no need to think about dinner.

He was sweeping up the crumbs from the chocolate-chip cookies when he heard singing in the kitchen. It was a moment before he realised that the sounds were emanating from his own lips: ' "When I was a lad I served a term/As office boy to an Attorney's firm./I cleaned the windows and I swept the floor,/And I polished up the handle of the big front door . . ." '

He couldn't remember the last time he had broken spontaneously into song. Certainly not since Caroline had died. In his early days at the Bar he had performed Gilbert and Sullivan, much of which he knew by heart, on stage in the Middle Temple concert. His noisy renditions drove Caroline mad. She used to hold her hands over her ears in mock horror. Running the broom methodically over the linoleum, he wondered whether she could see him now. He moved the chairs and collected the crumbs which had fallen beneath the table, just in case she could. Returning the broom to the cleaning cupboard he took out the dustpan and brush.

' "I polished up that handle so carefull-ee,/That now I am the Ruler of the Queen's Navee!" '

Going up in the cage of the creaking goods lift to the Wapping warehouse which had once been a grain store, Topher's carefree mood vanished as suddenly as it had appeared. He remembered Jo Henderson's words, concerning his daughter's relationship with David Cornish, and wondered whether during the course of the evening there would be an opportunity to talk seriously to Chelsea about the unsuitability of her lover.

While she was occupied with the dinner, Topher stood with David by the window overlooking the dirty river.

'Good health, Sir,' David raised his glass. 'How are the criminals? Still giving crime a bad name?'

'It's no good asking him about criminals.' Chelsea's voice wafted from the kitchen. 'I don't suppose he's ever actually met any.'

'You don't need to be a chef to judge an omelette, darling.' David said.

'Thank God someone's on my side. I did spend twenty years at the Bar, but I have never been able to convince Chelsea that the lives led not only by judges, but by other successful professionals, do not preclude them from the knowledge of what the ordinary man, whoever he might be, is thinking, nor how he is likely to react. We spend a great part of our day listening to the ordinary man. We have every opportunity of testing our opinions about a case against those of the jury, and of making up our own minds about the character of a witness. We'd have to be extremely stupid not to absorb – from what is constantly being acted out before us – a sense of the ordinary man's attitudes in the situations with which the law has to deal. In Chelsea's book all criminals are misunderstood members of the lower classes, just as all judges are disagreeable bullies with their minds rooted firmly in the nineteenth century.'

'Present company, of course, excepted.' Chelsea came in with the wooden salad bowl.

'Her notions are not only based upon stereotypes but are as ill-conceived as they are unjust.'

David put an arm round Chelsea.

'I didn't mean to put the cat among the pigeons.'

'It's all right, David,' Topher said. 'Intemperate abuse of judges is punishable as contempt of court. There's no doubt that, in the old days, there were some extremely unpleasant judges. Many of them were politicians. The English distrust politicians, just as they are suspicious of academics and make jokes about civil servants. Since the last war the judiciary has changed considerably. It is now composed, by and large, of unremarkable men with unsensational private lives. Critics – such as the one you have your arm around – are living largely on legend.'

'I think this critic had better get back into the kitchen if we're to have any dinner,' Chelsea said.

'Don't tell me you're actually *cooking?*' Topher sat down on the white canvas sofa.

'Heating up the spare-ribs. David brought a take-away.'

When she had gone Topher said, 'Chelsea's a different person when she has you around.'

'I do realise how hard it is on her,' David said, coming to sit next to him. 'As you know my wife is a manic-depressive. If I'm not there she doesn't take her drugs. It's impossible for me to leave her. I've tried not to mess up Chelsea's life. We've both tried. You see – ' he looked at Topher – 'the trouble is . . . it's quite simple, really. Chelsea and I love each other.'

'It's good of you to discuss it with me.'

David looked towards the kitchen. 'I couldn't manage without Chelsea.'

'What have you two got your heads together about?' Chelsea weaved her way round the Edwardian birdcage with a pile of plates. 'Whatever it is, you'll have to break it up. I need my butler.'

'For spare-ribs?' Topher said.

Chelsea kissed the top of his head.

'I can't help it if I was brought up properly.'

Chapter Fifteen

'Olga, you morning-star,/Godchild of Aphrodite,/Miracle of beauty,/
How accustomed you are/To sting with a caress . . .'

Topher, his mind only partly on the poem, wondered in what weak
moment he had agreed to go with Lucille to *Cats*. *Cats*! She had
called to say that she was spending the day in Hendon with one of her
girl-friends who would give her a lift to Hampstead at around six. She
was looking forward to seeing Topher again. Politely, Topher had
returned the compliment. But he was not looking forward to seeing
Lucille. He would much rather have spent the evening battling with
Pushkin and listening to the Beethoven Late Quartets. Ringing Jo
Henderson to say that he was unable to come down to the cottage, he
had been unable to bring himself to confess the true reason.

'I'm afraid I'm tied up on Saturday night,' he had said, lamely. Jo
had not pressed him further. She had re-issued the invitation to
Badger's for the following week-end when there should be some
'amusing people'. Topher was relieved to discover that he was not to
be the only house-guest.

He tried to concentrate on his translation, but was listening for the
sound of the front-door bell. In Lucille's honour he had put a decanter
of sherry and two glasses on a silver tray. At the back of the larder he
had found a packet of peanuts (the 'sell by' date long past) and had
tipped them into one of Caroline's engraved glass finger-bowls.

Lucille was late. An impeccable time-keeper himself, he did not
take kindly to unpunctuality in others. Drumming his fingers on the

side of his armchair he tried to work out the Russian for 'priapic folly'.

When Lucille finally arrived she was all apologies.

'Sorry I kept you waiting, love.' She embraced a decidedly edgy Topher. 'There must be something on at Wembley. We were sat sitting more than thirty minutes at Hendon Central. You've never seen such jams! What a smashing house. I'm dying to spend a penny.'

She was wearing a dress which might have looked right at a rave-up in Bingley but was, even to Topher's untutored eyes, a bit over the top for *Cats*. The grotesque diamond, spanning two knuckles, was set off by the black lace. Topher showed Lucille the way to the downstairs cloakroom. On her return to the sitting-room she looked at the sherry decanter and the time expired peanuts. Her face fell. Topher fetched the whisky bottle from the top of the fridge.

The drive to Drury Lane was not auspicious. The entire population of North West London appeared to be heading for the West End. The traffic was snarled up at Swiss Cottage and again at Euston Road.

'It's all my fault,' Lucille wailed. 'It's not one of my days!'

'Optat supremo collocare Sisyphus in monte saxum.'

'Come again?'

'"Someone up there doesn't love me".' Topher hooted angrily and uncharacteristically at a driver who was attempting to cut him up.

'You're ever so clever, aren't you?' Lucille said. 'I like a man with brains.'

It took fifteen minutes to find a parking place. Another ten — because of Lucille's stiletto heels — to reach the theatre.

'You must be cursing me,' Lucille said, taking three tiny steps to Topher's one. 'If there's one thing I hate it's a bad time keeper.'

'We should just make it,' Topher said gallantly, with more conviction than he felt.

Outside the theatre the queue for returned tickets regarded them hopefully. In the foyer, usherettes in *Cats* tee-shirts directed them to the escalators, urging them raucously to 'Pass along quickly please' as the performance was about to commence.

Topher bought a programme and a souvenir brochure for Lucille. The auditorium resembled a giant rubbish dump. Dustbins, an abandoned car, tyres, bicycles, and discarded Christmas decorations littered the stage and were suspended from the dress-circle. Apologising for the disturbance, Lucille and Topher squeezed past a line of knees. An American tourist in a plaid sportscoat removed his raincoat from Topher's seat.

111

'Hi!'

'Hi,' Topher said, without enthusiasm, as the house-lights were extinguished and a trumpet blast from an unseen band threatened to shatter his ear drums.

Above his head a thousand cat's eyes twinkled through the gloom. An old boot, hurled from the wings, landed with a thump in the centre of the stage. The four rows of seats, at the back of which Topher and Lucille were sitting, began slowly to revolve.

'It's the moving platform,' Lucille hissed. 'I was very lucky to get them.'

Topher, who was prone to motion sickness and never went on boats if it could be avoided, wondered for how long they were going to rotate. He became disorientated in the darkness and began to feel queasy.

'Smashing, isn't it?' Lucille said. 'We end up right round the other side. My friend told me.'

When they finally stopped, Topher had the sensation that the seats were still moving. He shut his eyes. When he opened them again the stage had filled with cats. Male and female bodies, taut leotards leaving no detail of nipple or crotch to the imagination, moved in erotic, feline rhythm to the hypnotic thrum of the orchestra. Wigged and whiskered, ginger and marmalade, multi-coloured and tabby, Thomas Stearns Eliot's *Jellicle Cats* enacted their anarchic rituals and belted out lyrics of which Topher could make neither head nor tail, because long before they reached him they were swallowed up by the music. Feeling decidedly alienated, and distinctly uncomfortable, he wondered what on earth had possessed him to come.

A sideways glance at his companion confirmed that his misgivings were not shared. Lucille – in company with the rest of the audience – was drinking in every movement, seemed to be able to distinguish every word. Topher considered Chelsea's contention that the habits you were trained in, the people with whom you mixed, led you to have certain ideas of such a nature that, when you had to deal with other ideas you were unable to be as impartial as you might wish. Perhaps Chelsea was right. If he was unable to share the evident pleasure of those who surrounded him, to raise the least fervour for what they were so patently lapping up, how could he be expected to give a sound and accurate judgement to the man in the street?

A number on the naming of cats preceded the information that, together with the Pollicle Dogs, the Jellicle Cats were preparing

112

themselves for the Jellicle Ball. Topher had never heard such arrant nonsense.

A glance at his programme, illuminated by the overspill of lights from the stage, told him that there were ten more acts to sit through before the interval. In them he would have the opportunity to meet The Rum Tum Tugger, Bustapha Jones, Old Deuteronomy, Mungojerrie, and Grizabella the Glamour Cat. Resigning himself to the fact that, in the interests of courtesy, all escape routes were barred, he sat back to let the sights and sounds of the production wash over him.

Bustapha Jones, a muscular black giant whose private parts seemed in imminent danger of rupturing his skin-tight hose, rolled his eyes, rotated his pelvis, and finally leaped from the stage to sit on the laps of several delighted ladies in the auditorium.

Old Deuteronomy, a senior (cat) citizen, solemnly decreed that — come the dawn – one lucky cat from those assembled at his feet, would be selected for the Journey to the 'Heaviside Layer'.

The lights were again doused. An oversized moon appeared in the sky. Grizabella, a mangy, spindle shanked, has-been of a glamour-cat, tottered into the spotlight in her high-heeled shoes. Softly, throatily, she crooned into the silence.

'Midnight, not a sound from the pavement . . .'

Topher sat up.

'Has the moon lost her memory . . . she is smiling alone . . .'

Something in her voice touched a chord within him. Grizabella's melancholy face was time-ravaged beneath the tousled hair.

'*I remember . . . the time I knew what happiness was . . .*'

Topher remembered too. It seemed a long time ago now.

'*. . . Let the memory, live again./Every streetlight seems to beat a fatalistic warning . . . someone mutters . . . and a street lamp gutters . . . and soon it will be morning.*'

Grizabella's song, reinforced by its injection of hope, grew stronger. It swelled to fill the auditorium. Made its way, uninvited, into Topher's head.

'*. . . If you touch me . . . You'll understand what happiness is . . . look, a new day, has begun. . . !*'

Topher refused to believe that there was a lump in his throat, tears in his eyes. Who was it who had said 'in the hands of a genius even a musical comedy can become a masterpiece'?

He felt a hand on his, pulling him to his feet.

113

'It's the interval,' Lucille said. 'I'm dry as a bone!'

The second half of the show passed more quickly. 'Gus: The Theatre Cat', 'Growl Tiger's Last Stand', 'Skimbleshanks', and the rousing choruses of 'Mr. Mistoffeles'. Finally, it was Grizabella who was chosen to ascend (in a red cloud) to the Heaviside Layer from where – lucky moggie – she would eventually be re-born.

'Outside the theatre Lucille said: 'Wasn't it smashing? I could see it all over again.'

While, in the second half at least, the show had not been as bad as Topher feared, he could not exactly share Lucille's sentiments. The thought occurred to him that he should have booked up somewhere for dinner.

Lucille was waiting expectantly.

'How about something to eat?' Topher hoped that she would decline the invitation and he could go home. He would just be in time to hear the end of the Late Quartets.

'I'm starving,' Lucille said.

She seemed always to be either dry or starving.

They walked to Soho, Lucille clinging to Topher's arm. Outside a strip club she pulled him to an abrupt halt.

'Just look at that!'

'That' was a photograph of a naked and well-endowed female manipulating a snake in a manner which left very little to the imagination.

'You don't see many of those in Bingley,' Lucille said.

A person of indeterminate sex, wearing evening dress and heavy make-up, informed them from the brightly lit doorway that they would be just in time for the second show.

'Shall we?' Lucille said. 'Just for a laugh.'

Topher was appalled. SEX SHOW CIRCUIT JUDGE . . .

He pulled his companion away from the photographs of the snake charmer and other redoubtable, moist-lipped ladies who inclined towards the camera at such an angle that their inflated bosoms threatened to shatter the lens.

'Not even for a laugh.'

In the quasi-Italian restaurant they faced each other across the bread-sticks. Over a large vodka (she was absolutely parched) Lucille opened her handbag to show Topher the souvenirs she had bought in the interval at *Cats*. A black tee-shirt from which stared two green cat's eyes, six *Cats* coasters, a *Cats* record, a *Cats* poster, and half a dozen *Cats* badges for her nieces and nephews.

With the first course of sea-food (which when it came looked more like an aquarium) they shared a bottle of white Villa Antinori. Assisted only marginally by Topher, who had to drive home, Lucille managed a *carafe* of the house red with her breaded veal escalope (captivating the waiter who hovered with the giant pepper mill), and a Tia Maria with her *zabaglione* which was itself laced with Marsala.

Sucking delicately on the sponge finger which she had dunked into the amber froth in its tall glass, she said: 'This stuff takes me back. I used to make it for Harold.'

Topher guessed that Harold must have been one of her husbands. He was not sure which one.

Before he had a chance to enquire, Lucille, an expression of sadness coming over her face, said quietly: 'Harold was my last husband. I was married when I was seventeen. Straight from school. To get away from home I suppose. That was Walter. 'Walter . . . Walter . . . lead me to the altar . . .' Walter led me to the altar all right but that was about as much as he could manage. He was a captain in the army. He should have married Stanley. Stanley was his batman. He did everything for Walter, bar get into bed with us. He would have done that too given half a chance!' Lucille scraped up the last of the *zabaglione* with her long spoon.

'After Walter it was Micky. Nothing suspect about Micky. Six foot two in his socks and the spitting image of Marlon Brando. I thought he loved me. He did really. It was just that he had a funny way of showing it. What he didn't know about women wasn't worth knowing. After Walter I thought this is it, Lucille, everything is going to be OK. It was for a bit. Then Micky started with the rough stuff. He had this terrible temper. I don't think he could help it. Afterwards he'd be as sweet as pie. My father used to tell us, if a man ever raises a hand to you girls — there were five of us, I was the youngest — you've to open the window and tell the whole street. I didn't know what he was on about. I never did what he said. I was too ashamed. Sometimes I was in a right state . . .' Lucille put a hand to the back of her neck. '. . . I never let on though. Not to anyone. People always said how sweet Micky was. He did have a lovely way with him. We were married for fifteen years.

'I think I'd still be married to him if Harold hadn't come along. I used to work in Schofield's, that's a big department store in Leeds. I was the fashion buyer. Harold manufactured dresses. As soon as I saw him . . . I couldn't help myself. Neither of us could. We used to see each other every Wednesday – Harold's wife went to Rug Making and Micky played poker. Harold took a little *peed-à-terre* for us. One Wednesday the pipes burst so Harold came to my place. Unfortunately Micky had a migraine – he suffered from them – and came home early. He almost killed Harold. It was all over the papers. Anyway, that was that. Harold and I got married. We had five years together and shall I tell you something?'

Topher waited.

'I'd never known what it was to be happy. It was like . . . Well, it was like nothing on this earth. We had a nice little bungalow and lived very quietly. Just a few close friends. Harold's children used to come. Harold did the garden. We didn't go away much. We were planning to go round the world when Harold retired.'

The waiter was standing by the table.

'Coffee?' Topher said.

'I'd love some . . .' Lucille said as if from miles away. '. . . and a teeny *crème de menthe*, if that's all right. Harold never did retire. He came home one day and fell over the front door step. I thought he'd just tripped. Then he walked into the glass door on to the patio. Soon after he began to complain of a terrible smell of burning rubber. Of course there was nothing burning. When he started to go blank in the middle of a conversation, I knew that something was wrong.'

She paused, lost apparently in thought.

'To cut a long story short, in three weeks Harold was dead. Tumour on the brain. They did operate but he never recovered.' She reached for the wine bucket and up-ended the empty bottle over her glass.

'You're not going to believe this, but before Harold died I never touched the stuff.'

Over the coffee she said: 'I don't know what got me started on that rigmarole. I'm sure you're not the least bit interested.'

'You've had a bad time.' Topher looked at his companion with new eyes.

'If it hadn't been for Tina I don't know how I would have managed. She's a wonderful woman, your sister. Which reminds me – she made a cake for you. It's back at the hotel.'

They were crossing Oxford Street in the car on the way back to the Mount Royal, when Lucille shrieked. Topher slammed his foot on the brakes.

'What is it?'

Lucille held up her hand.

'My ring!' Her outstretched fingers were bare. 'It's gone.'

Topher noticed that her speech, not surprisingly considering the amount she had drunk, was slurred.

'I've lost my ring!'

'You were wearing it when you arrived,' Topher said, 'I remember distinctly.'

'I always wear it. Harold gave it to me. It's a bit showy but I'm not bothered.'

'Did you have it on in the theatre?' Topher said.

'I don't remember.'

'Think carefully.'

'I'm trying to.'

'When was the last time you noticed it?'

'I don't know.'

'Did you take if off for any reason?'

Lucille was looking distractedly in her bag, pulling out the tee-shirt and coasters.

'Cast your mind back,' Topher said. 'Did you at any time. . . ?'

'It's no use coming the judge with me.' Lucille said, hysterically. She was emptying out the contents of her purse now into her lap. 'I can't even think straight.'

Topher had pulled up outside the Mount Royal and switched off the engine when he recalled that, on her arrival at his house, Lucille had paid a visit to the cloakroom.

'Do you take your ring off to wash your hands?' he said.

'It's not even insured. Harold said if I wear it all the time . . . or else I have to keep it in the bank . . .'

Switching on the ignition Topher headed for Hampstead.

Chapter Sixteen

In the cloakroom, on the wash-basin next to the soap, lay the ring with its over-sized diamond. Putting it in the palm of his hand, Topher held it out to Lucille who was sitting despondently on the chair in the hall.

The Koh-i-noor itself could not have inspired a more dramatic reaction. Lucille took the ring, slipped it on to her finger, jumped up and hugged Topher so tightly that he was almost strangled.

'You're an angel.' Releasing him, she held the ring up to the light. 'An absolute angel. I remember now. I took it off and put it on the side of the basin.'

She followed Topher into the kitchen.

'This calls for a celebration.' She eyed the whisky bottle which Topher had replaced on the top of the fridge. 'I really thought I'd lost it.'

'It's almost one-thirty. By the time we get back to the Mount Royal . . .'

'Just a little one.' Her eye was still on the bottle, her voice coaxing.

Topher poured her a very small whisky. She could not be much more the worse for wear.

When she had finished it she slumped forwards on to the table with her head on her arms, Harold's ring sparkling in the light.

'I'm really tired . . .' She sounded as if she was almost asleep. 'Can't I stay here?'

There were three spare bedrooms, not counting the top floor.

Topher could think of no good reason why Lucille should not spend the night in one of them.

'I'd better take you back to the hotel.'

Lucille opened one eye.

'I'll be no trouble.'

Topher pulled her to her feet. Her head fell heavily on to his shoulder. If she was going to get back to the hotel it looked as if he would have to carry her there.

'I promise to be good,' she pleaded.

Removing her arms from around his neck, Topher thought that she was in no state to be anything else.

'I'll cook you the most smashing breakfast.' Lucille sat heavily on the chair again. 'Harold used to say I was the best cook for . . . the best cook for . . . Sunday mornings we'd get up late . . . it was more of a brunch really . . scrambled eggs . . . and sausages . . . once in a while I'd make a kedgeree, Harold loved my kedgeree . . . or a Finnan Haddie with a poached egg on top . . . and we'd read the papers . . . sometimes we'd go back to bed again . . .'

'You can sleep in Penge's room,' Topher said. 'Just for tonight.'

He was woken next morning by the sound of music.

'Midnight . . . not a sound from the pavement . . .'

He thought that he was still dreaming and that he was at *Cats*. Then he remembered Lucille.

There was a tap on the door which was opened before he could answer it. Lucille came in with a cup on a tray. She was wearing her tee-shirt (a green cat's eye on either breast) which came down to the tops of her bare thighs. In the half-light, without her make-up, she looked like a young girl.

Putting the tray down on the bedside table, she started to dance round the room in time to the music which was loud enough to rouse the entire street.

'"Daylight . . ."' Her voice was not at all bad. '"I must wait for the sunrise . . ."'

Topher hoped that she was wearing something beneath the black tee-shirt which barely covered her bottom.

'". . . I must think of a new life . . ."'

She twirled over to the curtains.

'". . . and I mustn't give in."'

The mid-morning light flooded into the room.

'"When the dawn comes, tonight will be a memory too . . ."'

119

Lucille waltzed over to the bed and collapsed on top of Topher.

'"and a new day . . ."' Her voice was husky. '". . . will begin."'
She looked into his eyes. 'I'm sorry about last night.'

'That's all right,' Topher said magnaminously. Lucille was heavier than she looked and he had difficulty in breathing.

'I drink too much. There's nothing I can do about it. It's not a pretty sight. I made you a cup of tea. I didn't know about the sugar. There's two lumps in the saucer. Would you like me to hand it you?'

'I can manage,' Topher said, thinking that he could if Lucille would remove herself from his chest.

She ran her fingers over his face. 'You remind me of Harold in a way. You have nice ears. I like ears. There's not many people notice ears.'

Topher struggled to sit up.

'I didn't leave it there on purpose,' Lucille said.

'Leave what there on purpose?'

She was talking in riddles.

'The ring.'

'I didn't think for one moment . . .'

'Would you like me to pop into bed?'

'No,' Topher said. And as soon as the answer was out of his mouth he realised that it was not strictly true.

Lucille slid a hand beneath the covers.

Topher caught his breath.

As she leaned towards him he saw that she was not wearing a thing beneath the *Cats* tee-shirt.

'Lucille!' Topher said sternly.

He was just about to remove her blonde hair with its dark roots from his face when the doorbell rang insistently.

'Do you *have* to?'

Topher got out of bed and drew the curtain aside until he could see the front porch.

'Topher. . . ?' April was standing on the step looking up at him.

'I'm locked out. I went to post a letter and I posted my door keys by mistake. They slipped out of my hand. Marcus is in Brussels.'

'Who is it?' Lucille hissed.

'A neighbour. She's locked out. I've got her spare house-keys.'

Topher opened the window and stuck his head out. 'I'm coming down.'

'I hope I didn't wake you,' April said, when he'd put on his

120

dressing-gown and opened the front-door. 'I know you're usually around by now.'

'I must have overslept.' Topher feigned a yawn. April followed him into the kitchen and sat at the table while he looked for the keys. She cupped her hands round the teapot. 'Ouch!' She looked at Topher.

'Would you like a cup of tea?' he said quickly, listening with one ear for sounds of Lucille and wishing April would go away.

'I might as well keep you company. I wanted to pick your brains anyway.'

Topher poured out the tea and offered her the Fairy Cubes from the box on the table.

'Sugar?'

April shook her head.

'I don't. I didn't think you did.'

'Now and then,' Topher put one lump into his cup, rendering it undrinkable. 'What is it you want to ask me?'

'I've got this client,' April said. 'An Iranian. He asked me to decorate his flat while he was in the States. He didn't want to make any decisions. Money was no object. Everything had to be of the finest quality. Inez and I worked extremely hard to get the place finished on time. We did a fantastic job. When the client came back he took one look at it and started picking holes in everything. We'd put in white baths and he wanted navy-blue baths. We'd used plain mirrors and he wanted peach mirrors. We'd made blinds and he wanted festoons . . .'

'Festoons?'

April opened her mouth to answer when there was a crash from upstairs.

'What was that?'

'I left a pile of books.' Topher looked at the ceiling. 'They must have fallen off the bed.'

'Sort of drapey curtains . . .' April said.

Topher heard the flush of the lavatory cistern. He coughed loudly.

'Are you all right, Topher?'

'I think I've got a bit of a cold coming on.'

'You do look a bit odd. Why don't you go back to bed? I'll bring you up some breakfast.'

Topher looked at her in horror.

'You haven't finished telling me about the festoons.'

Praying that Lucille wasn't going to make any more noises, Topher

121

tried to pay attention to the end of April's story which was that the Iranian had refused to settle his account until she had redecorated the entire flat. April poured herself a second cup of tea while he advised her how to go about the recoupment of her fees. When he had finished April stood up.

'Thanks for the keys.' Picking them up from the table she looked at Topher. 'Marcus will be back at lunchtime. Would you like him to pop down?'

'What on earth for?' Topher remembered his cough. 'I don't think that will be necessary.'

In the bedroom Topher found Lucille, wrapped in his bathrobe, on her knees, trying to remove a tea stain from the carpet with a towel.

'I'm ever so sorry. I knocked the tray over. I think it's all come out.'

'Don't worry about it.' Topher pulled her to her feet.

'I took a shower.'

'I heard you.'

'I thought she'd never go.' Lucille moved towards him. 'My friends are picking me up from the Mount Royal at twelve. We're going to Windsor for the day.'

'We'd better be making a move then.' Topher removed her arms from around his neck.'

'I've got to change. I can't go to Windsor in my black lace.'

She drew away from him suddenly as if she had been electrocuted.

'What is it?' Topher said.

'I heard something.'

Topher noticed that the bathrobe had come untied. He found it hard to concentrate on some imagined noise.

The front door closed unmistakably and there was the sound of a bicycle being dragged along the floor.

'It's Penge.' Making for the door he held a finger to his lips. 'She has the key.'

Downstairs, Penge, in a loose white dress and sandals, a bunch of wilted marguerites in her hand, was eyeing the cups on the kitchen table.

'April was just here,' Topher said. 'She posted her keys in the letter box.'

Penge looked at him strangely and held out the flowers.

'She came to collect the spares. Are they for me? How kind.'

He filled a vase with water. The flowers were all lengths. Penge

122

seemed not to notice. She followed him into his study where he set the marguerites on the corner of his desk.

'What's that noise?'

Thinking immediately of Lucille, Topher listened. He could hear nothing.

'A sort of buzzing.'

Topher followed her gaze to the table near his armchair.

'I must have left the stereo on.'

Penge beat him to it. She put her head on one side to read the label on the record.

'*Cats*?'

Her face was incredulous. She waited for her father to speak. He couldn't think of a thing to say.

'*Cats*?'

'Don't keep saying *Cats*.'

'Is something the matter with you?'

'I could be getting a cold.'

Topher took his handkerchief out of his dressing-gown pocket and blew his nose. He tried to make his voice sound hoarse.

'If you don't mind I think I'll go back to bed for a bit. Marcus is coming to see me later.'

'I'll bring up some honey-and-lemon,' Penge said, 'like Mummy used to.'

Topher looked round in desperation trying to extricate himself from the hole he had dug. He had a sudden inspiration.

'There aren't any lemons.'

Smiling triumphantly Penge went into the hall. Topher followed her. From her saddle-bag she produced a lemon.

'I stopped at Camden Lock.'

Refusing to allow Penge to bring the honey-and-lemon upstairs, Topher had no choice but to drink it in the kitchen. When she wasn't looking he poured a slug from the bottle on the fridge in to the glass.

By the time he had got rid of her it was eleven-thirty. In the bedroom Lucille, fully dressed, was looking out of the window.

'Pretty girl,' she said. 'I don't know that she should be riding that bicycle. When's she expecting?'

'Expecting what?'

'Her baby.'

'Who?'

'Your daughter.'

'What *are* you talking about?'

'When is she expecting her baby?' Lucille said, enunciating clearly.

'Penge?'

'Do you mean to say you didn't know?' Lucille let the curtain fall. 'Hasn't she told you? Hadn't you noticed?'

'Are you sure?' Topher said. 'She often wears those loose things.'

'I may have left school when I was sixteen, but I do know a pregnant woman when I see one. I'm sorry if I gave you a turn.'

They drove to the Mount Royal in silence. Stunned by Lucille's revelation, Topher was unable to get the image of Penge out of his head. The more he thought about it the more he realised that Penge had indeed been acting strangely lately. He had attributed the long silences, the moodiness, the excessive touchiness – Penge had always been quick to take offence – to Caroline's death. But pregnant! Penge. That would make him a grandfather . . .

'Those signals were red, love,' Lucille's voice broke into his reverie. It was hardly surprising that he was distracted. What would Penge do with a baby? He presumed that it had been fathered by the minor poet, whom as far as he knew Penge had no intention of marrying. Plato had asserted that there should be no such thing as marriage. That children should be brought up by the State. Much as he admired Plato, Topher was of the firm opinion that the result of such misguided equality would be the death of civilisation which had, from time immemorial, been built upon a sound family life. He had never imagined that a daughter of his would become an unmarried mother, a present day statistic. Caroline would not have liked it the least little bit. She would, however, have know what to do. Marriage equipped one to cope with the anxieties of life, which sprung, uninvited, from the least likely corners.

An illegitimate grandchild was going to prove mildly embarrassing in the Judges Dining-Room. He wondered what Jo Henderson would say. He realised that he was being old-fashioned. Judge Cabot's son had been on a drugs charge while he was still at Eton. Stacy-Pratt's only daughter had done time for persistent shoplifting. A photograph of Jeremy Rowbotham's youngest (found soliciting in a public convenience) had been on the front page of every newspaper. Their Honours had survived. None of it had seemed anything to get steamed up about. Unless of course, he presumed, you happen to be Cabot, or Stacy-Pratt, or Rowbotham. He wondered why Penge hadn't said anything, and if Chelsea knew . . .

'Come up and I'll give you the cake.'

They were outside the Mount Royal. Topher had quite forgotten Lucille.

He hoped he wouldn't run into anyone he knew, as he escorted her, in her black lace, her diamond securely on her finger, through the lobby.

Her room was on the fifth floor. It looked out onto the well.

'Sit down a minute,' Lucille said. 'The cake's here.' She indicated a tin on the dressing table next to a half-empty vodka bottle. 'But there's a note somewhere from Tina.'

There were clothes on the armchair. Topher sat down on the bed and put his head in his hands.

'Drink this,' Lucille had poured some vodka into a tooth-glass.

Topher did not protest. Lucille was turning out her suitcase for Tina's note. Finding it, she put it on top of the cake-tin.

'You all right, love?'

It was the third time that morning that the question had been put to him.

Lucille kicked off her shoes.

'My friends will be here in a minute. I don't want to keep them waiting.'

She put a hand over her shoulder to undo her dress and turned her back to Topher for help.

There was a swimming sensation in his head. Remembering that with all the morning's goings on he had had no breakfast, he reached for the zipper. Lucille's skin was remarkably young. It seemed to burn his fingers. She stepped out of the dress and moved to the wardrobe.

'Don't go . . .'

'I'm not going very far. I'm only going to get my trousers.'

She came back to the bed and cradled his head against her belly, against her flesh coloured body stocking.

'Don't go to Windsor,' Topher said.

'What'll I tell them?'

Topher didn't answer.

The telephone rang. Lucille answered it.

125

A garbled voice came through the receiver. Topher couldn't make out what was said.

'Will you give them a message, love?' Lucille looked at Topher.

'Tell them . . . Tell them I can't make it. Say I'm not feeling very well. And that I'm really sorry. And that I'll be in touch.'

Chapter Seventeen

'Are you all right, Your Honour?' Mrs Sweetlove set his apple-juice on the desk. 'You look tired.'

'Perfectly all right,' Topher barked. Seeing his usher flinch, he added more gently: 'I've a bit of a headache.'

It was of course a lie. From Mrs Sweetlove's remark he gathered that the effects of his afternoon with Lucille at the Mount Royal were reflected in his face.

Lucille had hung the 'Do Not Disturb' notice outside the door. As she did so, something within Topher had snapped. It was as if all the nights, all the days, all the loneliness which he had experienced in the past months, had become focussed into a single sensation of anguish. He had pulled Lucille towards him. There had been a pause during which Lucille had removed her false eyelashes and put them on the dressing-table. What happened next he was not absolutely sure. When it was all over, not only the king-sized bed but the room itself looked as if a bomb had hit it. He was lying, with his feet on the pillow, gazing shamefacedly at Lucille. Her mouth was bruised, her lipstick had patterned her cheek, and she had been crying black mascara tears. Topher braced himself for her just reproach.

'I was wondering should we cut in to Tina's fruit cake,' Lucille said. 'I'm starving!'

Over the fruit cake, which they had eaten in crumbling chunks from the tin, Topher had apologised for his unbridled behaviour.

127

'Will you forgive me?' he stroked Lucille's freckled arm.

'Whatever for?' Lucille, sitting up beside him, picked out a *glacé* cherry and popped it into Topher's mouth.

Topher was silent. He knew that absolution would have to come from himself.

After the fruit cake he had fallen into an exhausted sleep. When he woke up, Lucille was sitting on the bed watching him.

'Feeling better, love?'

Topher felt as if he had been re-born. He had showered and dressed, and taken Lucille down to the coffee-shop for breakfast. At the table Lucille had put her hand, with its long red nails, over his.

'Don't feel badly,' she said. 'There's nothing like a good . . .'

'Lucille!' Once more in control of himself, Topher looked round to see if anyone was listening, but the coffee-shop was empty.

'You are a card.' Lucille winked at him. 'But ever so nice.'

Driving away from the Mount Royal, Topher thought that 'nice' was not an epithet which he would, in the circumstances, have applied to himself. He had behaved abominably. It was just as well that Lucille was to catch the early morning train back to Bingley.

He was waiting at the lights, at the junction of Gloucester Place and Marylebone Road, when he had remembered his impending grandfatherhood. Anxious to give the lie to what he hoped would turn out to be idle speculation, he made not for Hackney, where Penge herself could admit or deny the allegation that she was pregnant, but for Wapping.

Chelsea was watching a re-run of *Citizen Kane*. She expressed her surprise that her father was visiting her twice in one week.

'There's half a pizza in the oven,' she said. 'It might be a bit dried up.'

'I've just had breakfast.' Topher saw Chelsea's mouth drop open. 'I mean dinner.'

She looked at him suspiciously.

'It's about Penge,' Topher changed the subject.

'What about her?'

'Don't you know?'

Chelsea's face was blank. The two girls had always stood by each other.

'Is she all right?'

'As far as I know.'

'You know what I mean, Chelsea.'

'Do I?'

Orson Welles, alias Charles Foster Kane, alias Randolph Hearst, was running amok in the boudoir of his estranged wife.

'Can't you turn that thing off?'

Obediently Chelsea pressed the button on the remote control. The picture faded. 'Something bugging you?'

'Penge is pregnant. That's what's bugging me.'

'Did she tell you?'

'It's perfectly obvious,' Topher lied.

'What do you want me to say?'

'I want you to stop playing games with me.'

'Don't you think you should be discussing this with Penge?'

'You're the oldest . . .'

'Father, this is not a communal pregnancy.'

'So it is true?'

'She was afraid to tell you.'

'How long did she think she could keep it a secret?'

'You know Penge.'

As a child Penge had been prone to walk round the house with her eyes closed in the firm conviction that no one could see her.

'When is she. . . ? How long has she. . . ?

'Seven months,' Chelsea helped him out.

'You mean. . . ?'

'Mummy was too ill.'

A life had ended and a new one was coming into being. Topher acknowledged the poetic inevitability of the situation.

'Your sister is only a child herself.'

'She's twenty-five.'

'You know what I mean.'

Penge had always been babied. Both by himself and Caroline, and by Chelsea.

'It would have been different if it were you.'

Chelsea looked away. Topher realised that he had been tactless.

'I'm sorry.' He seemed to have spent his day apologising to women. 'I should not have said that.'

'I shall never have children.'

Distressed by the despair in her voice, he tried to steer the conversation back to Penge.

'Has she seen a doctor? Is she looking after herself?'

Chelsea, busy with her own thoughts, had clammed up.

'Look, don't you think all that would come better from Penge?'

By the time Topher had left Wapping it was too late to go to Hackney. A flapping poster on a deserted pavement news pitch caught his eye: NEW AIDS VICTIM. HOLLYWOOD MOURNS STAR. He thought back to Arthur, and their conversation in the kitchen.

'When you're pulling a bird,' Arthur's son had said, 'you got other things on your mind'. Thinking about Lucille, and his afternoon at the Mount Royal, Topher almost drove the car onto the pavement. HER MAJESTY'S JUDGE LATEST AIDS VICTIM . . .

When he got home he had had a hot bath. Then headed for the whisky bottle. Then, although it was after midnight, he had phoned Sally.

'Did I wake you?'

'What is it, Christopher?' It was obvious that she had been asleep.

He could hardly confess to Sally his fear that, as a result of his licentious behaviour with Lucille, he might have precipitated his own early death.

'It's Penge. She's going to have a baby.'

'Congratulations! That's wonderful.'

He failed to see what was so wonderful about it.

There was silence on the line. Sally was waiting for him to speak.

'I'm sorry if I woke you.'

'It's not every day you find out you're going to be a grandfather.'

'Don't!' Topher groaned.

He had a sudden urge to see Sally. The subject of literature, she had said, is the relation of human beings to each other. It occurred to Topher that it was largely the subject of life too.

'When can I see you?'

'Any time.'

'Tomorrow,' Topher said. 'After I've spoken to Penge.'

Despite the afternoon's exertions, he had been unable to sleep. He had prowled restlessly round the bedroom picking up and putting down Caroline's silver birds. The swallow and the nuthatch were cold and unresponsive. He replaced them on the table and made for his study.

There was a record already on the turn-table. The arm swung smoothly into position.

'Midnight, not a sound from the pavement . . .'

He did not want to think about Lucille.

'Has the moon lost her memory . . .'

130

In his embrace all her brittleness, all her brashness, had disappeared. He had spoken to another Lucille and that other Lucille had answered him.

'All alone in the moonlight . . .'

'To share, to give, to make other people happy was part of a woman's nature . . .'

'I was beautiful then . . .'

. . . he couldn't remember who it was who had said it.

'I remember the time I knew what happiness was . . .'

'Human beings have no right to be happy, nor should they be.' That was Thoreau.

. . . 'Let the memory, live again.'

He had turned off the stereo and slept like a log. Overslept. Now his head seemed disagreeably heavy.

'I've got a couple of Anadin in my handbag,' Mrs Sweetlove interrupted Topher's thoughts. 'Mr Sweetlove used to swear by them.'

Topher declined the panacea. With the same gesture he dismissed the usher from his robing room. Mrs Sweetlove did not go away. Topher looked questioningly at her. She was wearing her red fly-away glasses.

'I just wanted to say, Your Honour . . .'

Topher waited.

'I'm a mother, as you know . . .'

The scent of a not very expensive perfume assailed Topher's nostrils. It emanated from Mrs Sweetlove.

'If there's ever anything I can do . . .'

Topher wondered if Penge's pregnancy was written on his face.

Mrs Sweetlove swallowed.

'It can get very lonely . . .'

Topher sat up horrified as he recognised what he suspected was a proposition.

'I appreciate your kindness,' he said, fixing Mrs Sweetlove with a judicial smile and deliberately misunderstanding her, 'but I find that the general tendency of headaches is to cure themselves.'

The morning's case was a paternity suit. A pregnant schoolteacher (ironical) was trying to prove that the man with whom she had had a steady relationship for the past two years, was the father of her expected child. The man, a used-car salesman, admitted that although he had indeed had a relationship with the schoolteacher, he was not her boy-friend and he had, in fact, given the plaintiff money in return for her favours. Prosecuting counsel challenged the used-car salesman's assertion that their affiliation was purely a sexual one, with reference to joint outings to the cinema and the seaside. He was trying to demonstrate, with the help of diary entries, that they had in fact lived together, as a couple when Topher – who was experiencing some difficulty in keeping his eyes open – had felt himself nodding off. He managed to rescue himself, just in time, from the brink of unconsciousness and, like Dickens' Mr Justice Stareleight, 'immediately looked unusually profound to impress the jury with the belief that he always thought most deeply with his eyes shut'.

'The diary, Your Honour!' Mrs Sweetlove, hissed, handing the exhibit up to Topher.

Taking it from her, Topher dismissed from his head *The Pickwick Papers*, the afternoon with Lucille, and Penge and her pregnancy. He applied himself to the cross-examination of the used-car salesman, and to the case before him.

In the purlieus of North London, on his way to see Penge, Topher remarked the number of up-market shops which had unexpectedly mushroomed in what had once been a spurned and moribund area. Penge's street had, so far, escaped the gentrification. The garden of the Victorian house where she had lived for the past twelve months was overgrown, and the path was strewn with rubbish. A young man with a black moustache, wearing a plaid shirt and sporting a single earring, answered the door to Topher.

He was taken aback when the fellow, who wore a plaid shirt, said: 'You must be Judge Osgood.'

Penge's bicycle in the hall reassured Topher that he would find his daughter at home.

In the front room the minor poet sat at the table writing. With his pale face, his prematurely receding hair, and his damp hand (which he extended in greeting) he did not look, Topher thought, capable of fathering a child. Having enquired after each other's health and commented on the weather, both Chad and Topher looked out of the window, which was so grimy that you could scarcely see across the street. The young man in the plaid shirt, whose name was Robert, went upstairs to fetch Penge. She had been washing her hair and came down wrapped in a grey bathrobe, which Topher had discarded many years previously and which had once been pale blue. He averted his eyes from the girdle which was tied around Penge's middle but did not define her waist. Mystified, she greeted Topher and the four of them stood staring at each other awkwardly, as if about to embark on some bizarre quadrille.

Penge broke the silence. 'Is everything all right?'

'I wondered if I might have a word with you?' Topher said.

'You'd better come up.'

Contemplating the bedroom – shared presumably with the minor poet – Topher hoped that the house-proud Caroline, from her metaphysical existence, was spared the sight of it. Penge cleared the chair of its tangle of unsavoury looking garments so that Topher could sit down. Blotting her wet hair with a thin towel, she perched on the unmade bed.

'What's the matter?'

Topher wondered what they used for fresh air.

'I thought perhaps you could tell me that?'

They eyed each other, Topher looking into his mirror image. The resemblance was uncanny.

'Chelsea has been shooting her mouth off . . .'

'Not at all.'

'Well. . . ?'

Topher was silent for a long time, watching Penge dab and squeeze the darkened fronds until they began to turn golden.

'I'm not much good at this.'

Caroline had always dealt with the more delicate situations. Penge put the wet towel on her lap and sat facing him, her hands unconsciously cradling her belly.

'You know.'

Topher nodded.

'Well, that's a relief. I did try once or twice but I couldn't bring myself to tell you.'

'Couldn't you have done something about it while there was still time?'

Penge stared at him.

'Chad and I have been trying for ages . . .'

'Are you thinking of. . . ?'

'Having a baby has nothing to do with marriage. We are very happy as we are.'

'You'd be better off with Robert.'

Penge started to laugh. 'You can't be serious!'

Topher recalled the coloured handkerchief spilling from the back pocket of the young man's jeans, the moustache, the earring. He had

133

opened his mouth to talk about responsibility and commitment, about finances and plans for the future, when he happened to glance at Penge. Her face beneath the long curling strands had the gentle gaze of a Madonna, the unmistakable and indescribable halo of motherhood. He went to sit beside his daughter on the bed. He took her in his arms and felt the damp hair against his face.

'I wanted to tell you,' Penge sniffed into his shoulder. 'I thought that you'd be angry.'

That was putting it mildly.

'I wish Mummy was here.'

Recounting the episode later to Sally Maddox, Topher said that it was the minor poet, to whom Topher had addressed himself over a mug of rose-hip tea, who seemed to have the situation in hand. He had enrolled with the Law Society, and was going to qualify as a solicitor.

'What made Penge pluck up courage to tell you about the baby?' Sally asked.

'Oh, she didn't tell me,' Topher said, without thinking. 'That was Lucille.'

Chapter Eighteen

Driving down to Berkshire, Topher thought what a relief it was to get out of London, away from his women. The episode with Lucille had sent ripples in ever widening circles across the erstwhile calm of his life. Monday morning had seen him in the florists, on his way to court, sending a guilt-ridden bouquet – through Interflora – to Lucille in Bingley. In the evening he had rung Tina, to thank her for the cake.

'I'm so pleased you took Lucille out,' Tina said.

Topher did not tell her that it was Lucille who had done the taking.

'She's a lovely person and she's not had a happy life.' In the manner of sisters, she added, 'Shall you be seeing her again?'

It was not a simple question to answer. Had Tina posed it a week earlier, he would have had no hesitation in telling her that he and Lucille, with her jangling jewellery, were not in the least compatible. Having known her (in the Biblical sense), however, Topher was by no means averse to doing so again.

'I can't say,' was his reply.

'It's not my business.' Tina said. 'Anyway, did you enjoy it?' Topher was speechless.

'*Cats*,' Tina said into the silence.

'Oh, *Cats* . . .' Topher repeated. 'Great.' He realised that he sounded like Penge, and borrowed once more from her vocabulary to elaborate. 'Terrific.'

135

'Lucille thinks you're the cat's whiskers.' Tina laughed at her own joke. 'She wants to know where I've been hiding you.'

Topher had discussed Lucille with Marcus.

'Even Her Majesty's judges are human,' was all Marcus had said.

'Suppose I get AIDS?'

'I don't think it's the fear of AIDS that's bothering you. It's your punishing conscience again.'

Marcus was right. All week Topher had wavered between bouts of self-reproach, and desire for Lucille. He had discussed his dilemma with Sally, although he had not told her precisely what had taken place between himself and Lucille.

'There's something on your mind,' Sally had said, when he had visited her after extracting Penge's confession.

'The prospect of becoming an unmarried grandfather, so to speak.'

Sally fixed him with her brown eyes.

'It's Lucille, isn't it?'

'"I confess nothing, nor I deny nothing."'

'It wasn't just *Cats*. *Cats* couldn't have that effect on anyone.'

'Like most judges,' Topher said, 'I tend to be very old-fashioned in my ideas.'

'That's what I like about you. I liked your reserve from the moment Marcus introduced us. I find it terribly sexy.'

'So it appeared.' Topher thought back to their first meeting.

The warmth of Sally's thigh against his on the sofa, made him not only want her to lay hands on him again, but conscious that were she to do so he would raise not the slightest objection. He imagined that going to bed with Sally would in no way duplicate his afternoon at the Mount Royal with Lucille. With Sally he would be tender, as she would be with him. Afterwards he would recite some Pushkin for her.

Standing up, ostensibly to look at the books which he was getting to know as well as he was Sally herself, it occurred to him that he might just be falling in love.

'I don't deny that I find you attractive Christopher,' Sally was privy to his thoughts as usual, 'but you don't need to worry.'

She stood up and made for the tiny kitchen.

'I bought a couple of lamb chops. I'll stick them under the grill while you tell me about Penge.'

While Sally cooked the chops, Topher told her not about Penge, but of his ambivalence concerning Lucille.

136

'I can't understand it. She's not my type at all.'

Sally opened a packet of frozen peas and took a *baguette* from her shopping basket.

'"My father's house has many mansions".'

It was what she had written on one of her first postcards to him.

'Was *that* what you meant?'

'Didn't you know?'

After dinner – the chops and the peas and the French bread, followed by coffee and a box of Turkish delight consumed mainly by Sally – they got round to the subject of Penge and her expected baby.

'She needs Caroline,' Topher said.

Sally looked at him. 'She's not the only one.'

'At a time like this a girl needs her mother.'

'She'll manage. Women have an instinct for these things.'

Topher told Sally about Chad and his decision to embrace the law.

'He doesn't seem to be such a bad chap.'

'He must have something going for him. You have to give your daughter a little credit. I expect you make him nervous.'

'I make most people nervous. Not you.'

It was true. Talking to Sally was like talking to himself.

On Wednesday Lucille had telephoned to thank him for the flowers. 'I could come down on Friday,' she said tentatively.

Topher told her that he was going to the country. He omitted the fact that it was to stay with Jo Henderson. It was not exactly a lie.

Lucille was disappointed.

'How about the week-end after?'

A disturbance on the line saved Topher from replying.

Two days later a clumsily wrapped package had arrived. On the back of it was the name of the sender, 'Lucille Moss', in a spidery hand. Topher was ambivalent about gifts. Books chosen by others depressed him, and the ties, given to him by his family over the years, were generally not quite right. Winding the string into a neat butterfly, and folding the brown paper, for what was obviously not the first time, he opened Lucille's parcel.

It *was* a book: *Man in the Kitchen*. On the cover a jolly chap in a business suit executed some sort of war dance, while he nonchantly tossed a pancake with one hand and whipped up a *soufflé* with the other. Lucille had written on the fly-leaf. 'You must look after yourself, love Lucille!' Eighteen kisses (such as Chelsea and Penge had appended to their postcards as children) followed the signature in which the 'l's' were looped extravagantly and the dot over the 'i' composed of a small circle. Touched by Lucille's concern, he put the book on the shelf next to Caroline's ageing copies of Elizabeth David, the only culinary authority she had acknowledged.

Considerably lighter of heart than when he had left London, he slowed down in the sleepy village of Woodspeen to take a final look at Jo Henderson's directions (which had arrived together with a small map) on how to reach Badger's Cottage.

He and Caroline had never had a second home. Topher felt that if you always went to the same place it quickly became a habit, rather than a distraction, and Caroline maintained that worries about beds and plumbing could convert the most desirable of country residences into a nuisance.

He didn't know what he had been expecting. Possibly a terraced artisan's dwelling (such as Marcus and April had in Norfolk) or a converted barn, similar to that of Caroline's brother, Mathew, by the river Hamble. Badger's Cottage, a sprawling farmhouse set in grounds which extended as far as the eye could see, was not a cottage at all.

Parking his car on the sweep of gravel between a vintage Bentley and a Land Rover, Topher wondered whether he should perhaps have packed his dinner jacket.

The door was opened by a white-coated manservant. He took Topher's small grip from him, and informed him that Lady Henderson was on the terrace, and was expecting him. Traversing the drawing-room, Topher noticed that not only was it large enough to accommodate a tennis court, but that it had an open brick fireplace and was furnished with a great many chintz-covered armchairs.

Jo Henderson left the small group of people which surrounded her to greet Topher. He tried to repress the unbidden image of her breasts, now restrained by a striped shirt, which she had exposed for his benefit on the occasion of their last meeting. As she embraced him, her perfume (which had lingered so long in his car), took him back to the evening at Le Mazarin.

Taking Topher by the arm she made the introductions. There was a newspaper owner, wearing a yellow waistcoat, whom Topher associated with the Bentley, and a very young farmer, who never took his eyes off Jo, who had definite affiliations with the Land Rover. A flaxen-haired Fiona, in cream riding breeches (so close fitting it seemed a miracle that she had got into them), and an older woman with a disgusting smelling cigarette in her mouth, who seemed to be drinking a pint of gin, completed the group. Topher's fear – despite Jo's assertions to the contrary – that he was to be the only house-guest were immediately assuaged. The newspaper man's name was Giles, and the farmer's Sebastian. It should, Topher thought, over his Bucks Fizz, have been the other way round. They were waiting upon a Tilda and a Scott (*Lost Weekend?*) to complete the party.

Luncheon was served at a refectory table capable of seating at least twenty people. Despite the fact that Sebastian had been hanging upon her every word, Jo Henderson had seated Topher on her right. Sitting beneath the exposed rafters, the thought suddenly occurred to him that not one of the assembled company had known his late wife.

'Play polo?' Giles, his napkin tucked beneath his chin, asked from the far end of the table.

Topher realised that he was being addressed.

'Unfortunately, no.'

'Lucky man!' Giles leaned back while his glass was filled with Chablis. 'More expensive these days than keeping a mistress.'

'I'm too old,' Topher said.

'Are you referring to the polo or the mistress?' Giles chortled.

'Both.'

'Nonsense. Can't speak about the mistress,' Giles winked at Jo, 'but as far as polo is concerned all you need is co-ordination, a sense of anticipation, and the ability to think quickly.'

'I imagine it helps if you can ride,' Topher said.

'There's nothing like a brisk chukka to help you forget your worries.'

Privately Topher preferred the therapeutic qualities of Pushkin. 'I like to keep my feet on the ground.'

'Are you a High Court Judge, like poor Henry?' The woman next to him, whose name was Flora, and who had had the effrontery to light one of her filthy cigarettes, drawled, appraising him through half-closed eyes.

'Good Lord, no.'

'I've never understood exactly what it is that judges do.'

'Judges expound, direct, and administer the law,' Topher said. 'Or as Bacon put it: "The parts of a judge in hearing are four. To direct the evidence; to moderate length, repetition or impertinency of speech; to recapitulate, select and collate the material points of that which hath been said; and to give the rule or sentence."'

'"God in his heaven".' Flora exhaled. 'It must be nice to be always right.'

'It would be a very arrogant judge who imagined he was *always* right.' Topher ostentatiously waved away the smoke that was blowing in his direction. 'If absolute certainty was the pre-condition for decision, the judicial process would be paralysed.'

'Surely the judge does have to be right in a high percentage of cases?' Jo Henderson joined the conversation. 'Otherwise he would lose credibility.'

'If you are confronted with two conflicting stories and little else,' Topher said, 'you know very well that you have to base your decisions mainly — if not entirely — on your impression of the witnesses.'

'There's only one way to reduce crime. Reduce the number of criminals!' Giles almost choked at his own wit.

Jo signalled for the plates to be cleared away.

'Offenders, please Giles, not criminals. And they no longer commit crimes, they "breach regulations"!'

Coffee was served in the drawing-room. Taking his *demi-tasse* to the window seat, Topher was aware of an unaccustomed feeling of tranquillity. There were no echoes, such as those in his empty house. No books to be read, no music to be heard, no translations to struggle with by way of occupational therapy. From the low murmur of conversation at the far end of the room, Giles' laugh and the pleasant timbre of Jo Henderson's voice were distinguishable. Looking out of the window at the countryside, which it would need a palette of paints all in some degree green to capture, Topher had the ridiculous impression that he was monarch of all he surveyed, that he had come home.

After the coffee, Giles and Sebastian changed for the highspot of the week-end, the polo game. They went off in the Land Rover, (which surprisingly belonged to Giles) taking Fiona with them. Tilda (a dress designer much in the news because she was patronised by the young Royals) and Scott (who had been in records but now ran the business side of things for her), unable to keep their hands off each other, retired to their room. Flora set out for the village in search of cigarettes. Jo offered Topher a tour of the estate before taking him to watch the polo.

Accompanied by two Rotweilers, Topher walked beside his hostess over the cobbles, through the disused farm-yard and the loose boxes. He thought how different she was from the Jo Henderson of the

Judges Dining-Room, or the Jo Henderson of Lowndes Square. On both previous occasions he had had the impression that she was almost as tall as he, but realised that it must have been her high heels. Today, in her wellingtons, she appeared considerably shorter. She seemed also less brittle, more relaxed. Following her through the over-heated greenhouses, he chivalrously admired the giant marrows and the cucumbers, the ripening grapes and the delicate orchids about which Caroline would have been sure to offer some intelligent comment. Jo showed him the formal gardens and the orchard, the paddocks and the dew-pond, the fields sown with rye-grass and with rape.

'It was Henry's dream,' she said, leaning against a fence beyond which cows with swinging tails grazed ponderously. She turned to look at the colour-washed elevation of the house with its tiled roofs. 'He bought the old farm soon after we were married. We modernised it and, bit by bit, extended it. Henry was putting in some new milking plant,' she pointed to a partially completed building in the distance, 'when he had the accident.'

'I'm not a country person,' Topher said.

'I didn't think that I was. There's something very compelling about Badger's. I wouldn't like to give it up.'

'Why should you?'

'It's an enormous headache. Too much for one. It needs a man about the place.'

'Anyone in mind?' Topher thought of Giles or Sebastian.

'As a matter of fact, I have.'

Jo took his arm and led him back over the dried ruts of the path which bordered the field, towards the house.

'There's one thing I think you should know about me.'

She stopped. Facing Topher, she fixed him with her green eyes. In the Berkshire air they looked clearer, even more translucent, than they had in London.

'I *always* get what I want.'

Chapter Nineteen

The remainder of the week-end had passed pleasantly enough. No, that was not true, Topher thought, recalling it. With the exception of the polo game — of which the rules seemed incomprehensible and the action always to take place on the far side of the field — he had positively enjoyed it.

Dinner on Saturday night, presided over by Jo in a close-fitting black dress with spaghetti straps, which slipped perpetually from her shoulders, had been pleasingly relaxed. Tilda and Scott (with bags beneath their eyes) regaled the table with stories of thinly veiled royal idiosyncracies. Giles (feeding Fiona tit-bits from his plate and nibbling her ear) went over a blow by blow account of the afternoon's polo with Sebastian (who had sprained his elbow and had to eat with a fork in his left hand). And Flora (now into Panatellas) told tales of her beloved Kenya, where she had owned a coffee farm until she was chased out by the Mau Mau. After dinner, at which they had all drunk too much, they had played charades. Topher had led his team, comprised of Jo, Flora, and the injured Sebastian, to victory. In the small hours, after the night-caps, he had been escorted to his bedroom by Jo.

She had switched on the lamps for him, and with her hands on his shoulders kissed him goodnight, brushing his cheek with hers.

'Have you everything you want?'

The scent of her warm skin and her now familiar perfume adding to his general intoxication, Topher hesitated for only a second: 'Yes, thank you.'

142

Jo had kissed him again. This time in earnest. He was just beginning to enjoy it when she pulled away from him abruptly, replacing the strap of her dress on her shoulder.

'My room's through here.' She opened a door on the far side of the room. 'Sleep well.'

Topher had not been able to sleep at all. He was not sure whether it was because of the unaccustomed silence, broken only by the hoot of an owl and the recognisable cries of Fiona (which sounded as if she were spurring on a indolent horse), or the image of Jo Henderson in the adjoining room. During the night he thought that he heard foot-steps along the corridor, the creak of a door, the sound of Jo's low laugh. He had been trying to sort out the conflicting messages which were assaulting his mind, when he had become aware of the barking of dogs and the light filtering through the curtains, and realised that he must have dropped off.

His appetite at breakfast suggested that he had in fact slept quite well.

Jo, Sebastian, Giles and Fiona were out riding. Tilda and Scott had not yet appeared. Topher was left with the effluent from Flora's ever smoking chimney to season his grilled kidneys.

'You didn't know Henry of course.' Flora eyed him from across the table.

Topher shook his head.

'Delightful man. Everybody loved Henry. Jo was devastated when he died.'

Topher raised an eyebrow.

'I've known Jo a long time. You mustn't be taken in by her act.' Her cigarette hanging from her lips, Flora reached for the silver coffee pot.

'You know something, Osgood. You remind me of Henry.'

Topher had spent the morning walking. And thinking. Both about Jo Henderson and her night visitor — who could only have been Sebastian — and perhaps that the country was not such a bad place after all. Back at Badger's Cottage they had been joined by neighbouring farmers for cocktails which went on until two o'clock in the afternoon. At lunch, at Jo's request, Topher had carved the beef. As he wielded the knife, he had half expected to hear Caroline's voice from the table. 'Penge likes the crispy bits,' and 'No fat for Chelsea.' When lunch was over they had all slept (Giles with his arm round Fiona, her breast in his cupped hand) amidst the sea of Sunday newspapers, until it was time to go home.

Thanking Jo for the week-end, and realising that this was the second occasion on which he had enjoyed her hospitality, Topher promised to contact her in town so that he could reciprocate.

'Only if you want to.'

He looked into the green eyes.

'I do.'

On the motorway, his problems, relegated to the far reaches of his mind during the week-end at Badger's Cottage, came flooding back. Lucille, and what to do about her. It wasn't just that he had to make reparation. He *wanted* to see her. She made him laugh. He hadn't done too much laughing of late. He would call Lucille and tell her that he was free next week-end. To be on the safe side – he prayed it would not be a case of shutting the stable door after the horse had bolted – he would take suitable precautions to protect himself.

The next problem was Penge. It was all very well that the minor poet had elected to eschew poetry for the law, but it would be years before he qualified. Topher reckoned that *he* would now have not only to subsidise his daughter but also his grandchild. In response to Topher's enquiry as to where she would be having the baby, Penge had told him that she would be staying where she was. The birth would be attended by the District Midwife, by Robert, who had had experience of such matters, and Chad (who looked to Topher as if he would pass out at the mere mention of childbirth) who had not. Caroline, Topher was sure, would not only have disapproved of the arrangement but would not have countenanced it. Chelsea had promised to have a word with her sister.

Chelsea had her own worries. The anguish in her voice as she said 'I shall never have children' had grieved Topher. She adored children (as a child she had played mothers and fathers, setting up home with her dolls) but she had firm views about parenting. There would, he was sure, be no unmarried motherhood for Chelsea. He wished there was some magic with which he could cast the mote of David Cornish from her eye.

When he got home there was a postcard from Sally on the mat. She reminded him (he had not forgotten) that he was to be her guest on Wednesday at PEN. The picture, a Rembrandt etching, was of the Garden of Eden. Watched by the serpent, a naked Adam – looking uncomfortably like himself – reached for the apple held by a middle-aged Eve with hair round her shoulders, who bore more than a passing resemblance to Sally. Although the couple were both overweight, and

144

decidedly past their prime, the statement was categoric. Romance, desire, love, passion, were not the exclusive province of the young.

With the postcard on the kitchen table, Topher had opened a tin of sardines. After his supper he had taken the etching with him into his study. He kept it on the arm of his chair, while he wrote a reserved judgement. On Monday morning, his response to Mrs Sweetlove's customary query as to whether he had had a good week-end, brought home to him just how much he had appreciated Badger's Cottage. What if he and Caroline had been wrong? It apparently did one good to get out of London, to experience a change of environment. It had certainly made him feel more amenable. He had already treated the empty house to the first act of *Patience*, and was not aware of the least flicker of resentment at Mrs Sweetlove's enquiry.

'I had a splendid week-end, Mrs Sweetlove,' he said, cracking his knuckles before he remembered how much it annoyed her. He added, 'I trust you did, too,' before he realised his mistake.

'Yes, thank you, Your Honour.' Mrs Sweetlove slotted the video-recording of the events of the past two days into the play-back mechanism of her mind.

'My sister came over from Purley on Saturday, with her husband and the children. It's not that they're badly behaved, they're lovely children really . . .'

Topher picked up *The Times*. He tried to concentrate, against the monologue which floated over the newspaper.

Mrs Sweetlove had got as far as Sunday. 'I always do a bit of gardening on Sunday. Dennis was really the gardener. Salvias. He loved salvias, Dennis did . . .' when Topher decided that she had stretched his tolerance (induced by the week-end in the country) to the limit. He dispatched her, still nattering about slug pellets and John Innes compost, with a trumped up message to the Crown Prosecution Service.

The PEN club met in a house in Dilke Street. Beneath a frieze of members of the London Sketch club (whose premises it was), depicted in silhouette, the long tables were set for dinner. Bringing a bottle of Fleurie, his contribution to the evening, Topher had picked Sally up from her flat.

She had embraced him warmly. 'I missed you. I hope you aren't going to make a habit of going away for week-ends.'

It was said lightly, but Topher thought that he detected a note of jealousy in her voice. His suspicion was confirmed when Sally, ostensibly tidying away the pages of the novel on which she had been working said: 'I went to the hairdresser's on Saturday. There was a picture in the *Tatler*. "Lady Henderson at the Save the Children Ball . . ." Saint Laurent from head to foot.'

Turning to Topher she looked down at the sprigged dress she was wearing.

'What hope have *I* in my Laura Ashley?'

In the car, Topher, omitting certain details, recaptured the week-end for Sally. Perhaps to compensate her for the Laura Ashley, he said: 'It must be immensely satisfying to write a book.'

'". . . we beat out tunes for bears to dance to, while all the time we long to move the stars to pity"'.

'What would you say makes a *good* writer?'

'A built-in, shock-proof, shit detector.'

Startled, Topher stopped at the zebra crossing on Lower Sloane Street. The home-going crowds laid hands on the bonnet of his car. One never knew with Sally.

He had never been amongst a group of writers before. Squeezed into the tiny bar of the PEN club, he wondered was there a collective noun for them. A paragraph? A synopsis? Sally introduced him to an emaciated biographer who had recently published a seminal work on Goethe. He wore a spotted muffler beneath the open neck of his shirt, and bemoaned the lack of charity amongst reviewers. An unlikely looking author of best-selling children's books greeted Sally warmly, and bought Topher a gin and tonic. He wasn't sure what he had expected writers to look like. Pens for fingers? Full stops for eyes? Taking in the company, unassuming in both demeanour and dress, it was hard to credit their gifts for transmuting the everyday into works – if not always of greatness – at least of art.

At dinner he was seated next to Sally. On the other side of him was a nondescript young woman who looked as if a fat royalty cheque would not come amiss. Topher put on his half-glasses to read her place-card. Ann Barker. It meant nothing. Opposite, a red-faced man with a white beard had already made considerable inroads into his bottle. A younger man, in a suede jacket, glanced nervously towards the door. An ancient member, who looked to Topher like one of Caroline's more exotic birds, twitched her head, winked her beady eyes, and picked at the bread roll on her plate with red-tipped claws. Quivering with indignation, she leaned across the table to tell Sally

146

that after forty years she had changed houses. She refused to be published by a conglomerate.

At the top table, the speaker, a writer of thrillers, was already seated. Since there seemed to be no Grace, or other formality, Topher picked up his knife and fork and attacked the square of *pâté* on the plate in front of him.

Ann Barker looked at his place-card: 'Guest of Sally Maddox'.

'Do you have a name?'

'Christopher Osgood.'

'What do you write?'

Topher was taken by surprise.

'I couldn't write to save my life. I envy those who do. I'm a judge. You, of course, are a writer?' He noticed that she had bitten fingernails.

Ann Barker nodded.

'Do you write under your own name?'

He realised that he had fallen into the trap.

Ann Barker was shaking her head.

'"Tania Roxbury".'

Topher swallowed. He could not believe that his dinner partner was the author of the explicit titles, with their titillating jackets, to be found on every bookstall.

'You're shocked?'

'Surprised. I imagined "Tania Roxbury" differently.'

'I suppose you won't talk to me now. You think I write pornography.'

Topher picked up the bottle he had brought.

'Pornography, surely, is in the mind of the beholder. I'm not certain exactly what it is. Would you care for a little red wine?'

Ann Barker held out her glass.

'Most men,' Topher went on, 'if they were honest with themselves, would be perfectly happy to look at page three of the *Sun*, although they mightn't *buy* the newspaper for that or any other purpose. Pictures or descriptions of attractive, naked women are appealing. To suggest that they are not – or should not be – is hypoctrical.'

The young man in the suede jacket, who had been listening to the conversation, leaned forward.

'Ah,' he said, 'but where would you draw the line?'

'Why should the line be drawn at all? I am not convinced that one's attitudes could be changed for the worse by what one read or saw in a book or film. Every adult must draw the line for himself, every parent for his child. I don't deny for one moment that some of the material which is brought to my court disgusts me, but what disgusts does not necessarily harm.'

'Not even the young and weak minded?'

'In a free society we have to concentrate on the proper education of children – by the parents, not the state – and take that risk.'

'When Mrs Whitehouse catches up with me,' Ann Barker said, 'I hope my case comes before you. There can't be many judges who share your views.'

'Don't misunderstand me,' Topher said. 'The attitudes and notions that a permissive society propagates have been responsible for a very great deal of harm. But there's no legislation, that I could think of, which could put an end to it.'

Sally, who was standing up, was pulling at his sleeve.

'We have to help ourselves to the next course.'

'Forgive me.' Topher put down his napkin. 'I was getting carried away.'

'It was my fault, Sally,' Ann said. 'It all started because Judge Osgood thought I should either be exposing my heaving bosom – which would be hard in my case – in true stereotypical fashion, or writing Hampstead novels in which the misunderstood wife commits joyless adultery in the afternoons.'

'I didn't think it *was* adultery in the afternoons,' Sally said, making everyone around them laugh.

Topher stood back to allow the ladies to precede him to the buffet tables. Ann Barker took Sally by the arm and whispered, sufficiently loudly for Topher to hear: 'I like your boyfriend.'

148

Chapter Twenty

There was Coronation Chicken or vegetable *lasagne*, doled out in careful portions by two lady members of PEN. In the queue, Sally introduced Topher to a science-fiction writer, and an Armenian poet with whom Topher discussed Pushkin over the peas and carrots. The brought-in bottles of wine were beginning to have their effect. When Topher, carrying his plate, sat down at the table again it was difficult, on account of the low ceiling, either to hear or to be heard.

The man in the suede jacket – a literary agent – leaned over to ask Topher if he had come across his friend, a barrister, who would have been at the dinner but for the fact that he was nursing a cold. Topher enquired his name but all he could make out was Michael, the surname, on each of three occasions, getting swallowed up by the acoustics.

Ann Barker discussed the fickleness of editors with Sally, behind Topher's back, and inclining forward so that they could converse better, Topher became involved in a shouting match with the red-faced man with the white beard, who had finished his own wine and was looking hopefully up and down the table to see if anyone had any to spare. As far as Topher could make out he wrote books on what sounded like 'gravel' but was, Topher presumed, travel.

The Coronation Chicken was followed by a choice of lemon mousse or trifle. Holding out his small bowl Topher asked if he might have a little of each, only to be reprimanded for his temerity.

Before the coffee was served, the company was asked euphemis-

149

tically if it would like to 'make itself comfortable', prior to the serious business of the evening. The room, already clamorous with voices, was now further polluted by smoke. Turning his chair a little, so that he had a better view of the top table, Topher settled back to be diverted.

With a few carefully chosen words, dry with humour and fulsome with praise, a retired publisher, with silver hair, introduced the crime writer. Watching the speaker get to his feet and adjust the microphone, Topher thought how pleasant it was to relax while someone else sang for his supper. Being one of Her Majesty's judges had its flip side. Every week brought its requests. To be the guest of honour at a dinner. To address societies, bodies of magistrates, social workers, or others concerned with the law and its administration. Those invitations which in a weak moment he accepted, were for dates frequently as far as a year ahead. He deluded himself that they would never come round. When they did, he would sit in his study in the small hours, wondering what would amuse a gathering of City Liverymen, or hold a banqueting-suite of visiting American lawyers spellbound. He was a seasoned after-dinner speaker and well able to deliver a peroration of anything up to an hour's duration, fluently and without notes. Like the most accomplished of actors, however, his unruffled exterior on such occasions disguised a certain inner apprehension. Although he rarely sat down, other than to prolonged and enthusiastic applause, he was often unable to do justice to the usually excellent dinner which preceded such a discourse.

Tonight's guest of honour appeared to be master of the situation. He opened with the traditional, light-hearted, self-deprecating anecdote. Encouraged by the warmth with which this was greeted, he released his hold on the table, took a step back and, on a more serious note, exposed for the benefit of his peers his particular tricks of the trade.

Topher, who had read and enjoyed many of the speaker's books, was fascinated to discover how they were written. All the research was undertaken personally. Characters were allowed down no street the author had not trodden. The action took place in no country with which he was not familiar. *De nihilo nihil.* Nothing comes of nothing. A true professional, he earned every one of the megabucks with which he was reputed to have been rewarded. Half-an-hour – to the minute – after he had started speaking, the speaker took his seat (and his well earned drink of water from the *carafe* on the table) to deafening and extended acclamation.

'Did you enjoy it?' Sally asked on the way home.

Topher could not think when he had last been so taken out of himself.

'I had a splendid evening,' he said. 'Thank you so much for taking me.'

Driving amicably through the night silence with Sally by his side, Topher had the momentary illusion that they belonged together. He had almost forgotten that he must take her back to Jeffrey's Street. He wasn't at all surprised when Sally said: 'Independence is all very well but sometimes one gets fed up with going to places on one's own.'

It was not a question.

'I'm having a few people over on Saturday night,' Sally went on. 'Will you come?'

Topher was about to say yes, when he remembered Lucille, and how much he wanted to see her.

'Is it Lucille or Jo?'

He was trying to think of a tactful reply when she said: 'You can let me know.'

In Jeffrey's Street Topher followed her into the flat. As a matter of course.

Sally brought a bottle of Armagnac from the kitchen.

'I want to explain,' Topher said. 'About Lucille . . .'

'You don't have to.'

'Why are you so understanding?'

Sally, ostensibly absorbed with dispensing the correct amount of Armagnac into the glasses, was kneeling on the rug in front of the table.

'You want the truth, Your Honour, and nothing but the truth?'

Topher noticed with pleasure how the lamplight caught the contours of her cheek, as in a Rubens' painting.

Clutching the bottle, Sally looked up from her task.

'I love you, Christopher.' She sat back on her heels. 'So help me God.'

I love you, Christopher. So help me God. The words had haunted Topher for the remainder of the week. They danced and jigged before his eyes as he lay naked in the king-sized bed in the Mount Royal next to a similarly exposed Lucille.

'Penny for them?' Lucille lit a cigarette.

Saturday night had, in the end, offered four possibilities. Apart from Sally Maddox's *soirée*, Jo Henderson had invited him to a film *première*, and Chelsea and David – with an unexpectedly spare ticket for *Parsifal* – had asked him to join them. Topher had opted for Lucille. By way of preparation for the evening he had paid a visit to Boots. Standing before the counter – on which the contraceptives were brazenly displayed between the vitamin capsules and the vapour rubs – he was not surprised to find that there was, as with mustard and marmalade, a plethora of choice. In his youth, a word in the barber's ear as he put away his clippers, had been all that was necessary. He vacillated between heavy duty and gossamer. The thought struck him that Caroline would have known immediately just what would suit him. Avoiding the eye of a school-leaver behind the counter, he picked up an envelope (Lifestyles) and extended his purchase to a grey-haired woman in a white overall.

In bed with Lucille he could scarcely reveal the fact that his mind was on Sally. Her declaration of her feelings for him had been followed by a treatise on the nature of love. Following the traumatic break-up of her marriage, Sally had resolved never to have anything to do with love again.

'I was doing very nicely, or so I thought . . .' She looked at Topher. 'Until Marcus and April's.'

'When you publicly molested me.'

'I couldn't keep my hands off you.'

'That much was obvious.'

'Since that night, Christopher, I haven't been able to think clearly.' She glanced across at her typewriter. 'I have written nothing but crap.'

When he had kissed Sally goodnight, on her front step, Topher had experienced an overwhelming desire to shut the door, with himself on the inside, and to take her, without more ado, to bed. That he did not do so was due more to Sally's comment, whispered into his ear, that she had not the slightest intention of sharing him, either with Jo Henderson or with Lucille, than to his restraint.

He still ached for Caroline, was infatuated (however temporarily) with Lucille, and was becoming more than slightly attracted to Jo Henderson. He wondered was he turning, in his dotage, into some kind of satyr.

'Tina showed me a photograph of you.' Lucille's voice broke into his thoughts. 'In your army uniform. You were a handsome young man. You're not bad-looking now.'

'I could do with a bit more up here.' Topher smoothed the hair

152

which had become ruffled during the evening's exertions.

'I don't set too much store on appearances,' Lucille said.

'*Fronte nulla fides.*'

'What's that?'

'You shouldn't judge a book by its cover.'

'Or a sausage by its skin.'

Topher believed what Lucille had said. That she was indifferent to appearances. She seemed not to need constant reassurance from a mirror. She was at ease with herself, *bien dans sa peau*.

She lay back on the pillow and pulled the sheet up to her chin. 'If my mother – God rest her poor soul – could see me now. She would not believe her eyes. In bed with a *judge!*'

'What's so special?'

'You have to be ever so clever, for a start.'

'With a copy of *Everybody's Guide to the Criminal Law* – plus sufficient common sense to tell the difference between an honest man and a rogue – anyone could do it.'

'I was in court once. In Leeds. It was pouring with rain and I'd forgotten my umbrella. This poor little fellow, he didn't look as if he could hurt a fly, was accused of exposing his person. His *person!*'

'It's the jargon which holds the legal charade together,' Topher laughed. 'Until we hold our courts in the shopping precincts, so that people can just drop in on their way to the supermarket, the language is not going to be such that the layman will understand.'

'I used to think judges were stuffy.' Lucille stroked Topher's nose. 'You're not stuffy.'

'When judges didn't have so many cases to deal with, they could afford to be stuffy. These days we indulge ourselves less.'

'I wouldn't mind if you were, stuffy.' Lucille sat up, leaning on her elbow. 'Can I ask you something?'

Despite the grey roots at the base of her multicoloured blonde hair, despite the network of finely traced wrinkles about her eyes, Topher had a clear vision of Lucille as a young girl. He thought how pretty she must have been.

'They sent round this letter,' Lucille said, 'about how I'd won two hundred pounds, a fortnight in an English hotel, a set of cut glasses, or a video recorder. All I had to do was go to Leeds and watch a film about holiday properties – "Holiday Paradise" they called it. I go into Leeds every so often to get my highlights done. There's this wonderful man, I'd follow him to the ends of the earth. So I thought why not? I

153

sat through this film, two hours and a bit, and – you know me – I got carried away. Before you could say "knife" I'd got my prize – the video-recorder – and I'd signed on the dotted line. I was the proud possessor of a Timeshare Apartment. On the Costa del Sol. "Everything about it says Welcome." They kept very quiet about the annual maintenance fee, of course. Anyway, what I wanted to ask you, Topher, what I wondered is, love . . . My seven days is coming up at the end of the month. How would you like to spend a week on "beaches of ever-changing texture . . . in the natural charm of the Andalusian countryside . . . where the Atlantic is tamed by the Mediterranean and the sun shines for over 320 days a year"?'

Chapter Twenty-One

Topher was convinced that he was dying. He particularly wanted to be in Knightsbridge early, because he was in the midst of an indecency case, but he had woken up with a sore throat, the sensation that his body was on fire, and the realisation that it was only with the greatest difficulty that he could lift his head from the pillow. Marcus, having received his panicked telephone call, looked in on his way to the hospital.

'You look awful,' he said, from the end of Topher's bed.

'I feel awful. What's the matter with me?'

'I can't really say . . . I'm not that sort of a doctor. I don't even have a stethoscope.'

'You could feel my pulse.'

'I make it a rule never to touch the patients. I suggest you call your GP.'

'Do you think it could be pleurisy?'

'Hard to say.' Marcus picked up Topher's *Times* and turned to the city pages. He ran a finger down the stock-market prices. 'Bloody marvellous!'

'Or pneumonia?'

'You're not coughing, are you? I only have to look at a share for it to go down.'

'Don't change the subject.'

Marcus shut the paper.

'You're keeping something from me?' Topher groaned.

'Such as?'

Topher was silent. He wished his head would stop banging.

'I suppose you think you have AIDS?'

'It had crossed my mind.'

'Absolute rubbish.'

'How can you be so sure? You just said you weren't that sort of a doctor.'

'It's highly unlikely . . . By the way, how is Lucille?'

'You see, you admit the possibility.'

'Anything is *possible*. I suspect that what you're suffering from is a nasty dose of flu. I hope I don't catch it. Tell me the number of your GP and I'll give him a bell for you. Then I must be off. I expect April will look in later.'

Topher directed Marcus to Caroline's bureau and the well-thumbed leather telephone book which Chelsea had given her mother for her fortieth birthday.

'McCormack, isn't it?' Marcus said. 'Would that be under *M* or *C*?'

'Hard to say.' Topher felt too ill to explain the idiosyncrasies of his late wife's filing system.

Dr McCormack whom they had known for years but rarely troubled, was as likely to be under D (doctor), G (GP), P (practice) or T (Ted) his Christian name, as it was under either M or C. By the same token Mr Plant, who had made the curtains and cushion covers when they had last redecorated the sitting-room, could be found under U (for upholsterer), although he never actually touched upholstery, and the telephone number of Caroline's Bird-Watching society — known impiously as Twitchers — was listed between the Thames Valley Water Board and that of Mr Farquarson, who had been Penge's piano *t*utor.

Marcus, more by good luck than good management, had found the number he was looking for. He spoke to the receptionist of what was now a group practice.

'MacCormack's on holiday,' he told Topher, when he'd hung up. 'A Doctor Harrington will call.'

'Never heard of him,' Topher rasped.

'I'm sure he's quite capable of prescribing an antibiotic,' Marcus said, 'which is probably all you need.' He looked at his watch. 'My first patient is at eight.'

'Second.'

'A case of primary erectile impotence.'

'At least *he* won't get AIDS!'

Waiting for April, Topher fell into the febrile half-sleep of sickness and thought about Lucille.

It was three months since he had turned down her invitation to Southern Spain. Deeply tanned ('boobs and all', as she put it) Lucille, bearing a bottle of Marques de Cacères, and a bag of shellfish, had come straight to Hampstead from Gatwick to cook Topher a *paella*. The next morning Mrs Sweetlove had recoiled in horror from the smell of garlic on his breath.

It seemed natural that on Lucille's visits to London she should take charge of Topher's kitchen. His *rechaufée* dishes gave way to *daubes* and stir-frys, in accordance with Lucille's moods. He looked forward to her visits. He liked to watch her, bracelets jangling, saucepan or plate held unconsciously in mid-air, as she chattered away and waltzed between stove and larder in his kitchen where she seemed so much at home. Sometimes he wondered . . .

Lucille had thrown out hints. 'I'm up to here with Bingley, it's time I made a break.' Or 'It must be ever so nice living in London. There's always something going on.' Lucille never stayed the night. Their love life took place in the king-sized bed at the Mount Royal where Topher rejoiced at the renaissance of his virility. There was nothing feminist or militant about Lucille. She liked men. She didn't think that there was anything either demeaning or degrading about pleasing them. Whatever made Topher happy made her happy. He was in danger of drowning in Lucille's attentions.

Lucille had found an ally in Penge. She had wheeled her bicycle in one night when Lucille was putting a Shepherd's Pie into the oven.

'Sorry,' Penge said pointedly to Topher, appraising Lucille in her black halter-neck top and violet satin skirt. She prepared to wheel her bicycle out again. 'I didn't know you were entertaining.'

'I'm not *entertaining*,' Lucille said, laughing. 'I'm Lucille Moss from Bingley. I'm making your father a Shepherd's Pie – you really shouldn't be riding that bicycle in your condition, love – there's more than enough for three.'

Penge, her hunger overcoming her disapproval, had stayed for dinner. Over the washing-up Topher heard them discussing epidurals and breast-feeding (Lucille had a daughter in Canada), with animation.

Penge had grudgingly admitted later that she liked Lucille, and that Topher had to have *some* social life. She was unwilling to be drawn further.

157

Topher surprised himself at the ease with which he managed to juggle his engagements. His diary, which in the months following Caroline's death had been a monochrome of empty pages, was now so full of permanent-blue entries that he was hard put to find an evening when he was free. He had temporarily abandoned Pushkin (half way through *Mozart and Salieri*) and sometimes had to stay up into the small hours to write his judgements. Lucille usually came down on a Monday or a Thursday. If she was also in town at the week-end, his Saturday night spilled over into Sunday.

It was an unusual week when he did not see Jo at least twice. They dined out (Jo cheerfully confessed to her inability to boil the proverbial egg, the veracity of which statement Topher doubted), or went to the opera. Sometimes they did both. He was now greeted by name at Wiltons and Langan's. When he had escorted Jo to her goddaughter's wedding, their picture had been in *Harpers and Queen*. 'She's out to get you,' Chelsea had muttered. It was of course true. Jo Henderson made no secret of it. At Badger's she seated him at the head of her table and tried to involve him in decisions concerning both the cottage and the estate.

Sometimes, as he negotiated the long drive, he made believe that Badger's Cottage was his. He knew that he had only to say the word. Jo had not been to Topher's house. She was interested only in Topher. Sometimes he caught her watching him and had the distinct impression that the green ice of her eyes was melting. It was no trouble to convince himself that a life spent between Lowndes Square, the Royal Opera House, Badger's Cottage, the Palace Hotel at Gstaad, and Round Hill, Jamaica, was not too daunting a proposition. Returning, when he had a moment, to *Mozart and Salieri*, he wondered whether he had gone completely mad.

With Sally Maddox, Topher felt, there was a proper measure in things. *Est modus in rebus*. Although all that Sally got was what was left of the blank pages in his diary (what she referred to as the 'shitty end of the stick'), he was more at ease in her company than he was with either Jo Henderson or Lucille. Whether he was listening to Sally hold forth upon the novel, or he was attempting to unravel the spaghetti which featured frequently in her culinary repertoire (she did not pretend to be much of a cook), Topher was conscious of an almost marital familiarity, a lack of restraint, which made him look forward to his visits to Jeffrey's Street. Sally demanded nothing. He wondered sometimes if he did not give her very little in return.

His confused and semi-conscious thoughts were interrupted by the front door bell. It was over two hours since Marcus had left. Wondering why April hadn't used her key, he got out of bed and held aside the curtain. A young girl, her frizzy blonde hair tied with a pink ribbon, stood on the doorstep. Shivering, Topher opened the window.

'Yes?'

'Mr Osgood?'

'What is it you want? I'm ill.'

'I know you are. I'm Doctor Harrington.'

Ridiculous! Topher pondered the desirability of letting her into the house. Taking the line of least resistance – his throat was not up to doorstep dialectic – he threw down the key.

Face to face, Dr Harrington looked even less promising than she had from above. She seemed to patronise the same second-hand clothes shop as Penge, and not to have heard about stockings.

'How old are you?' Topher asked, rudely.

'Old enough.'

'That may be a very good answer,' Topher said, 'but it is not the answer to my question.'

He realised suddenly, and with horror, that he was not in court. Dr Harrington had reddened slightly.

'Forgive me. I'm accustomed to Dr MacCormack and I am not feeling myself.'

'We'll start again if you like.' Taking her stethoscope out of her case she approached the bed.

Topher was impressed at the seriousness and extent of the examination which followed. Dr Harrington took the history – during which he considered, and rejected, the advisability of telling her about his relationship with Lucille – and investigated him with an expertise which, after he had got over his first qualms, could only command respect. Palpating his abdomen she was firm but gentle. When she made a leisurely exploration of his testicles he tried to keep his mind on The Director of Public Prosecutions v Rogers 1953, *apropos* of the case he was in the midst of hearing. When the tips of her fingers encountered glands in his neck, he tried not to flinch. At the young lady's request Topher coughed, then coughed again. He opened and shut his mouth in accordance with her instructions.

'Well?' he said, when she had put away her stethoscope.

Dr Harrington's eyes were turquoise. Her mouth was wide, like a letter-box.

'Mumps,' she said from the end of the bed.

Topher's opinion of her took a rapid nose-dive.

'Don't be ridiculous!'

They looked at each other. Dr Harrington's gaze did not falter. Topher realised that he was not on the Bench now.

'What do you mean mumps?'

'Mumps. The parotid glands are just coming up. By tomorrow it will most probably be extremely painful for you to open your mouth.'

Topher thought of Chelsea and Penge with their grossly swollen faces when they were children.

'Grown men don't get mumps.'

'It is rare,' Dr Harrington conceded, 'but if there is contact and the resistance is low . . .'

'How long will I have to be off work?'

'Two weeks. Maybe three. The attack can be quite severe in adults.' Dr Harrington scribbled something on her pad.

'Aspirin when necessary, and I've given you something to relieve your throat. There's not much else I can do.'

She tore off the prescription and put it on Caroline's bureau.

'Your wife can take it to the chemist.'

Her unconsidered remark had the effect on Tophor of a physical blow. Dr Harrington might well be an expert in the diagnosis and treatment of infectious diseases but she still had a great deal to learn about diplomacy.

'My wife died almost a year ago.' Topher watched her face, guessing that it would become suffused with embarrassment when she realised her gaffe.

Dr Harrington's expression was one not of confusion but concern. She sat down by his side.

'How absolutely dreadful for you.'

Notwithstanding his fiery throat, Topher found himself reiterating the trials and tribulations of the recent months. He had the impression that Dr Harrington was not humouring a man old enough to be her father, but that she was actually listening to every word.

'Loneliness has been associated with a weakened immune system,' she said when he had finished. 'The stress induced by your wife's illness and death, could well account for the fact that you picked up the infection. Have you been away this year?'

Topher shook his head.

'I suggest that when you've recovered you take some time off.'

'A holiday?'

Dr Harrington stood up.

'Why not?'

When she had gone, letting herself out, Topher made a call to Knightsbridge Crown Court. He had to repeat 'mumps' three times to the disbelieving usher whom he instructed to terminate the indecency case.

Mrs Sweetlove was similarly disbelieving. 'Mumps, Your Honour!'

To Topher's horror she offered to visit him. She was sure she could be of help. He reassured her, although his mouth felt like the bottom of a birdcage, his throat burned, his pyjamas were soaked, and his bed a shambles, that he was being cared for by a veritable fleet of nurses.

'Just let me know, Your Honour,' Mrs Sweetlove said, 'and I'll be round like a shot.'

He had just fallen into a deep sleep when April, knocking gently and carrying a tray on which a jug of iced barley-water shimmered like a mirage, opened the bedroom door.

'I hope you don't catch it,' Topher said, feeling sorry for himself.

'Catch what?' April set the tray down beside him.

'Mumps.'

He told her about Dr Harrington's findings and about Dr Harrington. April reassured him that she had had mumps as a child. At her insistence, and against his better judgement, he went into the bathroom to wash, and change his pyjamas, while she tidied his bed. By the time he was back in it, and had dispatched some of the barley-water, he felt a great deal better. April was looking considerably dishevelled.

'It's time you thought about moving. This house is far too big. There must have been five hundred glasses in the cupboard when I went to look for one.'

'Caroline collected glasses,' Topher said defensively. They had rarely returned from a bird-watching trip without visiting a village junk shop or antique fair, where she would add to her collection.

'Poor Caroline,' April said, 'I think of her so often. What will you do?'

'About what?'

'About Christmas, for one thing.'

'Christmas!'

161

'I wanted to say – before you are inundated with invitations – that Marcus and I would be most upset if you didn't spend Christmas with us. You can bring Chelsea and Penge, and the baby of course. It's due any moment isn't it?

Topher did not want it to be Christmas. For ghosts and memories, momentarily displaced, to make their presence more poignantly felt.

'I'd be lost without you and Marcus,' he evaded the issue.

'I only wish you'd let us do more. I could find you a nice little flat – every other house in the street is being converted – and decorate it for you. You wouldn't have to lift a finger.'

'I'm too ill,' Topher groaned, 'to think about anything.'

'Of course you are. How very thoughtless of me. I'll shut the curtains, so that you can sleep, and take your prescription to the chemist. Do the girls know you're ill?'

'Chelsea and Penge have their own problems.'

Feeling that he knew April well enough for her not to be offended, he closed his eyes in dismissal.

Chapter Twenty-Two

David Cornish was free to marry. Chelsea had rung, the words falling over themselves, to break the news to Topher. An unexpected telephone call from David's wife had informed Chelsea that she had known all along that her husband was seeing another woman. She was prepared to give David up on one condition: Chelsea was to come to the house to fetch him.

'What do you think?' Chelsea asked Topher.

'I think that's . . . splendid.'

'You don't sound very pleased.'

'I've got mumps.'

'*Mumps?*'

Topher sighed.

'Is anyone looking after you?'

'A great many people,' Topher said through his teeth.

'Poor you.' Chelsea sounded relieved. 'Look I'll come over when I can.'

'There's no need. I'm managing very well.'

Which was, Topher thought, replacing the telephone on the bedside table next to the hothouse grapes from Jo, the understatement of the year.

He could not remember when he had last stayed in bed. In the manner of those of strong constititution (he had inherited his from his father) he had little patience with indisposition. He had been known to tell his family, firmly believing it, that the afflictions of which they

163

complained from time to time, existed no where so much as in the mind and could be banished by their own volition. In the grips of his own singularly inappropriate illness, he wondered whether his words might not only have been hasty but foolish. He felt wretched and had felt wretched for days.

A tom-tom in his head (which was reluctant to contain any cohesive thoughts) beat incessantly; his throat was raging; his neck and face (now distended unilaterally) were stiff; he had the greatest difficulty in opening his mouth which, when he did manage to do so in the interests of eating or speaking, caused him great distress. His chest hurt when he took a deep breath. Dr Harrington had started him on an antibiotic which upset his stomach. Each limb was a millstone. He shivered and shook. He was, by turns, unable to get warm, and afterwards consumed with such a fever that his bed-clothes were perpetually sodden. He felt extremely low, and had at times an absurd and atypical desire to weep with self pity.

There was no question that he had not been looked after. He had been churlishly ungrateful for some of the care which had been lavished upon him. Someone should write a book, he thought in his more lucid moments, about sick-room etiquette. Apart from Marcus, who blew in and made jokes, at which it caused Topher severe pain to laugh, he had been surrounded by women. Sally Maddox had been the first to arrive, with an armful of books. At lunchtime she had disappeared into the kitchen from which she had emerged (what seemed several hours later) with a plate of her spaghetti which Topher would have been unable to eat even if he had had the strength to distentangle the glutinous strands. Despite his irritation with her – he wondered whether he had in fact got something wrong with his brain – he was sorry to see Sally go. The minute he heard the front door close he wanted her to come back.

Lucille had brought books too. A plastic carrier of gold- and silver-embossed paperbacks. She had tried to jolly him out of his misery with her 'Come on, lamb' and 'You'll be all right, love', and 'I'll make you a nice *crayme caramelle*.' She had talked to him as if he were a child and, like a child, he had refused to eat her custard.

Jo Henderson had, in addition to the grapes, sent a dozen quarter-bottles of Moet Chandon (1981) and a jar of beef-tea. She had commiserated with him over the telephone.

'By the way we always have this enormous house-party at Badger's, darling.' She had taken to calling him darling. 'I didn't want you to lie there worrying about what you were going to do in the Christmas vacation.'

Christmas was the last thing Topher was worrying about. He had opened one bottle of the champagne. It had had disastrous effects on his salivary glands and had not been at all wise. When a bouquet of white lilies (Pulbrook and Gould) had arrived from Jo, he had serious doubts about the suitability of her choice.

Mrs Sweetlove had sent a card (with a rabbit on it) trusting that Topher would 'soon be hopping about again'. Tina had insisted upon coming down from Bingley. She had arrived bearing love from Miles, and a bag in which – apart from her overnight things – were a ginger cake and some Lancashire hot-pot.

'Who sent these gorgeous flowers?' She stood wide-eyed before the lilies.

'Just a friend.'

'Has Lucille been to see you?'

Topher nodded.

Tina put her nose into the lilies which had no smell.

'Lucille really likes you.' Tina roamed the room, setting it to rights with her customary lack of method, and putting everything away in the wrong place. 'This house is really too big, you know.'

It was the second time in a week that its unsuitability had been pointed out to him. Tina's solution to the problem was different from April's.

'Do you think you'll settle down again?'

'Get married, you mean?' Topher disliked euphemisms.

'I know it's early days. Lucille may be a bit brash but it's mostly because she's nervous. You won't find anyone better natured.'

'Why is it that women always feel they are obliged to *do* something about a man on his own?'

'For one thing, it's not tidy.' Tina picked up Topher's dressing-gown from the floor. 'You don't *like* being on your own?'

Topher had to admit that he was getting used to it. He also had to admit something which had come as a revelation to him since his widowhood. He liked women. He enjoyed listening to them. He was interested in their opinions. When he was with a woman, whether she was nineteen or ninety, he liked to give her his complete attention. Caroline had always told him that every woman he met, no matter what she looked like, was left with the impression that he wanted to go to bed with her. He had never believed it. The unspoken invita-

165

tion, if it existed, was inadvertent. It had something to do with his eyes. Feather-brained as she was, Topher even liked having his sister about him. He watched her move from one side of the room to the other, forgetting what it was she had intended to do by the time she got there. Women, he thought, gave a sense of meaning and continuity to life. An insinuation of pasts which had been, and of futures to come. Men were pinned down, two dimensional, unequivocally in existing time.

'I wanted to discuss Christmas,' Tina said. 'You'll come to Bingley. Evelyn's room is free and Lucille has offered to cook the turkey. She's a smashing cook. You can bring the girls. I won't take no for an answer.'

'I don't know . . .' Topher said.

'Of course you don't. Not when you're feeling poorly. I just wanted to say we're expecting you. You're going to notice it at Christmas, without Caroline.'

Topher did not need to wait until Christmas. While he had been in bed he had had time to think. One of the conclusions he had reached was that he had not sufficiently appreciated Caroline, who had possessed, he decided upon reflection, the finer qualities of Sally Maddox, Jo Henderson, and Lucille, rolled into one. It was a paradox of course that people died without knowing what those closest to them were thinking. He wished that it had not been so. He could not fathom how today's mercurial partnerships fared, when his relationship with Caroline had scarcely had time to mature in the cask of their life together. He regretted the fact that he had not expressed his indebtedness to her both more often and in more certain terms.

By the time he had recovered from the mumps, Chelsea had — or rather did not have — her lover and Penge had had her baby. Only one of them was ecstatic.

When Chelsea had let herself into the house on the day she was to collect David Cornish, Topher had been sleeping. His fever had abated and the swollen glands were subsiding. He was not only beginning to enjoy his convalescence, although feeling somewhat guilty at the attention he was receiving, but to believe that he might live. Never again, he vowed, conscious of the altered state to which he had been brought by his ailment, would he be unsympathetic to physical suffering. Opening his eyes, and expecting to find an animated Chelsea bursting with her good news, he was amazed to find his eldest daughter in tears.

For a long time she was unable to talk at all. She borrowed a large linen handkerchief, and sat blowing her nose noisily into it while Topher waited for her to speak. He pieced together the story which came out incoherently in between Chelsea's sobs. She had taken the day off from the BBC and prepared a celebratory dinner before going to Fulham to fetch David.

'Spare ribs?' Topher said, in an attempt to cheer her up. His words had the contrary effect.

'I b . . b . . bought a ph . . ph . . pheasant,' Chelsea howled. 'David adores game. And a p . . piece of his favourite Dutch cheese with the black rind . . and a bottle of Mouton Cadet.'

'My God!' Topher was impressed.

'Candles on the table, soft lights, sweet music . . .'

Topher waited while she took another handkerchief from his drawer.

'As soon as I got to Fulham I could see that something was wrong. She'd come off her drugs. David's wife, I mean. She'd absolutely flipped. The house was full of people and she had the stereo on. You could hear it half way down the street. 'I know you,' she said. 'Stupid cow. I've known about you all along. He's upstairs if you want him.' It was one of those tall houses with lots of floors. David was in bed . . .' It was some time before Chelsea could finish her story because she had burst into tears again. When she stopped crying she put Topher's handkerchief unthinkingly into her handbag and stood up, apparently to look out of the window.

'He was just lying there. When I came into the room only his eyes moved. There was a nurse looking after him.'

She was now in control of herself.

'He was unable to speak. Paralysed down one side. He'd had a stroke . . .'

By the time Chelsea had told the rest of her story, Topher's temperature had shot up again. David had collapsed on the squash court. His wife had lived for years with the knowledge that David had had a lover. This was her revenge.

Chelsea was inconsolable. The humiliation she had undergone in Fulham was as nothing compared with her heartbreak for David – whose bleak future she could not contemplate – and the loss of her love object. Her life was in ruins. She was tempted to dispose of what remained of it. Topher was in need of Caroline and Chelsea of her mother.

'Have you told Penge?'

'Penge is in hospital . . . That's what I really came to tell you. She's in labour.'

The following few days had all the ingredients of a nightmare. David Cornish's wife — who had become completely manic — had refused to let Chelsea anywhere near the house. She would neither let her see David nor communicate with him. Chelsea did not know whether he was alive or dead. She had gone completely to pieces and had been given sick leave from the BBC. Unable to face her own company, she had left Wapping and moved back into her old bedroom where she lay with her face to the wall. She refused to talk, even to Marcus, who said she was in a state of shock. Sally Maddox, who could generally be relied upon not to visit in the mornings, had come up against a writer's block and arrived to see Topher at the same time as Lucille. And Penge, after a stop-go labour, half-way through which she had been admitted to hospital, had finally managed to give birth.

Topher, whose life prior to the mumps seemed to have been straightening itself out, felt thoroughly confused by the events. Looking into the mirror he seriously considered that despite his still distorted face he did not look like a grandfather. He certainly did not feel like a grandfather. He had spoken on the telephone to Penge. In the manner of first time mothers she had managed to convince herself that she was unique. She was over the moon.

Topher enquired if the child had a name. 'Charles,' Penge said, 'If it had been a girl it would have been Caroline.'

It was such moments, Topher thought, rather than any material success or acquisition, that rendered the quiet desperation of most people's lives, tolerable. Because of the possibility of infection he had as yet seen neither his youngest daughter nor his new grandson.

Lucille, who had arrived with the largest teddy-bear Topher had ever seen, had opened one of Jo Henderson's bottles of champagne 'to wet the baby's head'. They were drinking the toast when Sally had played her distinctive melody on the doorbell. Lucille had let her in.

The encounter had been civilised. Lucille, as if she were holding a *salon*, had poured champagne for Sally who accepted it with only a *soupçon* of approbation for the older woman. Each of them had endeavoured to prove herself at home. Lucille had straightened his pillows with a proprietorial 'Lift your head up for me, love,' and Sally, who had brought *When we Very Young* (a first edition) for the new baby, had demonstrated her familiarity with the house by fetching *Cross and Jones* on Criminal Law at Topher's request, without having to ask him where it was located.

Watching the two women circling each other, like boxers in the ring (Sally having the slight advantage of having known of her rival's existence), the sudden thought struck Topher that he loved them both.

Chapter Twenty-Three

Topher, fully recovered from the mumps, was delighted to go back to work. In addition to Chelsea, who wandered round the house like a zombie and got in his way, he now had Penge and the baby to contend with.

Chelsea had been down the road unburdening herself to Marcus. Topher, glad to have the house to himself, was in his study listening to the sixth Brandenburg and trying to work out the Russian for: 'For three days Natasha/The merchant's daughter/Was missing', when Penge had appeared on the doorstep with what Topher thought was a bundle of washing, but which had turned out to be his grandson.

At the sight of her tear-stained face beneath the porch-light, he had groaned inwardly.

'We've been evicted!' she said in her Lady Bracknell voice. She handed her bundle to Topher and, to his dismay, picked up her suitcase from the step.

It was a story such as Topher heard every day. Penge's landlord had been granted a possession order. The tenants of the Hackney commune had been given notice to quit. Robert had found alternative accommodation. Chad was staying with his grandmother in Wales whilst working for his Law Society exams. The other occupants of the house had gone their various ways. Penge had come home.

Temporarily, she assured Topher. Until she and Chad got their act together. Meanwhile mother and baby were well and truly ensconced. Topher, who had on his own admission been lonely at times, was ambivalent about the new arrangements. There was no doubt that the house was large enough, but he did not care for the perpetual clutter (about which he had forgotten) left by his daughters in the kitchen, the havoc they wreaked in his now ordered housekeeping, the baby garments he pulled out of the airing-cupboard whilst searching for his underpants.

He could have overlooked the chaos were the household not in perpetual auditory and sensual motion. To begin with there was the crying. The sound had at first delighted him, as had the initial glimpse of his grandson. As he returned the inquisitive gaze, explored the minuscule limbs, an immense sadness had enveloped him as he realised that he could not share with Caroline his earliest impressions of this imprint they would leave upon the sands of time. Charles Sheridan Beerbohm (poor little mite) Osgood-Jones.

The novelty of having the little chap in residence had now worn off. His stertorous yells disturbed Topher in the night and awoke him in the morning. The small noises, breathing and scuffling, from the Moses basket in his study (where Penge was prone to dump her son in the evenings), distracted him.

It was not only the baby. When Topher wanted to use the telephone it was to find that it had been appropriated – on what seemed a permanent basis – either by Chelsea or by Penge (whom he could not disabuse from the impression that Plynlimon was a local call). When the line *was* available there was little privacy.

When Topher was well enough to go out again in the evenings, both Penge and Chelsea, the parental role reversed, enquired where he was going. They waited up for his return and demanded to know where he had been. Apart from the domestic disorder, he had to contend with Lucille on Sally Maddox, and Sally Maddox on Lucille.

'Known her long?' Lucille said in the Mount Royal coffee-shop. Topher's libido seeming to have been affected by his illness, they had spent the evening in the cinema. The film had been a transatlantic gangster epic about the notorious Al Capone, whose appalling lack of table manners had led him to fracture the skull of a dinner guest with a baseball bat. The sepia-toned streets of Chicago (peopled by extras and traversed by vehicles exhumed from motor museums) had been intended to evoke the days of Prohibition. They succeeded only in making it more difficult, as did the clumsy plot and distorted sound-track, to suspend, even for a moment, disbelief. While brains were blown out, and blood spouted from machine-gunned viscera – to spread over Persian carpets across which dying victims dragged themselves towards final acts of redemption – Lucille fed herself popcorn from the carton on her lap. Topher, narrowing his eyes to see its face in the semi-darkness, looked frequently at his watch. When the film was over and they made their way over the rubbish-strewn floor towards the exit, he reflected sadly that the cinema seemed not only to be aimed at society's lowest common denominator but also at the very young.

When Lucille, with both hands round her coffee cup, had enquired how long he had known Sally Maddox, Topher was still lamenting the decline of the silver screen.

'Sally is a good friend.'

'See much of her?'

'I suppose I do.'

He realised afterwards that what Lucille had been seeking was not an assessment of how many times a week he saw Sally Maddox, but reassurance. Women did not always say what they meant. It was the expression on Lucille's face, as she uncharacteristically refused a second chocolate *éclair*, which alerted him to the fact that he had been tactless. He tried to redeem himself by dismissing Sally merely as an acquaintance. As soon as the words were out of his mouth he knew that he was not telling the truth. Over the past months Sally had become part of his life. He needed Sally as much as he needed Lucille.

He had been expecting to see Lucille again on the following Saturday. It wasn't until she called to say that she couldn't manage it, that he realised how much he looked forward to her visits.

Tina had telephoned soon afterwards.

'What have you done to Lucille? All the stuffing seems to have been knocked out of her.'

'Nothing,' Topher lied.

'I thought perhaps you'd had a row or something. Lucille's ever so miserable. Of course it's not my business . . .'

'No it's not,' Topher sighed.

Feeling guilty, he had called Lucille.

'It's stupid to get upset over Sally Maddox . . .'

He could hear her sniffing.

'You know I love you.'

As soon as he'd said it Topher was appalled. He didn't even know if it was true. He wondered if his brain – although it was not his brain

172

Dr Harrington had been worried about – had been affected by the mumps.

Lucille had been slightly mollified by his declaration.

'I can't help it if I'm jealous.'

'Of course you can't. But there's no need to be.'

'Sure?'

Topher was saved from replying by Penge bursting into his study, demanding to know whether he had seen the baby's rattle.

'See you next week?' he said to Lucille, shaking his head at Penge.

'Do you really want me?'

'You know I do.' He only slightly evaded the issue. Penge was turning over the papers on his desk in search of the rattle. He did not return Lucille's telephone kiss.

The appeasement of Sally had proved more difficult.

'She's very nice,' Sally said, over her sesame prawns.

Unable to face Sally's spaghetti, Topher had taken her to Mr Kai of Mayfair (to which he had been introduced by Jo).

'It would be easier if she wasn't.'

'Who is?' Topher asked, knowing very well.

'Your Lucille.'

'She's not *my* Lucille.'

'This is me you're talking to. Sally Maddox. Remember?'

He could not delude Sally.

'I like her,' Sally said.

Topher spread plum sauce on his paper-thin pancake, topped it with slivers of cucumber and spring onion, and searched with his chop-sticks for the succulent bits amongst the pieces of shredded duck.

'So do I.'

They ate in silence for a while.

'How's Penge managing?' Sally changed the subject.

'Very well indeed.' Topher was relieved to be shot of the spectre of Lucille which had come between them. 'Caroline would have been proud of her.'

Once he had got over the shock of seeing his daughter bare her veined and swollen breast publicly to stop his grandson's mouth, Topher had been astounded at the way Penge managed to cope with motherhood. True she never seemed to get dressed, and fed her child wherever she happened to be when he was crying. She was besotted with young Charlie, however, and ministered as if to the manner born to his not insubstantial needs. It looked as if the advent of her nephew might be the saving too of Chelsea. Sharing the baby's care with a perspicacious Penge had been the catalyst in rescuing her from her depression. There was talk of her returning to the BBC but as yet none of her going back to Wapping. Topher was looking forward to leaving the Community Care Refuge and Home for Unmarried Mothers (into which his house seemed suddenly to have been transformed) and getting back to the comparative tranquillity of the Bench.

'Do you go back to the County Court?' Sally, as usual, was tuned in to his thoughts.

Topher nodded. He had already been in to glance at the papers of his first case.

'Compensation. An old lady knocked down by a lorry.'

'I know all about that . . .'

Topher remembered the son who had been killed.

'Our action was in the Crown Court. I thought it was a crime. I've never been sure exactly what a crime is.'

Topher finished the last of his pancake. 'In attempting to define a crime one runs into serious difficulties. When Parliament enacts that a particular act shall become a crime, or that an act which is now criminal shall cease to be so, the act does not change in nature in any respect other than that of legal classification . . .' He looked at Sally. 'You're not listening.'

'I was thinking about Lucille.'

She took Topher's hand.

'You don't need Lucille.'

'Sally . . .' Topher said. 'Dear Sally.'

On his way to court Topher replenished his larder (which during his illness had become the dumping ground for alien cans and packages) with his familiar requirements. Next to the supermarket a colourful display of posters in the window of the Travel Agent's caught his eye. 'Fishing in the Lijang River.' 'Carnival in Shanghai.' 'Temple of Heaven: Beijing.' Unaware what impelled him, he went inside. The brochures were stacked at the back of the window, between the ski literature and the 'Short Breaks'. A slow boat to China. A little time on his own, away from Chelsea and Penge, and young Charlie, and Lucille, and Sally (who had made it clear she was expecting him to spend Christmas with *her*), and Mrs Sweetlove (who had telephoned him every single day of his illness), might be exactly what he needed to sort out the turmoil in his head. Dr Harrington had suggested a holiday.

The brace of young ladies in charge of the office were plugged into their telephones. They seemed not only uninterested in selling him a vacation, but indifferent to his presence. He helped himself to a brochure which he tucked beneath his arm. On his way to the car he wondered whether an inclusive tour to the People's Republic of China via Cathay Pacific, although not exactly a slow boat, might not be just what the doctor ordered.

In his robing-room a jam-jar of pom-pom dahlias had been put on his desk next to the apple juice. Mrs Sweetlove, fidgeting with her gown and perfuming the room with essence-of-something not very much to Topher's liking, was like a cat on a hot tin roof.

'We *are* pleased to have you back, Your Honour.'

Topher noticed that in his absence her hair had become a curious shade of plum. He grunted what he hoped was graciously.

'Mumps can be very nasty,' Mrs Sweetlove said. 'I remember when my sister had them. My younger sister that is, not the one that lives in Purley . . .'

'I need to look at the County Court Rules, Mrs Sweetlove.' Topher indicated the book-case. 'I wonder if you would be so very kind as to hand me the Green Book.'

It was a relief to be back in court. To conduct his own orchestra after being at the mercy of his body, which had seen fit to play such infantile tricks on him, and of his frenetic household. Re-invigorated by his enforced rest he found himself smiling benignly upon the most lumpen of witnesses, extending unaccustomed tolerance towards barristers seemingly in the grip of verbal diarrhoea, and listening with great patience to the most inarticulate of police officers. With his mind partly on Jo (who was taking him to a dinner party at the nether end of the day) he made a determined effort not to look at the clock even when it got towards lunchtime. He did not want to be accused, like Tolstoy's Court President, of being anxious to get through the sitting as early as possible, in order 'to call before six o'clock on the red-haired woman with whom he had begun a romance . . .'

The day – an injunction, followed by a committal, followed by a trial – went quickly.

He spent an agreeable half-hour playing with his grandson, before changing into his dinner-jacket and presenting himself at Lowndes Square.

Topher had not seen Jo since his illness. He thought at first that he had forgotten how attractive she was. Then he realised that she had made an extra special effort with her always immaculate appearance, and that something was afoot. Her neck and shoulders emerged, lotus-like, from a shimmering orange sheath with a matching bow on the hip. One leg, in its shadowed stocking, was visible to the thigh when she moved. The table was set for an intimate dinner for two and the candles matched her dress.

'Aren't we going out?'

'It's so long since I've seen you.'

'I thought you couldn't cook?'

Weighed down by his recent miseries, he realised how much he had missed the sound of Jo's laughter.

'Who said anything about cooking?'

The meal had been sent in. Caviar with the champagne, *consommé* with the claret, roast partridge on *foie gras* with the white burgundy, and peaches with the port. Having subsisted for so long on Lucille's caramel custard, Sally Maddox's spaghetti, Tina's Lancashire hot-pot, Chelsea and Penge's haphazard offerings, and the rapidly diminishing contents of his own larder, Topher savoured every morsel. He demonstrated his gratitude by making the coffee. Setting the cups down next to the double brandies Jo had dispensed while he was in the kitchen, he sat down (which was about all he was now capable of) on the sofa next to his hostess who was slightly out of focus.

'I must congratulate you.' Looking at the abandoned dinner table, Topher raised his glass.

Jo reciprocated with her brandy balloon.

'Better than going out?'

'Infinitely.'

'In which way?'

'In every way.'

'Name one.'

'Superb food . . .'

'How about the wines?'

'Incomparable.'

'Service?'

'Impeccable.'

'Ambience?'

'*Intime.*'

'Company?'

'Adorable.'

'Pleased you came?'

'Yes.'

'Glad we stayed in?'

'Yes.'

'Will you marry me?'

'Yes . . .'

Topher put down his brandy and looked at the orange blur.

'What's that you said?'

'Will you marry me?'

'I need notice of that question.'

He didn't remember much of the rest of the evening. Only that he had left his car on the Res. Park. in Lowndes Square and had gone home in a cab. He was grateful to find all the lights out in the house. Taking his shoes off in the hall in order not to wake young Charlie, he crept noiselessly up the stairs.

On his bed, scribbled across the dragon on the front of the unopened China brochure, was a note from Penge. 'Lucille wants you to ring her, no matter how late', and 'Sally Maddox phoned'.

Chapter Twenty-Four

'Passenger' for Guangzhou please board the plane. Passenger' for Guangzhou please board plane. Passenger' for Guangzhou please board plane. Passenger' for Guangzhou . . .'

The child, Delilah, was pulling at his sleeve.

Opening his eyes, Topher saw a column of Chinese travellers, hung about with parcels, moving resolutely towards the boarding gate. He tried to orientate himself.

Delilah's mother was assembling her formidable array of hand-baggage. She held out the bottomless bag of Australian sweetmeats which had sustained her daughter throughout the tour.

'Give the judge a lolly, Delilah. Your mouth gets very dry when you've been sleeping.'

'Passenger' for Guangzhou please board plane. Passenger' for Guangzhou please board plane . . .'

Through the window Topher could see that the fog had lifted and that the Ilyushyn had been turned round. It was now guarded by six emissaries of the People's Liberation Army, in oversized green over-coats, with bayonets fixed. He was amazed to find how long he had slept. His cracked mug, half-full of tea, was on the spit-spattered floor by the lumps of lead that were his feet. Delilah must have taken it from him.

Stamping to restore his circulation, Topher helped himself to a sweet. He remembered the riddle which Delilah had asked him before he dropped off.

'What time *do* you go to the dentist, Delilah?'

'"Tooth 'urty!" Get it?' She took his hand. 'C'mon, judge. We're going to Guangzhou.'

Beijing/Guangzhou, Guangzhou/Hong Kong Hong Kong/London. Topher was almost at the end of his journey.

His decision to spend Christmas in the People's Republic had been greeted with a variety of comments.

'All those Chinese!' Mrs Sweetlove had been appalled. 'Millions and millions of them!'

'I'll save you a piece of Christmas pudding,' Lucille had said. 'They say the food's not very nice.'

Jo was disappointed that he would not be spending Christmas at Badger's, and both Tina and his daughters were offended that he would not be sharing the festivities with them.

Sally had surprised him, although he thought, in retrospect, that he should not have been surprised.

'I'm so happy for you, Topher. It will do you good to get away.'

Her words had comforted him during the long flight to Canton. They had sustained him during the midnight wait in the steaming cauldron of Bombay. He had thought of them when he had introduced himself to the group of Australian teachers, newly arrived from Sydney, who were to be his companions on the trip.

The tour guide – young Mr Chen from Taiwan province – in his rimless glasses and his fawn anorak, had been delighted to welcome a visitor from England. Regarding Topher as curiously as if he had come from outer space, his first words to him had been to enquire politely whether he happened to know George Michael of the Wham. Confessing his ignorance of the pop singer, Topher wondered what he was doing, 12,000 miles from home, when he could have been in Bingley eating Lucille's Christmas pudding.

When he revealed to the school teachers that he was a judge, only the eleven-year-old Delilah, whose presence had at first made Topher apprehensive, had not been intimidated.

It was Delilah who sustained the spirits of the group in the less auspicious moments of the trip, while Topher, by virtue of his age and status, became its natural leader. When the hotels turned out to be unheated (the external temperature registering minus four) or dirty (peanut shells and mice droppings under the beds) and the food inedible (cold semi-fried eggs, in deference to the Western breakfast), they looked to him for guidance.

179

It was not until they reached Shanghai, where long-johns hung like ceremonial flags from the plane trees which lined the streets, and astonished faces were pressed to the windows of the buses at the sight of Occidental noses, that the thought crossed Topher's mind that perhaps he should marry Lucille.

The two days allotted to the city had been spent trotting after the indefatigable Mr Chen. He had taken them to see the Jade Buddha (carved out of a single piece of stone), the Site of the First National Congress of the Communist Party of China, and the Residence of Dr Sun Yat-sen. On the last afternoon Topher had made his own way to the water-front (familiar from the old movies), where he would not have been in the least surprised to have encountered a trilby-hatted Humphrey Bogart or the sinister bulk of Sydney Greenstreet.

Fascinated by the ships, and with trying to decipher their flags half remembered from his schoolday, he had remained for the evening in the vicinity of the Huangpu River. He watched a demonstration of students (agitating for better career opportunities and the chance to travel abroad) and ate an indigestible and unidentifiable dinner. Later on he had coffee in the Shanghai Peace Hotel to the accompaniment of jazz played by an enthusiastic band of elderly musicians left over from the Cultural Revolution. The nostalgic sounds of *Red Sails in the Sunset*, and *Won't you Come Home Bill Bailey* (pre-war Britain rather than Middle Kingdom) had taken him back to England and Lucille.

That Lucille wanted to become his second wife was plain. She made no secret of it. He had his doubts about how she would go down in the Great Hall of Lincoln's Inn, or at the Garden Party, but then one could not have everything. Penge approved of Lucille. Chelsea did not care. Tina, revelling in her role as match-maker, would be in her seventh heaven. Life with Lucille would not be life as it had been with Caroline, but it would not be dull. Lucille would see to that.

He was trying to superimpose the image of Lucille upon the landscape of his future, when he was roused from his reverie by the strains of *Auld Lang Syne*, not only played but sung by the six inscrutable members of the band. After this improbable finale, they put away their instruments, and the Coffee Lounge was summarily closed.

Topher removed from his pocket the instructions he had been provided with by Mr Chen – 'To return to your hotel please show this card' – and went out to the street. A grim looking, cloth-capped coterie, bolstered against the elements, stood on the corner by their antediluvian taxis. Putting his faith in the only driver who seemed prepared – after lengthy and unintelligible angry exchanges with his comrades – to take him, he was whisked off into the night.

At the railway terminal they followed Mr Chen to the Soft Seat section of the train that would take them to Wuxi, where they were to board the canal boat for Suzhou. As they were carried along the platform on the human tide, it was easy to believe that one person in five on the planet was Chinese. A great many of them, Topher thought, seemed to be on Shanghai station.

In Suzhou, their first port of call was the Embroidery Research Institute. A portrait of Prince Charles (with Princess Diana on the reverse side and not a knot in sight), so finely worked that the stitches were invisible, impressed even Topher. He was less impressed by the unheated sheds where the young embroiderers sat, with hot-water bottles on their laps, straining their eyes for eight months at a time over a single fish or cat or bird. The dead-fingered girls in the silk factory, their hands in hot water from morning to night as they teased the threads from the cocoons, were no better off.

Unable to face another sweatshop, where the monthly wage was less than the price of a glass of orange juice in his joint-venture hotel, Topher politely declined the sight of fans being carved from sandalwood, and made his escape. With Delilah clinging to his arm, dodging the bicycles, and stepping over the drying orange peel on the pavements, he led the way down-town, where she bought a tie for her father from one of the open fronted shops. The wizened shop-keeper, eating her lunch from an enamel bowl, took the money in her mittened hands, and put it into the canvas pocket of her apron, without interrupting the steady rhythm of her chopsticks.

To Topher's relief the next stop was a garden. With its rockeries and water-falls, its miniature trees and zig-zag bridges, it was – according to Chen – the perfect place for recollection. While the schoolteachers took photographs of each other, posed outside the Tassel-Washing Waterside Pavilion and Pine-Viewing and Painting Appreciating Hall, Topher sat on a stone seat in an arbour and thought of Sally.

She would not have needed much persuading to come to China with him. There had been several moments when he had wished that she had. It would be no hardship to be married to Sally. He liked her company. He liked her generous nature. He liked the fact that she was sincerely interested in his family, and had gone overboard about his grandson. He had reservations about her spaghetti.

Feeling a tickling beneath his chin, he realised that it was Delilah's fluffy white hat.

'C'mon, judge. Didn't you hear the hooting? Everyone's on the bus.'

A Jade and Mahogany Factory, in which he was not in the least interested, being next on the itinerary (the teachers' hold-alls had long been bulging with souvenirs), Topher asked Chen if he might visit a People's Court. He should have known better. Regarding him through the thick lenses, with eyes that seemed not to have blinked since the Long March, Chen assured him, without the slightest hesitation, that all the courts were shut.

Jo Henderson was the only one of his women who had actually proposed marriage. Topher left her, as well as his shopping, for Beijing. Unpacking his lunch-box on the plane – after an uncertain take-off, during which the seats jerked backwards, overhead lockers crammed with new television sets and electric fans, flew open, and the arm-rest of his seat came off in his hand – he vowed never again to complain about British Airways. The free gift, a tinny key-ring, presented ceremoniously by the cheongsam-ed stewardess, did little to compensate either for the stale roll and the 'beafmeat', which passed for a meal, or the speed and – what seemed to Topher – utter recklessness, with which they shot from the clouds to land in the sub-zero dawn of the capital.

Since he seemed to be in imminent danger of losing his ears from hypothermia, Topher's priority was to buy a hat. Given that the entire population seemed to be suitably kitted out against the bitter cold, he did not think that it would prove too difficult.

With his head down, his hands in his pockets, and his exhaled breath visible, he went in search of a gentlemen's outfitters. A solitary overcoat and a pair of gloves in a steamed-up window, caught his eye. Inside the shop, from around a central brazier at which they warmed their hands, a circle of well-wrapped up Chinese suspiciously measured his approach. Recalling the charades he had last played at Badger's, and feeling not a little ridiculous, Topher mimed 'hat'. Getting no response from his dour audience, and unable to see anything which remotely resembled a hat in the glass display counters, he moved on. By the time he actually found what he was looking for, he had grown accustomed to the scrutiny, and his ears had almost dropped off.

Dwarfed by the vast expanse of Tian'men Square, and assaulted by the icy wind (courtesy of Outer Mongolia) as he waited with his group to visit the Mausoleum, the unhappy thought occurred to Topher that had he been a Chinese judge, under the banner of Mao Zedong in the late sixties, he would almost certainly have met his death on that very spot at the hands of the Red Guards. Summoned by Chen, and infiltrating the patient queue of Chinese work-units who stood politely aside to allow the foreigners to pass, they stepped on to the red carpet and entered the building. Hurried along by grim-faced attendants, they shuffled in pairs – 'Two to the right, two to the left, hats off, no talking' – past the crystal sarcophagus where, draped in a red flag and preserved in eternal slumber, lay the waxen remains of Chairman Mao.

The Great Hall of the People ('the Great *Whore*'), with its 10,000 seat auditorium, impressed with its size and construction, as did the Mausoleum with its solemnity. But for Topher it was the visit to the Great Wall, which made its way through five provinces and two autonomous regions, which was the apotheosis of the journey. He had not imagined that it would be so vertiginously steep or so treacherously slippery, or that there would be so many Chinese – each one of whom stopped open-mouthed to stare at him, climbing it. The sight of the Great Wall, snaking into the distance from the fortress where he paused for a moment to regain his breath, gave him the same sensations of euphoria as did the green acres of Badger's. He was not sure whether his elation was due to the fact that on Christmas Eve he found himself at the height of some 1000 metres, suspended between the *Shanhaiguan* Pass and the Gobi Desert, or the thought, provoked by the grandeur of the landscape, that he might do very much worse than marry Jo.

The idea of accepting Jo's proposal remained with him as clinging unceremoniously to the guard rail, he slithered in his unsuitable shoes down the more hazardous reaches of the descent. By the time he rejoined the group which was waiting anxiously for him in the car-park (Delilah, wearing an 'I climbed the Great Wall' sweat-shirt) he had convinced himself that the prospect of life with Jo, shared between their Monday to Friday judicial interests and the asylum of week-ends at Badger's, might not be all that bad.

On his last afternoon in Beijing Topher, having so far managed to avoid them, visited his first Friendship Store. With the help of Delilah, he chose scarves for his daughters (trying to dismiss from his mind the wrinkled fingers of the girls in the silk factory), a diminutive Happy-Coat for Charlie, and a fan for Mrs Sweetlove. Eschewing painted ashtrays, mahogany coasters, and other local arts and crafts, he traipsed the aisles in a panic of indecision before settling on a marble seal for Sally, engraved with her name in Chinese characters, and a scarlet kimono for Lucille. Recalling the *objets d'art* which decorated Jo's sitting-room, he could see that she was going to pose more of a problem. He settled on a jade necklace, and wondered if the number of *yuan* he spent on it reflected Delilah's extravagant taste or his predilection for Jo. He was walking away from the jewellery counter when he was stopped in his tracks in the art department. A painting was displayed on an easel. *Morning Song*. A dozen sparrows, delicately brushed-stroked, huddled together on the bare brown branches of a water-coloured tree.

'It's only a load of old birds,' Delilah, pulled him towards the refreshment counter. 'Who wants a load of old birds!'

Chapter Twenty-Five

Topher stood on the balcony of the Barbican flat, which would have fitted comfortably into the two ground floor reception rooms of his Hampstead house, and looked out on to the peaks and spires that traced the graph of the London skyline.

Whilst his whistle-stop tour of China had been in many ways unsatisfactory, it had enabled him, on his return, to regard his *modus vivendi* in a new and improved light. To say that after three weeks he understood China, would have been no more intelligent than to assert that he could get a very fair idea of Christianity by looking at the dome of St. Paul's.

Chaperoned by Chen, and cocooned for the most part in his group, he had paid homage to the landmarks and to the sliver of life he had been permitted to glimpse behind the recently lifted curtain. He had, with the help of his guide book, committed to memory the dynasties from Xia to Qing. He had tasted (and rejected) jelly-fish, and white-fungus, and lily bulbs, and had swallowed a mouthful of 'sea cucumber' before Delilah had informed him that he was eating slugs. He had cruised on the longest canal in the world, trodden the only man-made structure visible from the moon. From the window of the train he had watched the countryside transmute from the dull olives of the plains to the brilliant emeralds of the paddy fields. Guangzhou, Shanghai, Suzhou, Beijing were now more than place names on a map, but he knew that even if he were to live among the Chinese for half a lifetime he would not be able to claim that he knew a single one of them. It was not only a question of nationality. It was a matter of ancestors, an attitude of mind, a spiritual concept which was totally and permanently exclusive.

His welcome home had been gratifying. His presents variously received. Chelsea and Penge (who had had sufficient *nous* not to dash out for a Chinese take-away) had collaborated in a formal dinner in the dining-room, at which his grandson, whom he scarcely recognised, had worn his new Happy Coat. More gratifying even than the dinner, was the fact that Charlie (who according to Penge was being poisoned by the noxious wastes of Hampstead) was about to be taken to his father in the Welsh countryside, and that Chelsea had her bags packed in the hall.

With the help of Marcus she had reconciled herself to the misfortune which had overtaken her lover, and was now able both to go back to Wapping and to deal with her predicament in practical terms. It was a subdued Chelsea who rested her head for a long moment on Topher's shoulder before returning to her warehouse.

'Thank you for having me,' she said. 'I know it was a bit of an imposition.'

Topher opened his mouth to tell her that while he expected to wait for an invitation to visit his daughter in Wapping, this would always be her home. That no matter how old she was, how independent, she would always have the inalienable right to return. Eloquent as he was in his summings-up, his reserved judgements in which he was never at a loss, he could not find the words. Caroline, who had a veritable arsenal of good sense in her armoury (she was fond of talking about doors closing and others opening) would have known exactly what to say.

'It's been a pleasure,' Topher said, as if his eldest daughter were an acquaintance blown in from New York. 'Look after yourself, Chelsea. And keep in close touch.'

He hadn't thought that it would be such a wrench to say goodbye to Charlie. He had grown attached to his grandson and swore that in return he had been acknowledged with a toothless smile. He had taken Penge to the station. After holding Charlie tightly to him for a moment, he had handed the baby to his mother in the carriage. As the train pulled out ('Say goodbye to Grandpa,' Penge had said, animating the small hand at the window) Topher, waving inanely after it from the empty platform, was disturbed to discover that there was what could only be described as a lump in his throat.

186

The welcome with which Sally had greeted him had been rapturous. As he fell willingly into her arms, the thought occurred to him that people of mature years were subject to exactly the same emotions as their children (and grandchildren). He was more pleased to see Sally than he had imagined. He kissed her face and her hair and both her hands, and they had talked – and it was not only about China – far into the night.

'God how I missed you,' Sally said. 'There can't have been a moment when I didn't think about you. You are the light of my life.'

'I kept saying to myself,' Topher confided, thinking back to the Children's Palace (*Jingle Bells* sung in Mandarin by five year olds) and the Temple of Heaven, 'Sally would have liked this.'

'Next time . . .' Sally looked at the marble seal he had brought her, which stood next to her typewriter. 'India, Africa . . . Where shall it be?'

Raising his head from where it rested on her shoulder, and looking into the face, the image of which had accompanied him to the markets of Wuxi and the gardens of Suzhou, Topher thought that it would take very little effort on his part to make Sally Maddox his whole world.

Lucille, with no hesitation, had removed all her clothes to try on her present. For the first time – and he wondered whether it was significant – Topher had taken her to his own bed. Celibacy, he decided, did not suit him. As if to make up for his lost three weeks, and despite the jet-lag which had caused him to nod off from time to time on his first few days on the Bench, he had made love to Lucille with the vigor and potency of a very much younger man.

'You're good for me,' Topher said, when they were resting amicably, side by side.

'We're good for each other. Don't tell me you haven't realised that?'

Forbidding Topher to move, Lucille had gone down to the kitchen for a tray of tea and hot-buttered toast, over which he had told her about his trip. She wanted to hear every little bit. He started with the Temple of Six Banyan Trees in Canton and did not stop until he'd reached the Forbidden City.

He had left Lucille cooking dinner for them both while he went to his court to fetch some notes. When she opened the front door to him in her scarlet kimono, framed in the light from the hall, it was as if the house, which had been inanimate for so long, had sprung into new life.

He had been looking forward to going down to Badger's, but when he opened the curtains on Saturday morning, he was greeted by an ominous quiet. The view from his window was transformed by a deep blanket of newly fallen snow.

'You're not to attempt it, darling,' Jo said, on the telephone. 'The roads are treacherous, and we're completely cut-off.'

His house was echoing once again now that the girls, together with Charlie, had gone. He had spent most of the week-end with Sally, who had smiled wryly at his dilemma but had good-naturedly taken him in.

By the time he saw Jo, the pavements in Lowndes Square were ankle-deep in slush. Jo was not yet home. The porter let him in to her flat. He helped himself to whisky and switched on the television to watch the disaster pictures which a few days ago had been of snow ploughs rescuing stranded cars, but were now of floods. When Jo swept in, in her fur coat, about which Penge (who campaigned against mink-farming and the killing of Pilot Whales) would have had something to say, her cheeks were flushed and her nose red.

'Sorry, darling.' She shed brief-case, handbag and umbrella as she came towards him. 'I had to wait for a taxi. It was Wally Matheson's goodbye party – he's been posted to Brussels – you don't know anyone who wants a Barbican flat?'

Topher waited until the end of the evening before giving Jo the necklace. Over dinner – it was so long since he had seen her that he had almost forgotten how much he enjoyed just looking at her – he discovered that she knew a great deal more about China than he. She knew about the Sui and the Tang, the Boxer rebellion and the fall of the Qing; that it was the melting snows of the Tibet-Qinghai plateau that fed the Yangtse and the Yellow rivers, and about the hundred year life cycle of the bamboo.

She even knew, when he fastened his gift around her neck, that jade was the Chinese symbol of nobility, beauty and purity; that it was a guardian against disease and evil spirits; that it had once been used to plug the orifices of a corpse to prevent the life force escaping.

'It's beautiful, Topher.'

He stood behind her as she fingered the green of the beads

against her black sweater, admiring them in the Chippendale mirror.

Topher cupped his hands round her firm, strong breasts.

'So are you.'

She turned to face him. Seeing that she was surprised by his gesture, he said: 'There's nothing wrong with me.'

She looked at him.

'I know.'

There was something in her voice.

'What do you mean?'

Jo sat down in the armchair.

'One night, at Badger's, the door was open. I heard you call out in your sleep.'

'What did I say?' Topher sat down opposite her.

It was a moment before she spoke.

'Lucille.'

Topher could not think of anything to say.

'I presume the lady is the reason I haven't had an answer to my proposal. I'm not used to being turned down.'

Topher could not explain that Lucille was only one of the reasons that Jo had not had her reply. He was not ready to tell her of the decision he had made, the revelation which had come to him in the shadows of the Ming Tombs.

It was through Jo that he had found the flat in the Barbican, but it was April who was dying to get her hands on it. She wanted to enlarge it with a *trompe l'oeil* panel (a column set in a pedimental niche), to drag the woodwork, and rag-roll the walls. The decision to move had not been made all at once. Out of curiosity he had agreed to see the flat. He had dropped into the local estate agent's on his way home one day, to get an opinion as to the market value of his house. The estate agent had arrived poste haste in his white Porsche. A property developer had arrived hard on his heels. He was not interested in the fact that from Chelsea's window, when the trees were bare, you could just see the Heath. Or that you could bang away in the Piano Room to your heart's content without disturbing the neighbours. Or that in the conservatory, created by Caroline at the back of the house, the sliding doors could be opened to admit the birds. He made Topher an offer so astronomical that he was hard put to refuse. Encouraged by Marcus and April (despite the fact that they would miss him desperately), by

189

his daughters, keen to see him make a new life for himself, and by Tina (on the telephone from Bingley) who thought that until he got away from her shade he would not get over Caroline, he had, with more than a little trepidation, agreed to sell the house.

He refused either to be hurried or to allow anyone to help him as he sorted out his *lares* and *penates*, the testimony in porcelain and in glass, in blankets and in linen (Caroline must have accumulated a hundred pairs of sheets), to his married life. He had had many offers of assistance. He did not want Marcus telling him which pictures he must keep. Penge and Chelsea's opinion as to a piece of Wedgwood, which to them was nothing but a fruit-dish but to Topher was poignant reminder of a week-end in the Fens. He spent the winter evenings, not unhappily, going through a lifetime of papers and sorting out his books.

Sally had thought his decision a healthy one. Lucille was a little bit sorry. She had grown to like the big house. It made no difference to Jo.

There were, inevitably, adjustments to be made. Instead of leaving his car in the garage beneath the house in the evenings, pausing to smell the lilac or the roses on his way back up the path, Topher would have to leave it in the underground car-park where the attendant, darting from his glass booth, greeted him with 'Your Honour this', and 'Your Honour that'. His obeisance reminded Topher of Mrs Sweetlove, who was appalled at how he would manage without a garden and thought he must be out of his mind to move.

The flat was ridiculously small. He refused to let April touch it. He would see to it himself in his own good time. There was no room for a study, but he would line every wall with books. To reach his possessions in the single living-room (the concert grand from the Piano Room was going to Wapping), he would have only to stretch out his hand. The kitchen was no more than a cupboard, the bathroom little larger. He would not need an Arthur — with his never-ending demands for slug pellets and fertiliser — to make inroads into his whisky. There was scarcely need for a Madge. He would at first, he had no doubt, miss the commodiousness of his old home. Lucille had pronounced the new flat 'ever so cramped'. But the spacious house and the green sward of its garden had been designed to accommodate a family. If he wanted fresh air he had only to step out on to the windswept balcony, on which he now stood.

The Ming tombs, where the Emperor Wan Li was buried together with his royal spouses, had been a disappointment. Topher thought he might just as well have visited a bank vault. Standing in the semi-darkness he had experienced a surge of homesickness, and wondered, once again, what on earth he was doing in this underground cavern, surrounded by strangers, on the far side of the world. The feeling of alienation had been followed immediately by one of exhilaration. He was aware of a glorious sensation of what he could only describe as liberation, as the pieces of his life, fragmented by Caroline's death, cavorted suddenly into place.

Chen, huddled into his anorak was explaining with as much enthusiasm as he could muster, that it had taken the Emperor half a million workers, a heap of silver, and six years to construct his necropolis. Topher, stunned by the vision which had come to him, was not listening. He was repeating, in his head, the words on the record which Lucille had given him, the song from *Cats*.

'Daylight, I must wait for the sunrise./I must think of a new life,/And I mustn't give in./When the dawn comes, tonight will be a memory too, and a new day will begin.'

It was paradoxical that the long night, in the shadows of which he seemed to have existed for so long, should end so abruptly in the murky resting place of the Emperor Wan Li. That the nightmare — in which he denounced all responsibility for his actions — was finally over. It was as much as he could do not to take Delilah in his arms and dance her round the sarcophagus.

If the particles of his existence had come together in the catacombs, his decision had been made as they emerged into the sunlight from the subterranean tomb.

'If you touch me you will understand what happiness is/Look, a new day, has begun.'

He would be like the swan, the *Cygnus melancoriphus*. The *Chenopis atrata*. He would not take a second mate.

The melody of a skylark, ascending almost vertically over the city — recalling spring days on the downs of southern England, moors and peat bogs alive with the self-same sound — brought him back from the Ming Tombs to his balcony. He had no need of Caroline's binoculars to see Wordsworth's 'ethereal minstrel', to follow the flight of his 'pilgrim of the sky'. With his naked eye he could make out the white tail feathers, the streaky brown of the body, the small crest along the trailing edge of the wing. The bird, in full-throated song, hovered high in the bright morning air, poised motionless for a moment, then with a flap of its wings, soared confidently away into the distance.

Topher laughed aloud.